Eaten by Wolves

Richard R DiPirro

Bacon Cake Books

Published by Bacon Cake Books

Cover design and photography by Hillarey H. DiPirro

ISBN #979-8-9857078-1-6

http://richarddipirro.com

PART 1

THE MURDER

1

UP THE MOUNTAIN

ON A FLAT ROCK, a few feet off the trail, a blue-tailed skink lay still, soaking in the late morning sun. Its long, splayed fingers clutched the warm stone. "Hey Will, look at this guy!" Van Ryan crouched down and stared at the skink. Brown and light-tan lines ran down the creature's back like racing stripes, stopping abruptly before a long, thick, bright blue tail. Fat hind legs were spread out and coiled beneath it. As Van looked at it, the skink turned its head up and offered him a toothless grin.

"What's wrong?" Will Snowden sat on a downed tree, shaking a stone out of his boot.

"Nothing, man. Just ... check this guy out. He's smiling at me. Look at his face!"

"We've got to move if we're going to make the falls by noon. Come on." Will tied his boot tight, slung his pack on his back and set off up the trail, leaving Van to follow.

The trail wound up around the periphery of the mountain. It was the same trail Van had hiked with his father when he was a boy. Van would spend the day stealing glances at the wilderness and scenery while his father trudged along, grunting at him to keep up. The old man had an objective, a timetable, and he wasn't going to be slowed down by his surroundings, or his son. "Fun takes work," he would say when Van asked him to stop, or slow so they could enjoy their surroundings. The forest flora inhabitants called to Van as he hiked, inviting him to sit, to feed on the sunlight, to grow. His father had been dead almost ten years, and now, as Van and Will made their way up the mountain, Van was free to call back to the trees, the flowers and weeds as he hiked.

Their destination was always the same campsite, six miles up from the trailhead. The site was flat, clear of brush and relatively free of roots and rocks, and there was a small creek running nearby they could fish if they felt like it. They used to knock the hike out in three hours or so with full packs, tents and sleeping bags, but it had become more like four or even five hours now, with Will dragging Van along. Van was still in shape, he just seemed to find more to look at now along the way. He didn't always jump up after they had rested, and sat instead with his eyes closed, listening to the flies buzz around his head, little men in his brain being fried by the sun.

Van pulled a water bottle from the side of his pack and sipped while he walked. Will plowed ahead as usual, a steady twenty yards ahead. He was a machine, piston legs pushing him forward. Will carried the finest camping and hiking gear money could buy. He had the sportiest, lightest internal-frame pack; the most rugged, waterproof boots; and a sleeping bag and tent which could keep him warm at the south pole. He carried most of the cooking equipment and food on top of his own gear, but it never slowed him down. Van could have thrown his own beat-up military pack and gear on top of Will's and climbed on top of that, and Will would have hauled it all without noticing.

Van had his own rhythm now. His boots picked their way around roots and ruts on their own, and he leaned forward to keep the pack's weight from holding him back. It was a beautiful, late August morning in north Georgia, and a steady breeze brought cool air through the trees, loosing rogue leaves too eager to wait for the season to change. Van smiled at the constant flickers of motion at his peripherals while he hiked, things skittering under cover or scampering along branches as the men walked by. An hour or so passed before Van realized it.

"Yo, brother! You alright up there?" He called ahead.

"I'm good. Come on!"

Will already had his boots off and his feet in the water when Van made it to the falls. The water plunged from twenty feet above into a dark pool and fed a stream that wandered off to join other streams further down the mountain. Van slipped his feet in and marveled again at how rejuvenating the cold water could be. The miles melted away. Even sitting downstream a few dozen yards from the waterfall, the spray wet his hair and cooled his steaming head.

Will threw pebbles in the stream, like Van did as a boy. Van sat quietly, looking at the water, bold minnows nibbling his toes. Waiting. Will threw a bigger stone.

"You alright? What's up?"

"You know, I never had a chance. You know I never had a chance, right? How the hell did he get that close, man?" Will and his wife had been carjacked a few days prior. Someone had run up to them while they were stopped at a red light and put a gun to her head, ordered them both out of the car and drove away with it. "The whole thing took less than a fucking minute man! What was I supposed to do?"

"You couldn't do anything, brother."

"By the time I knew what was happening, it was over!" Will stood up and started pacing along the bank of the creek. "He already *had* her; you know? One squeeze of that trigger and she was done, man! For what? At the fucking intersection of where? On goddamn Who Gives a Shit Boulevard, right? Son of a bitch."

"They find your car yet?"

"Hell no. Worthless bastards. Probably in a hundred pieces by now."

"But you're still here."

"Yeah." He sat back down, next to Van. "What was I supposed to do, man? I can't be everywhere! Why didn't she see him? He came from her side! She could have said something, and I would've taken off, you know?" Van was silent. "Now she's telling me she doesn't feel safe! What the hell am I supposed to do? I keep her safe! Who could have predicted that shit? She should have seen him coming. It's not my goddamn fault!"

They each kicked their feet around in the water. Van looked at Will. "You okay?"

Will nodded, and the nod turned into a shrug. "I don't know, man. I was fine at the time, but after ..." He shook his head. "I mean, I know you've been through shit like that, right, but ... yeah, it's been messing with me, you know? I admit, I was scared, man. And then she's giving me a hard time ..."

After a few minutes, Van dried his feet, put his boots back on and stood up. "Come on, brother. Let's move." Will nodded and wiped his eyes. He got ready and they both slung their packs on their backs and headed on up the trail.

Van let Will take point again. It only took a handful of yards until Will was pounding the trail with his boots again, chugging on like a broken-hearted locomotive. Tree limbs and random leaves and twigs lying across the trail fled from his approach. Ferns coiled back into themselves, and flowers turned away from the sun. Nothing could stop him once he got going. It was what Will needed, sweat and adrenaline. Van followed behind, trying to comfort the trail as they passed.

They were about an hour from the campsite when Van first heard it, behind the rustling of dead brush and the rub of leaves and branches. It was a human voice, he was sure. Far away. Like barely hearing someone yelling at you on a windy day.

"Will! Ssh! Hold up!" Will stopped and Van caught up with him. "You hear that?"

Will tilted his head. "I don't hear anything."

"Come on!" Van took off up the trail.

"Whoa! Hang on, man!" Will yelled, but it didn't matter. Van was gone. The voice was there, someone was there. It called again every time Van stopped to listen. After a few hundred yards the voice changed direction and Van took a hard left off the trail and plunged into the woods. "Yo! Van! No man! Stay on the trail!" Van ignored him and charged straight ahead, perpendicular to the path up an incline thick with fallen branches, debris, roots and rocks. Van knew it was a bad idea to wander around off trail. The ground was covered with leaves, dried and decomposed, and rocks and holes hid everywhere. Snakes and broken legs loved this terrain. But every time Van slowed or second guessed his pursuit, the voice would call again, and he would charge ahead.

Fifty yards of climbing and the hill crested. The way became clear and steady. Van was breathing heavy now and his legs burned. His pack was getting heavier with every step. Will caught up with him. "Van, what the actual fuck man?!" Van turned to face him and waved ahead. "You hear it, right?" His face was flush and damp, and his eyes burned with excitement.

“I don’t hear shit, you idiot.” Will said. He leaned over and put his hands on his knees while he took deep breaths. He stood up and Van was gone again. “Goddamn it!”

2

A Meadow's Meal

VAN HEARD HIS NAME called again. The voice had been faint and far away when he first heard it, but it was getting closer now and it was calling him by name. All other noise had stopped, save for the daredevil leaves that lived on the very top branches, rustling in the breeze. Birds, squirrels, frogs, sounds that should have been all around him were quiet. Just his name in the air, very close now.

He crested another hill and froze. He stood at the edge of a small clearing surrounded by thick, old trees. A hundred yards away stood an earthen mound about twelve feet high, covered in wet soil, moss, wild grass, and fallen branches. The mound backed up to a rock wall looming two hundred yards straight up, its face dark and shot through with striations telling the history of the Blue Ridge mountains. Small boulders and pieces of rock lay piled against the sides of the mound, where they must have broken and fallen from the wall above. Water dripped and stained the rock face, and patches of moss clung heartily to the damper crevices. Behind him, off to his right, Van heard Will enter the clearing and stop still.

Van remained frozen, willing himself to be small. A deer stood in front of the earthen mound, and it stared directly at him. Van was exhausted, his legs were shaking, and he was trying hard not to gasp for air. The deer, a good-sized whitetail doe, looked at him intently. Ever so slowly, Van stood up straight, wiggled out of his pack straps and took several long, deep breaths. The doe stood steadfast. Van took a tentative step forward. Then he took another. He didn't know why exactly, but he felt compelled to approach the creature. He crept in comic slow motion, in the clear without the slightest cover. Step. The deer stood confident and curious, its ears and tail twitching back and forth. Van had never been this close to a deer before. Step. He had seen hundreds over the course of his life. As a child he had fantasized about befriending and riding a deer or keeping one as a pet, but always the slightest movement sent them leaping away. Another step. This deer was beautiful. Her flanks were light brown with faded white spots. Her dark eyes stared right through him. She was a young adult, and her thin coat hadn't yet started to darken and fill in for winter. Van was so close now. If he reached out his arm, he could just about ...

"Van Ryan!" Van recoiled immediately, drawing his hand back as though he had touched something hot. He snapped his head toward Will, but Will was still standing straight, motionless, his pack still on his shoulders.

"Van Ryan." The voice was clear and strong and came from directly in front of him. It was the same familiar voice he had heard on the trail. He stood still while interest turned to panic and the scenery around him shimmered. He turned his head left and right, his eyes darting around the clearing, searching for the speaker. "Here," the voice came softer this time. "In front of you." The doe took a small step toward him. "Here." And with that word, Van realized with certainty that the deer talking to him.

He fell straight backward, onto the soft grass. "Will!" He yelled, but there was no answer. Van looked at the deer. She shook her head slowly, gently.

"No, Van Ryan." Van continued to scramble backward. "This is real. I am real." The deer's voice was familiar. Van flipped over onto his hands and knees and crouched in a runner's stance, prepared to sprint his way down the mountain and back to his home some seventy-five miles away. As he looked up though, he found himself staring directly into the eyes of a large wolf. The wolf's head hung low, in line with Van's, and its mouth was pulled back to show bright red, healthy gums and perfect, pointy yellow fangs. A low rumble came from somewhere deep in its powerful chest, like thunder waking up. Van knew it was hopeless to run. Even if he could somehow evade this creature, he knew these beautiful killers never traveled alone. As though the pack had heard him, two more wolves stepped silently out of the tree line. Van crawled back one pace, back toward the center of the clearing. The wolf stalking him lost its cruel sneer and looked at Van as bemused predator to prey. His pack mates spread out on either side, cutting off any possible escape route.

"They will not hurt you," the deer's voice said. "I have called them here. Be still." Van slowly stood again and turned around to face the deer. He saw that three more wolves had joined the group, two sitting at the ends of the earthen mound at the far end of the clearing. Another huge wolf with reddish-grey fur had positioned itself regally next to the deer, its ears high and pointed, its chest thrust out, the alpha of the pack.

"They ... they won't hurt me?" Van finally addressed the deer directly.

"They will not," the deer replied. Again, a shimmer at the edges of Van's vision. He noticed for the first time a slight humming sound behind the deer's words. It seemed to fill the space inside the meadow. "Do not attempt to leave this clearing." Van and the deer stared at each other for some moments while Van tried desperately to get his breathing under control.

"Okay," Van said, when he could. "What ...? What is this? What's going on? Deer? You're a fucking deer!" He used his shirt to wipe the sweat from his face. "Please tell me this is some fucked up dream or something. I fell and hit my head, right?"

"This is real, Van Ryan."

"What the goddamn hell ..." Suddenly there was a choking, gagging sound from behind Van. He turned and looked at Will and for the first time realized that Will was trying to move, trying to speak. He wasn't just frozen in shock; he was being held in that position involuntarily and he was trying to call Van.

Van turned back to the deer. "What ...?"

"Van Ryan! Watch." The deer's familiar voice, loud, in Van's head. The humming.

"What? Why?" Van was breathing hard, and his chest was quivering. Something terrible was happening.

"Van Ryan!" The voice, in his head. Louder this time. "Your path and your friend's have parted now. Stand, and observe."

"Will!" Van took a step toward him.

"Van ... NO!" Will choked out two words. His eyes strained to turn toward Van. They were as wide as sledding saucers.

With no warning or sound, the large red wolf left the deer's side. With two effortless bounds, the wolf hit Will in the dead center of his chest with its forepaws, knocking him off his feet. Wolf and man flew several yards in the air, and the alpha's mouth was around Will's throat before they hit the ground.

Van tried to help his dying friend but the wolf closest to him turned to block his path with a threatening sneer. There was no glorious expiration for Will Snowden. No final words or grand gestures. Just a long hike up the mountain and the last of his blood watering a quiet meadow.

Van could see the exact moment Will was gone, the fingers uncurling, the wax-model face and body going limp. He tried to reach his friend again and was again blocked by one of the pack. Two of them quickly dragged what was Will Snowden away into the shadows around the perimeter of the clearing, and he was gone. "What?!" Van turned toward the deer in disbelief and astonishment. It had all happened so fast. "What the …? What …? Who the fuck are you? They killed him! They fucking KILLED him!!" Van slowly dropped to his knees. "Will!"

The deer spoke in the same familiar voice, "It was necessary for you to witness that."

"He was my best friend …" Van's mind spun.

"His time was over. This was his end."

"What the is that supposed to mean? He was fine! We should have been heading down the fucking trail tomorrow and he would have gotten on with life. I've known Will Snowden since I was eight years old, you asshole deer … You FUCKING KILLED HIM!" How could Will be dead? Van's thoughts ran down and up the mountain trails, leaping over cold streams and stabbing everything with pointy dead tree branches, like he had as a boy. His mind was broad and angry, broken splashes of pain and color.

"Why? Tell me why?"

"His time was over. And we needed you to witness his death."

"What the does that even MEAN? His time wasn't "over!" He was going to be a goddamn millionaire! And have fucking *kids*! And play softball with other middle-aged assholes until his knees gave out." Van closed his eyes and shook his head violently. "Who are you? Why…?" He rocked forward and pressed his forehead into the scrub grass and moss. His hands lay flat on grass so soft and cool and soothing he wanted to tear it from the mountain's face like flayed skin. His bloody palms could feel the mountain below and around him. Insects, worms and reptiles and small mammals slept and worked underground. Larger creatures prowled. And ate.

"You're a goddamn talking deer, and my friend's dead and I … and I'm imagining this entire thing! Boom! There it is. Will's at home right now with Yip and I'm …. alone somewhere. I'm here, in the woods, having some kind of psychotic break, or acid flashback or something."

"No, Van Ryan. This is all real. This is real and your friend is dead. They can bring his body back if you find it is necessary, but it would be unpleasant. They have been making use of it."

"No … please," he pleaded, "who are you? What is happening?"

"It is complicated, Van Ryan. It will be difficult for you to understand. First … we are not the creature you see before you."

"What?"

"We are not this deer before you. These animals obviously do not possess the capacity for human speech."

"Wait …"

"The conversation we are having is taking place entirely inside your mind." The deer paused. Van stood and began walking in a tight circle with his hand on his forehead, trying to force his mind to concentrate, to comprehend.

"Yes! I know that! I know!" Van felt almost relieved. "This is all bullshit. Where's Will?"

"THIS IS HAPPENING, VAN RYAN!!" The voice was a drill instructor's ringing through the early morning squad bay. "You must come to terms with that fact. The voice you have been hearing is manifesting in your mind, yes. But this is really happening." Van was deflated. He held his hand out uselessly in front of him.

"But the deer ..."

"Human beings respond better to a familiar, recognizable form addressing them rather than just an ethereal 'voice in their heads,' so to speak. Disembodied voices are easier to dismiss. The deer in front of you has no idea what is occurring right now. She exists in something resembling a waking coma. The wolves are also in the same state. They are under no distress at all, and they move and act without knowing they are under our control." The alpha wolf approached Van and lay down in front of him. It rolled over to reveal its stomach and wagged its tail like a domestic dog who needed his tummy rubbed. The wolf's tongue lolled happily from its bloody mouth. "Enough," the coma-deer said, and the wolf sprang instantly back to its side.

Van stood quietly for several minutes, staring first at the deer, then the wolf, then the cloudless, late afternoon sky above them. At last, he stirred, and walked slowly in a circle as he spoke. "Well, what are you then?" He waved his tired arms at every corner of the clearing. "If you're not the goddamn deer, then *who* are you? *Where* in the hell are you?" He walked to the closest oak tree and kicked it. "Here?" He picked up a thick, dead branch and broke it over his knee. "Is *this* you?" He turned back to the deer. "Goddamn it! Tell me!"

"'I' and 'you' are words that mean nothing to our kind. There is only 'we,' and *we* are many. My kind arrived on this planet a long, long time ago." The deer paused again, letting each new course digest. Not *deer*, Van told himself.

"An ... alien, then?" Van stopped and raised his arms above him. "Great, we're at fucking aliens now! Well, why not? So, apparently, I am either in the middle of a shitty sci-fi alien murder mystery, I'm having some sort of latent psychological experience, or I have really and truly lost my mind!" Laughter came then, for the first time. It was painful and ugly. It came hard and long, and Van danced around the clearing, laughing and spitting and turning in circles and punching at the air. "ALIENS!! Ha hahahaha!! Mother FUCKER!!" He picked up a hand-grenade sized rock and threw it into the center of the clearing. "There, fucking Marvin the Martian. Marvin the deer! Make that rock move. Pick it up! Show me something other than a goddamn talking Disney character!"

"That is not possible, Van Ryan." Van had never wanted to punch an animal in the face before now. "My kind does not have the ability to manipulate physical objects."

"Well, what then? How do you have a goddamn deer looking like it's giving the Gettysburg Address and a wolf that just ate my best friend sitting next to it, waiting for me to throw a stick so we can play fetch?"

"My kind has the ability to manipulate what your species refers to as the "electromagnetic spectrum," although that is a very simplistic explanation. It is a small thing for us to influence the tiny electrical impulses governing these animals' thought processes and motor skills."

Van was quiet while he absorbed what the Not Deer was saying/not saying. "The voice ... is your voice then? You're projecting your voice into my head?"

"No, Van Ryan. My kind do not have a "voice" as such. We do not communicate vocally. Those parts of your brain which process auditory input are being stimulated by a small projection of energy. You are "hearing" the sound of your own voice. That is all." And that was it. The familiarity of the voice Van had been hearing. It was his own voice.

"So, I'm talking to myself. I hear voices in my head. How the hell can I not believe that this is all one huge hallucination?" Van closed his eyes and breathed deeply. "How much of what I've seen has been real today? If you can influence the electrical signals in my brain then you must be able to create visions as well, yes? Make me see whatever you want?"

"It is not as easy as ..."

"Make me do something! Make me recite Walt Whitman. Make me dance around this meadow like Julie Fucking Andrews!"

"That cannot ... "

"Yes! You can! You did it to Will. You froze him on the spot so your friend could eat him. He offered his goddamn throat like it was in a chafing dish on a buffet line!"

"I cannot do what you ask. We are proficient at manipulating the electrical impulses in the brain. That manipulation has its limits, however, and those limits vary from human to human."

"Why?"

"We cannot answer that, Van Ryan. It may be due simply to the chemical and physiological make-up of each individual human brain. Possibly the balance of serotonin to endorphins, or the constitution or viability of individual neurons. Why do psychotropic medications affect each person differently, at different dosages? Why do some humans develop mental illnesses and not others? Why does trauma affect individuals in different ways? In the entire time we have been among your kind, it is the one puzzle we have not solved. Your brains are a complex masterpiece of form and multi-dimensional function. Animals do not pose the same challenges. Perhaps it is that part of the human brain that has evolved the capacity for individual self-awareness that creates the randomness in the brain's function. We do not know for sure."

Van was aware of how hard he was working his own addled brain trying to understand. "You say you can't make me move, but you did make me hear things."

"Yes. A much less complicated manipulation."

"But you did freeze Will, yes? Before your minions ate him."

"Yes, we did, Van Ryan. Your friend's mind was much more accessible than your own."

Van sat then, hard. He breathed deeply and tried to settle his mind. "Can we make this deer go away, please? And these fucking dogs. This one still has something of Will's in its teeth." The deer immediately looked startled and twisted itself awkwardly to bound away from Van. Two long bounces and it was lost in the tree line. The wolves around Van's periphery faded into the trees like late-morning mist.

"Where are you then?" Van asked. "Physically. You're a voice ... my voice, in my head, but where actually are you?"

"We are all around you, Van Ryan. The bulk of our physical form lies in front of you, buried within a blanket of earth and forest detritus. Over the centuries we have existed here, we have also spread underneath the surface of the topsoil and into the structure of this part of the mountain. We are incorporated into the form of the highest trees you see, as we were in their ancestors." The voice was quiet for a moment. "Enough questions, Van Ryan. It is time to discuss why you were brought here."

"I thought you brought me here so you could murder my best friend."

"No, Van Ryan. We had the creatures end Will Snowden so that you would be convinced of our abilities. Anything less would have left you wondering if you had merely dreamed or hallucinated our meeting. Also, as we have said, this was his end."

Van's new grief for Will was swirled splashes and random blotches, multi-colored like paint on an artist's pallet. He wanted so badly to argue with the being, to list all the things Will had been to him. All the things he still had ahead. Guilt and loss, love and anger all painted a changing portrait of Will on the stretched canvas framed by his death.

"So, what is the point of you then? You all? All of you?" Van asked. "You've been here 'centuries' for what, exactly? Do you all just plant yourself on mountainsides? Hijack random hikers? Feed people's friends to predators? What, exactly?

"No," the voice said.

"No. No, what? What are you, goddamn it? Where ... how long have you been here?" Van felt himself running out of energy. The shock and adrenaline rush were wearing off, and he desperately wanted to understand what had happened before he passed out.

"We are from far away. And we have been here for a long ... a very long time." There was a pause. "Our initial purpose ... our primary function is to observe."

"Observe."

"Observe and report," the voice, the *alien* voice inside Van's head said.

"Report to who?" Van asked.

"To those who sent us here. Periodically, jointly, we send a transmission in the form of energy to a distant location. Our sense is that energy is then gathered with other information, from other locations, and then forwarded again. How many times it is rebroadcast is unknown to us. The final destination of our periodic reporting is also unknown."

"Alien spies. Why not? Taking deer? Alien spies! It all makes sense now." Van digested. "So, where the hell does one shitty little human like Van Ryan fit in? You've been here forever. You're all powerful. What could you possibly need me for?"

"Your use of sarcasm demonstrates a lack of seriousness, Van Ryan. You underestimate the gravity of this moment."

"How could I underestimate "the gravity" of the moment? My BEST FRIEND was just EATEN! I have been talking first to a fucking DEER, and now apparently to my fucking SELF!" Van felt an unsettling well of hysteria threatening to surface. "You have taken what was a normal, leisurely afternoon and turned it into a screaming, murderous, green nightmare that I will live over and over for the rest of my life! Most likely in a mental hospital. Unless I am there already, which is not impossible right now!"

"That is enough, Van Ryan. Be quiet now." And with that, Van's world slipped diagonally and blurred.

3

A Commission

AWARENESS BECAME SQUARE, FRAMED images in his mind. He stood still in the woods, on a mountain in a country, on a continent on a small blue planet and his eyes were wide open, but everything was too small to see. He felt himself untethered, weightless, surrounded by a meaningless infinity. He was himself and not himself, and he realized that the entity in front of him, in the meadow, was showing him something without words. Words were much, much too stupid to describe what he was seeing.

He was present in a limitless void, not floating, not suspended. Not up and not down. Motionless. Without motion. It was not black, as he had always been led to believe by books and movies and tv shows. Instead, brilliant color burst alive and swam and swirled everywhere he looked. Tendrils of distant color-blast nebulae reached out and danced with gasses and unlabeled forms of radiation from stars and dust clouds conceived before time existed. Space was not empty. It was majestic. It was stuffed full and dynamic and so very alive.

There was sound in space. The quietest whispers and hints of cataclysmic frictions, eruptions, explosions from millennia past and from distances beyond comprehension. Sound lived as subtle vibrations Van could feel around him, caressing him, joining with his own rhythms, projecting that on forever. His entire existence swam in the past. Everything he saw, every light that shown, every moment he occupied had come to pass eons ago. His knew now that his perception of the present, of time itself, was naïve. He lived his life as static as a mollusk, adhered to a rock beneath the water's surface, living a short, linear life as the big, beautiful universe ebbed and flowed all around and before and after him, always unaware of his presence.

Gradually, Van noticed forms around him at various distances that looked like each other. They were an undefinable color and their shapes were amorphous, yet they all resembled each other. They slowly grew closer; above, below and on every side of him. Van knew then that he was the entity, was also the same undefinable color as the forms around him, and that they were all of a like kind, linked as one. As he studied his relation to the other forms, Van realized that he and they were all hurtling through space, even as he had the sensation of stillness. It was only as they grew closer to other, larger objects that he had any perspective of his own motion and speed. Just then, as he had that thought, enormous familiar spheres began flying by. One looked like it may have been Neptune, a round flash tinged blue. Another blur and then definitely Saturn, then Jupiter. As all the other like entities drew closer to Van, it became obvious they were all on a joint trajectory toward Earth.

And there it was, a point of blue and brown, green and white. No reduction in velocity. A fleeting sensation of gravity and wind and a soft, quiet landing. Van felt a stretching out, a reaching, and a melding of his form into the young forest around him.

The late afternoon light of a faded day found Van on one knee, his arms embracing himself and tears and sweat mingling on his face and neck. As he came back into his new, normal self, he felt fear and disappointment. Confusion. Loss. His paradigm for 'Van Ryan' was gone, obliterated completely by the overwhelming totality of space and time, and the undeniable recognition of his own infinite smallness.

"Rise, Van Ryan," said the entity. Van stood, and his body felt like it weighed a thousand pounds. "You have a task to perform."

"I ... have so many questions."

"Of course you do, Van Ryan. There will be plenty of time for that later."

"Please ..."

"My kind exist as one. A collective consciousness. We are physically spread out across great distances, but we remain always in contact with each other, and in this way, we function as one. With this composition, we perform our primary mission."

"Collecting and transmitting." Gone was Van's skepticism, his anger. He sat in awe of the being in the meadow.

"Correct. Recently, however, there has arisen a problem. One of our kind, one component of our whole, has disappeared from the collective. We are unable to contact this part of us, and it is a cause for concern. This has never happened before. We have always assumed that our longevity was perpetual, our connection incapable of interruption. The physical composition of our being is invulnerable to heat and cold, and climatic fluctuations and meteorological occurrences have no effect upon us. We do not "age" or atrophy, to our knowledge, and our ability to camouflage ourselves has been without flaw."

"I don't understand. What does this have to do with me?"

"We need you to travel to the location of this component and aid us in returning it to the collective ..."

"I'm sorry. I don't ...I don't understand."

"Be quiet, Van Ryan and allow us to explain. We are going to provide you with a small quantity of our physical substance. You are to transport that substance to the component in question and merge it with the form there. That should remedy whatever problem there is. Do you understand?"

"Yes? I think so."

"Good. We have reduced the density of our substance significantly in one specific location at the top left of the mound you see before you, to the rear, adjacent to the wall. You should be able to climb on top of the rocks next to the object in order to reach the spot we are indicating. You must first dig there until you reach our physical form, and then use something to strike the surface. Do you understand?"

"I ...I don't ...what should I use to ...?" Van's mind was swirling mass of confusion. He felt like a surfer caught and pounded by a tidal wave. *I can't ... I can't ...*

"VAN RYAN!" The voice rang and resonated through his head. "Understand this: time is of the essence. We cannot perform our primary function without this missing component. This needs to be attended to immediately. Do you understand?"

"Yes ... yes."

"Now, use something to dig a hole at the top left area of the form you see before you. To the rear. Do it now."

"Yes. I understand." Van walked toward the mound. He managed to climb on top of a small boulder, no doubt a piece of the rock face that had broken off long ago, and then onto a larger one laying alongside the mound. This gave him access to the top. He cleared some branches and wet leaves from the area the alien/entity had indicated. The first six or eight inches of soil under the leaves was damp and loose and he dug through that with his hands. Fat earthworms and various grubs and beetles fled the destruction of their home as Van clawed through the dirt. Finally, he reached a layer that he couldn't break through with his fingers alone. He searched around, first among the debris on top of the mound, and then along the meadow's tree line for something to assist in the excavation. He found a branch, about as big around as his wrist, that looked like it hadn't fallen from its tree very long ago. There was a pointy split at one end, and Van used that to dig out clumps of older dirt from the hole.

After ten minutes of excavating, Van's stick hit something much harder than the dirt he had been digging. The stick fractured immediately the moment it broke through the dirt and made contact with the object buried beneath. Van dug desperately with the stick, and then again with his hands, until he had uncovered approximately a square foot of the object. He gazed at it in wonder. It was a dull, pinkish color, with streaks of red and violet running through it. As Van watched, the small ribbons of color pulsed and shimmered as they traveled in indeterminate directions. The surface of the object was smooth. It appeared solid and non-porous. When Van touched it hesitantly, it was warm, but not hot. The heat throbbed gently along with the bands of color.

"That is good, Van Ryan. Now you must strike the surface very hard, two or three times. You will notice a small area appear to liquify. At that moment you must place your hand on it. Keep in mind, we have lessened the density of our form in that one area, but it will still take a series of powerful blows to affect the change."

"Place my hand ...?"

"That's right. Do not worry. It will not cause you any discomfort."

"Okay..." Van said. He reached down and pulled his hunting knife from its sheath on his belt. He raised it above his head and brought it down hard, pommel first onto the exposed area of the object. The effect of the blow was so jarring it knocked Van off balance and he fell backwards off the rock he was standing on. He managed to twist his body and land on the ground on his knees without hurting himself. "Son of a bitch!" He could feel the vibration still in his wrist and elbow. He climbed back up and looked. There was the slightest scratch in the surface of the object. He could barely see it. He looked at the pommel of his knife and saw that it was dented slightly on one side. "Well, that's not going to work," he said to himself. "What the hell ..." He scanned the meadow slowly, looking for any possibilities; any sharp rocks or ...

Will's pack. It was still on the ground on the far end of the meadow, where it had fallen from Will's shoulders as he was dragged away ... *don't think about that.* Van knew that Will carried a small axe with him when they were camping. They used it to drive tent stakes and chop and split firewood. Van walked quickly across the meadow, trying to reach the pack before his resolve disappeared. The axe was hooked to the outside, and Van willed himself to ignore the blood splatter on the pack while he freed the axe. It was secured with a nylon strap and a plastic quick-release clip, but the strap had gotten twisted underneath the handle of the axe, and Van couldn't get the clip to open. He tried to work it with his fingers and then tugged it and pulled it more forcefully. He didn't want to have Will's pack in his hands. He started to pull on the axe more frantically. He picked the whole pack up and slammed it on the ground repeatedly until at last the strap snapped and the axe was in his hands. The pack fell to the ground and Will's tent and his wet weather parka spilled out of the opening. Van had been with Will the day he bought that parka.

Van tore himself away from the scene, strode back to the alien mound and climbed back on top of the rocks. The axe was small, but had weight to it, and one side was blunted, like a hammer. Van climbed on top of the mound this time and positioned himself to be able to deliver the strongest blow he could. He raised his arm and brought the blunt side of the axe down on the object's exposed surface. His arm and wrist shook like a bell being rung, but Van could see that he had struck a significant gouge in the surface.

"Yes, Van Ryan! Good! Again!"

Van repeated the action and again the bones in his arm felt as though they would shatter. He struck two more times, and suddenly the entire area of the form he had uncovered shimmered, and then melted into a thick, liquid substance. Van tossed the axe to the ground.

"Now, Van Ryan! Do it."

Van drew a deep breath and lay his hand flat, palm down, in the liquid before him. There was no pain, although the liquid was hot and pulsed with a steady rhythm as it engulfed his hand. His skin tingled, not unpleasantly; a sensation somewhere between a tickle and a light itching.

"Very good, Van Ryan. Now lift your hand away."

Van did as he was told. His hand was covered in a very thin layer of the substance. It clung to his skin like wax. He brought it up to his face to look at it, and as he watched, the substance quickly disappeared into his skin, sucked into each individual pore until his hand was left clean and dry. "What the *hell?!*" He looked back at the surface of the object. It had turned solid again, with no sign that it had been disturbed at all.

"It is alright, Van Ryan. There is nothing for you to worry about. A very small bit of our substance has been absorbed into the skin of your hand. The substance is inert and poses no threat to you. We determined this was the most effective means of transport to the objective."

"Well, I'm glad I could be your 'most effective means' ..." He turned his hand over, examining it. There was no indication there was anything different about it. "So ...what now?"

"You have one purpose now, Van Ryan. One task. You must travel to the location of our silent component and join it with the bit of us you now carry."

"Where is this component? How will I find it?"

"You will be provided with further instructions and information as you travel along your journey. For now, however, there is approximately one hundred and sixty minutes left of daylight. You must start down the mountain immediately."

"But ...but what about ..." Van indicated Will's pack.

"Will Snowden is no longer your concern, Van Ryan. We told you before, his time is over. His life is over, and now his death has passed. *You* must get down the trail before it becomes dark. It is time for you to go."

So, Van slung his pack back on his back, took one last look at the spot where his oldest friend died, and at the meadow which had drunk his blood and dried in the sun. The grass stretched out, content with its life of sunshine and rain, rot and growth. Van struck out the way he had come, back toward the familiar trail, which felt much less familiar than it had only a few hours before.

4

Deployment

HE LAY IN THE corner of a dark room in a dilapidated farmhouse, trying to stay asleep as a loose shutter slammed against tired wood shingles. A storm was coming. Peeking through barely opened eyelids, he could see, through the room's dirty windows, an angry confluence of grey and dark clouds. The wind pushed the clouds toward the house playfully, remorselessly, and Van could feel the hairs on his neck and arms trying to wake him. A reckoning approached, heralded by the slam, slam, slam of a broken shutter.

The knocking on the front door was rhythmic and relentless. Van sat up and tried to make sense of where he was and saw that he was in his own bed, fully dressed. His t-shirt was soiled with blood and dirt, and the knees of his pants were dirty and grass-stained. Next to the bed were his muddy hiking boots. He knew he couldn't answer the door in those clothes, so he threw on a fresh shirt and a pair of exercise shorts. Van's apartment opened onto the street. Peering through a front window he could barely make out the form of his landlord, a middle-aged black man in a well-fitting suit, standing on his doorstep. He sighed as he opened the door. “Good morning, Mr. Wilmer.”

The man’s suit was charcoal grey, his tie was burgundy, and the knot was perfect. His shoes were brown and highly polished, well-worn but uncreased. Van had only ever owned one suit, black, for court and funerals, and cheap dress shoes made of stiff leather that felt like cardboard boxes on his feet. “Van Ryan,” the man said. “These are for you.” He had a paper sack in one hand and held it out in front of him.

Van reached in the greasy bag with a skeptical look and pulled out a warm donut. He looked at the man. “They are donuts, Van Ryan. You need to eat. You need to be on your way.” Van took the bag from the man and looked inside. There were, indeed, a half-dozen fresh donuts, made at the Blue Egg bakery, the best in town. His stomach cheered. “You need to be on your way now, Van Ryan.” The man was looking directly at Van with no expression on his face at all.

Van squinted at the morning sun as it tried to creep in the front door. The street was alive and moving, busy with traffic. It was already warm outside, and cars cruised by with their windows open, lousy music from stereo speakers banging on front doors up and down the street. Dogs crapped where they wanted while the humans they walked looked the other way. Van scrutinized the landlord further, and something in the man’s lack of focus seemed familiar. Like a deer he had once met.

“Okay, wait ... wait a minute,” he said to the man. “You’re ... you know. From ...?”

“Yes, Van Ryan. We met yesterday. On the mountain.” And over the irresistible smell of fresh-fried dough, scenes of the previous day came flooding back to him.

“Fuck.” Van’s shoulders slumped. “Get in here. Come in.” Van waved the man into his apartment.

"There's no time for that, Van Ryan. You need to be on your way." Mr. Wilmer, the landlord, was sweating, although the morning was cool. A dark stain was spreading around the collar of his shirt. Van wondered if any part of the man was conscious right now. Was he watching Van from behind his own eyes? Hearing the alien's words spoken in his voice? Or was he mercifully asleep, unaware that he had been kidnapped? Van hoped that was it, that he would simply come to whenever the entity left him and wonder why his shirt was soaking wet and he had donut crumbs on his jacket.

"You just woke me up! Where am I going?" Van was angry. The memories from the day before were slowly filtering in, memories of the clearing on the mountain, memories of ... "Oh Will. Oh no. What about Will? What about him? What am I supposed to tell his wife? Shit, I left him up there!"

"Nothing. You will tell her nothing, Van Ryan. You did what you had to. Nothing more and nothing less. Will Snowden's death will become known, in its time. That is not your priority. Right now, you need to gather your things and get on your way."

"Fuck that. I'm not going anywhere right now. I need to do something about Will ..."

Mr. Wilmer crossed through Van's small living room and into the kitchen and began opening and closing drawers until he found what he was looking for. He removed his jacket and held up the one decent chef's knife Van owned. "You will pack what belongings you need for one week of travel, and you will get in your vehicle now." And the man pushed up the sleeve of his sweaty shirt and slowly drew the sharp blade of the kitchen knife across his forearm. The blood did not spurt or gush from the fresh wound, but began steadily flowing, dripping onto the stained linoleum floor.

"What?!" Van slapped the knife out of the man's hand. He grabbed a dish cloth hanging from the oven handle and wrapped it around the wound on the man's arm. He held the bleeding man's good hand and pressed it against the wound. "Hold that, you son of a bitch!" Van dug into one of the kitchen drawers and came up with a half-used roll of duct tape. He wrapped it around and around the dish towel as tightly as he dared, until the bleeding slowed to an acceptable ooze. When he was done, he looked at the man's face. Mr. Wilmer, the landlord, had begun sweating again, but he gazed into Van's eyes like a model on a taxidermist's shelf. "Come on," Van said. "We'll go get you fixed up, you poor bastard." He put his arm around the man's waist and began to steer him toward the front door.

"That won't be necessary, Van Ryan." The man turned again toward Van. "You must gather what you need and begin your journey. Now. We may not be able to control you directly, but as you see, there are many ways to compel you."

Van covered his face with his hand and battled quietly with the anger and helplessness he felt. Finally, he opened his eyes and said calmly, "Fine. Okay. Where am I going?"

"Memphis, Tennessee. There you will meet someone who will guide you to the silent component's location. You will receive additional guidance along the way. You must go now."

"Yes! I got it. I must go now," Van felt beaten. Tired. "Will you take this man to get medical attention? Please? You won't feed him to your fucking wolves or bears or whatever, will you? Because if that's what we're dealing with here, I'm not cooperating. You can just send them my way instead."

"There is no reason to kill this man, Van Ryan. He has served his purpose, and our point has been made. We will leave him at the nearest medical facility." Van nodded. He opened the front door and waved them both out into the sunny day.

Van strode around the apartment cluelessly, trying to pack for a trip he had no hand in planning. He had no idea what he was supposed to be doing, or how long it would take him. The landlord/entity had said one week. Okay. Toothbrush, deodorant, razor, whatever. No problem. He looked around the apartment. Suddenly, nothing looked familiar. He went into the bedroom and started throwing things on the bed. Shirts, pants, shoes. They looked like someone else's clothes. *Those couldn't possibly fit me.* He thought. *Who the hell bought this ugly pair of pants?* His backpack was on the floor, leaning against the wall, but Van couldn't touch it, didn't want to acknowledge it. Instead, he grabbed an old duffel bag out of his bedroom closet and started stuffing clothes into it. He opened the top dresser drawer and grabbed underwear and socks and stopped. In the back of the drawer was a worn photograph of Yip.

He touched the photograph as he had a hundred times. Her hair so soft, her cheeks flush, her eyes laughing at the camera. He touched her two-dimensional image gently, knowing he could never touch her in this world. Except once, one kiss, so long ago, forgotten by one of them. He looked at the picture, and he knew how her hair smelled, how her lips tasted, and he was grateful for that one kiss, although the memory of it haunted him every day. She was Will's girl then, and she was Will's wife now, and Van loved her more than Will did.

The front room of Van's apartment served as both a living room and an office. A shelf lined with books hung along most of one wall, above an old desk Van had saved from a thrift store. Historical fiction, adventure novels, spy books, graphic novels were lined up and stacked haphazardly along the length of the shelf. Some of the books Van had bought at book sales at the local library. Others were still on loan; most of those were late. Van had long ago figured library late fees into his monthly budget. He looked now for a book to return, any book, and he saw *Slaughterhouse Five*, which he had finished at least a month earlier. He leaned on the desk and as he reached for the book, it slipped through his sweaty fingers and fell on the computer keyboard. The screen lit up, displaying a news story he had been reading the morning before. Images of angry people with badly painted signs in some small town in Arkansas. The headline read, "*The Most Racist City in America?*" Van had been struck by that headline. Was there really a "most racist" city? Weren't there racists in *every* American city? According to the article, folks in this town seemed totally at ease expressing disgust for and abusing folks unlike themselves. Billboards on the way into this town proclaimed love of the white race, and hatred of others.

Van found that sort of impersonal hatred morbidly curious. What sort of person lives in a town like that, grows up in that world? Were the people there actually villainous? Did they shuffle through town in dark cloaks pointing bony fingers at those not like themselves? Or white cloaks, more likely? What happens to someone raised in an environment devoid of empathy? Can they still grow to love and care for strangers, or is their lot cast with their neighbors?

Van realized Will had still been alive when he read that article. He grabbed the Vonnegut book and the duffel bag, took one look around what now felt like a stranger's apartment, and headed out. All that was missing was the sound of a starter's pistol.

5

Late Fees

IT WASN'T A FANCY library, but then Canton, Georgia wasn't a very fancy city. No grand pillars or concrete lions guarding the entrance. Just a stand-alone metal book-drop and double glass doors with flyers for children's book readings taped on the inside. Van made his way in and was faced by the perpetual display of new releases. Books from today's *"Most Popular Authors"* were all carefully arranged three-dimensionally on a skirted table. Super Most Popular Author's thirteenth original *"one-of-a-kind best seller"* was flanked by political noise written by celebrities, and "autobiographies" of wealthy people ghost-written by faceless talent. You had to push through racks and shelves of this and religious taffy to reach the circulation desk.

It was in the darker stacks, in the back corners of the library, that the timeless stories lived. Shelves and shelves of current mythology hidden in plain sight. There you could find sharp-talking gum shoe detectives slapping tough guys around. Wily spies serving good-guy countries behind enemy lines. Cops catching bad guys. Heroes vanquishing villains. Destinies fulfilled. Tales of the world as readers *want* it to be.

Then there are other stories, in between those. Stories of heroes losing. Of evil crushing the weak. Stories of war, of bad choices and regret. Questionable heroes pulled along by forces outside their control. People dying ignobly, unavenged and unredeemed. Villains that scare readers the most: the villains within themselves. These stories are bound in unworn volumes, their covers new and unstained. The bindings are fresh, and crackle when they are opened. These books live their lives mostly unread. They are tales of the world as it *is*.

Yip was sitting behind the check-out counter, staring at a computer screen. She was the antithesis of a made-for-tv librarian. She wasn't mousy or matronly. She didn't wear glasses or dress in conservative clothes. Her hair wasn't tied up in a bun or a tight, dark ponytail. Her hair was short and fearless, and today it was dyed a light, bright blond. She wore a loose-fitting blue sundress that revealed nothing and somehow suggested everything. The color of the dress easily complemented the subdued blue of her wide eyes. Van stood behind a spin-rack of well-read paperbacks, watching her.

He wondered, as he often did, what it would be like to wake up next to her. Not in a sexual way necessarily, but what would it be like to open his eyes and see her face on the pillow next to his? If she were his, he would wake himself up early every morning, earlier than her, so that he could lie and watch her sleep. Listen to her breath. He would take his time watching the gentle rise and fall of her chest while she slept, her eyelids twitching while she dreamed.

"Hey there, you." She smiled at him. "Unless you've developed a thing for Fabio, I think you're in the wrong section." Van looked at the books in front of him and saw he was facing a spin rack of creased and well-loved Harlequin romance paperbacks.

"Oh shit. Yeah, not my thing really." He stepped out where she could see him.

"You guys just get back? How was it?"

Van was struck mute. He stared down at the worn carpet beneath his feet. *How was it? Will got fucking eaten by wolves, Yip. But other than that ...* Van couldn't make the words come out of his mouth. "Okay. It was okay," he managed.

She was distracted by whatever she was working on. "Well, that's good." Van watched her freckled arms as she typed on her keyboard, longing to gently run his hand along the fine, light hairs growing there. Behind Yip, Mrs. Ingles, the old head librarian, slowly wheeled a cart of books past.

Fuck it, Van decided. She deserved to know what happened to Will. He took a deep breath. "Yip, I have to tell you something ..." He looked up to tell her the whole, fucked-up story, and saw Mrs. Ingles standing behind Yip with one arm raised high over her head. In her long, veined hand she held a pair of scissors, open, with one worn blade pointing down toward Yip's neck. Yip didn't know she was there, and both women held his horrified eyes with their own. Mrs. Ingles' eyes were empty and emotionless, like Mr. Wilmer's had been, and the old lady moved her head slowly from side to side, silencing Van.

"What is it?" Yip asked him. "You okay?"

"Nothing, no ... Sorry." Mrs. Ingles' arm came down slowly, and Van saw her wake up behind her eyes and stare dumbly at the scissors in her hand. She walked off to finish re- shelving books, shaking her head and muttering to herself. Yip shook her head at Van and went back to her typing.

"Okay, well ..." Van said, backing away from the desk slowly, "I have to go." He turned and headed toward the exit.

"Hey, wait!" Yip called after him. "You got something for me?" She smiled and held her hand out. Van looked down and remembered the Vonnegut book. He stepped up and laid it on the return counter, trying hard not to touch her hand.

"You want me to see what the damage is this time?" She started typing again. "You might have to take a second job soon to pay these fees off."

"No. I'm sorry." Van turned again and started for the door.

"Hey, it's not a big deal. Are you okay? Van?"

"Sorry!" He yelled as he pushed through the glass doors. He turned and watched her return to her work. In a quiet, choking voice he whispered to her through the glass, "I'm so sorry." He ran to his truck, slammed the door, and laid his head on the steering wheel. His hands were shaking.

Life in Canton was over, Van knew. Gone. His apartment, the bar, this library, the Blue Egg bakery and their delicious doughnuts ... all gone. All left on the mountain. Nothing would ever return to that grey stasis he had muddled along in for so long. He was beyond that life now, propelled *beyond.* His life existed now between his two hands, at ten and two on a worn steering wheel.

Van started his truck. It began to rain.

6

Defensive Driving

IT WAS ALMOST MIDNIGHT when Van passed through Birmingham. He meant to stop for the night here, but he was in the zone and he figured he had a couple hours of driving left in him. The night was quiet and wet, and the truck lights splashed sharp scene-cuts for Van as the road unwound behind him. He thought again about putting on some traveling music, but he couldn't figure a selection that would harmonize well with the lonely sound of the wind around his windows. He moved along, one mile and then another, cut off and too close to all the other cars around him.

He had called the bar and let them know he wouldn't be around for a few days. Erin, his manager, took the news in stride. Truthfully, Van hadn't been around much anyway. Even more truthfully, the place was going under, and everyone knew it. The staff all showed up and did their thing and made their money, and everyone was hi-fives and smiles when Van was around, but he was sure they were all looking around for their next gig. He had tried. He had tried to make it work. He schmoozed the customers and managed the staff. He checked the numbers and kept an eye on the inventory. It just didn't feel like *he* was the one doing these things anymore. He would be there, and things would get done, but Van didn't remember doing any of them. When he walked into the front door of the bar now, it felt like someone else's place, full of strangers he might once have recognized.

That numb feeling followed him around all the time now. It clung to his back, weighing him down. Breathing in his ear. Everything felt like too much work; brushing his teeth, grocery shopping, even reading felt like more effort than it was worth. When Will called and told him about the carjacking, and asked Van to join him on the mountain, Van saw an opportunity to escape the slow burn in his mind. Boots on the trail, a pack on his back and his knife on his hip – that was as real as things got anymore. Everything else was just noise. Static. Costume dress-up at the Canton Community Center. A masked ball, the theme being "Status and Responsibility." The mountain offered an escape from all that.

Thoughts of the bar, of music and stories and Yip visited Van's mind and were gone again, replaced by another handful of arbitrary images. The highway was infinite and straight. The wheel felt solid in his hands. Van loved driving, being in control of the truck and everything in it. His hand and feet worked in perfect synch. His mind wandered, though, drifted as it did when left unobserved. Thoughts moved along faster than the traffic, morphing one fantasy into another, one landscape into the next. It was a release, like freeing a tortured race dog from its cage. Movies he had seen lately and songs he loved, violence, shit jobs, dead plants he had left at home. Each image lasted five minutes or an hour, all mixed in with the soundtrack of four worn tires spinning, holding his world to the wet road.

A shift then, thoughts of a clearing, on a mountain. A talking deer speaking frankly only a few feet away from Van as wild beasts ate things from the inside of his friend. Smelling distance. Not the smell of damp seats and old French fries, but of warm salty blood and thick, pungent predator's fur. A feeling of helplessness like Van had never felt before. Van yelled at the vision louder than he thought possible, but he couldn't stop what was happening. He couldn't save Will.

Van shook the vision from his head and then watched the car to his right drift, slowly. Its speed matched Van's truck, around 70 mph, and it floated carelessly into Van's lane, as though it were strolling through a crowded mall, and it spotted something shiny in a store window.

Everything slowed. Van saw it all happening, saw what was coming but could do nothing to prevent it. He was boxed in. There was a solid line of cars in the lane to his left, and some asshole had been riding his tail for a dozen miles so he couldn't slow down. The lazy car, an older-model green Camry, didn't slam into Van's truck, it just nudged it some to the left. The driver of the Camry reacted violently, overcompensating, and as Van was pushed to the left, he saw the Camry out of the corner of his right eye spinning wildly out of control. Van glanced off the car to his left, sending it into the concrete median, where it planted itself as the vanguard of a dozen violent rear-end crashes behind it. Van steered slowly, serene in the knowledge that his own violent death was imminent. Now he held the wheel but had no control at all. He felt no fear. He thought he would never be afraid again. Light impacts left and right. His truck turned and careened some more, but it kept moving, slowly spinning across the wet highway. Seventy m.p.h. spinning. Loud crashing and rending all around him, glass breaking, his and others, colors and dark, flashing lights but his truck moved peacefully now this way, now that.

Spinning. He waited to flip; did he flip? Was that him, or did another vehicle jump over his, obscuring the sad, sad highway streetlights for a moment? He waited to come to that final stop, where inertia would carry his body on, crush him, tear him to pieces, but the truck meandered and spun across the field of carnage to the far-right lane, and then the shoulder, and he easily pulled himself onto an off-ramp. He fishtailed at the last, as he tried to slow down, and hit the end of a metal guardrail straight on, tearing it from its braces like a sheet of perforated paper. The length of guardrail folded on itself once and drove itself straight through the middle of Van's hood, his engine, and up through the windshield, missing Van's right ear by less than twelve inches. Steam spewed from Van's ruined truck, which was facing upward at 45 degrees, wheels spinning. Adrenaline struck Van at last when he realized that he had survived, and he leaned his face against the cool steel of his guardrail passenger as the world began sinking into blue and red. He wept some, and bled.

7

Dennis Ryan

VAN'S FATHER WAS A big man, bigger than Van would ever be. Dennis Ryan stood with a wide back, broad, thick shoulders, and forearms as wide as small trees. He towered over men six feet tall. He had worked as a merchant marine in his youth, and hard work at sea had made his arms and body as coiled and taut as the rope he handled all day. A favorite trick of his was lighting kitchen matches on the rough, rock-hard calluses on his hands. They were like a pair of cheese graters, and when Van was a boy, his father handled him like he was made of glass to avoid damaging him.

For all his bulk and brawn, Dennis Ryan was a quiet man. A soft man. Not "soft" in the sense of being weak; he had shown Van the extensive map of scars that covered him from head to toe, detailing for Van the assorted acts of violence at sea which precipitated each one. He was soft, rather, in a way that led to his stopping to save turtles trying to cross a busy road. Or caring for a bird that had fallen out of its nest. He was *soft* in the sense that he was *kind*. He cared about things. He cared about animals and insects and (sometimes) people.

During Van's childhood his father made his living as a carpenter, a builder. The story set between ship and hammer, about his leaving the sea for dry land, was his father's favorite, and Van had heard it countless times. As Dennis Ryan told the story, he woke up one morning, young and stupid and missing one eye, in a hospital somewhere in Georgia. There had been a car accident that may or may not have been his fault, but definitely involved alcohol. The first thing he saw when he opened his eye was Van's mother, trying to take his blood pressure.

"Good morning, Captain Morgan," she said to him with a smile.

"Where am I?" He asked her.

"You're in heaven, sweetie. Can't you tell?" She let the air out of the cuff with a loud hiss and wrote something on his chart.

"So that makes you an angel, then?" He smiled at her through swollen lips.

"If you want. Or could be I'm a demon." She shrugged.

"Guess I'm going to have to keep my eye on you then." He pointed to his uncovered, surviving eye, and according to Dennis, she giggled slyly.

And that was all it took. Dennis traded in his sea legs for a pair of work boots, and thus began the brightest-lit time of his life. Van's mother breathed beauty into Dennis Ryan's salt-washed world. Life before her had been bad food, back-breaking labor, and close living quarters with ill-tempered men. Van's mother was a ray of filtered sunlight, warming his skin after a long, long storm. They set up house in a suburb of Atlanta and had a son. Dennis read him pirate stories and adventures of brave captains battling the wild sea. Van's mother sang him old '70's folk songs. She collected yard gnomes and planted them around the edges of their world.

Van's earliest memories of his mother were the warm, cuddle-scented skin dreams all children deserve. Smiles and the sweet melodies of a happy mother's voice shined down from her face, and Van's young toddler world was contented and fascinating. As he began to walk, though, he saw her from a place outside of her arms, saw her whole, not just a face above his. He saw tears. He saw her sitting in her chair, staring out the window, ignoring him as he banged his empty sippy cup against her knees, pleading for more juice. Van saw his huge father kneeling on the floor next to her as she sat in her chair, his own face wet with tears, his voice quiet and urgent. While she stared out the window. Somedays still she held Van, too tightly, and whispered over and over that she loved him, that she was sorry, and she loved him. Her eyes inches from him, wet and alive, ringed with despair. His small hand touching her face. Those memories are fewer, and older. There are sharper images of her in her chair, looking out the window, her eyes as cold and unfeeling as raindrops.

One night, when he was five years old, Van's mother walked out the door after a quiet disagreement with Dennis, and Van and his father never saw her again. She never came back for her things, never withdrew money from their bank account, never wrote them a letter. The police couldn't find her. Dennis hired a private investigator to search for her, but she was truly gone. She had disappeared completely.

It destroyed Van's father. For Dennis, losing his life with Van's mother was like finding himself cast off, marooned in a suburban archipelago, his small crew looking to him every day for answers. The disappearance was immeasurably worse than if she had just been killed. At least then there would have been a body to mourn, a burial site to visit. A disease or an accident to blame, somewhere to direct all the anger and anguish instead of turning it all inside. Sadness became his world, became their world.

Several years after his wife's disappearance, Dennis built a workshop behind the house and began spending his evenings there shaping things out of wood. The first thing he produced was a fairy tale house, about gnome-sized, with a crooked window in the front and a high, peaked roof which sagged drowsily to one side. The siding and the roof were covered in small, irregular wooden shingles and Dennis had incorporated small twigs to serve as molding and trim. A rounded front door opened and closed on tiny hinges, and the entire thing was painted in five different, happy spring colors. Young Van loved the gnome house. His father left it on the back deck and Van brought a different toy to stay in it every night, imagining his dolls and action figures enjoying legendary visits in a multi-colored, magical castle.

A month or so later, there was another gnome house on the deck when Van got home from school. This one was slightly larger, and the roof drooped slightly lower. It had a yellow star on a twig sticking cock-eyed from the roof's peak. That night there was a big party for Van's toys to celebrate the new construction. After that, a new house appeared every few weeks. Soon they lined the perimeter of the deck and started creeping out into the back yard.

"Dad, you should sell some of these, you know?" Van said when he was older. "Let's rent a table at the flea market and I bet you could make a bunch of money."

"No," he said.

"Why not?"

"They're shit," he replied.

"Well, let's give some of them away then."

"No, I told you. They're shit."

Van loved them. As more of the gnome houses appeared, the nightly gatherings of figures and dolls and stuffed animals grew in size and attendance. Van found some old strands of Christmas lights in the basement and asked his father to run them around the deck and the yard. To the distant sound of tinny music coming from his father's workshop, characters danced and laughed and chatted the night away.

As Van grew older, so did his father. The houses generated at a much slower rate and eventually stopped altogether. They filled the yard, high and low. Van had taken to hanging some of them from low branches in the few trees in the back, and they swayed above older, earth-bound models circling the trees' trunks. The bright colors had long ago faded to an almost uniform light brownish/grey, and what shingles were still attached were warped and split. Not long before his father was killed, Van asked him during one of their few conversations, "Dad, the houses. The gnome houses, you know?"

"What about them?"

"You spent so much time on them, put so much work in. But I never saw you take any pleasure in it."

"Why would I? They're shit."

"They're not, though. They're amazing."

His father put his beer down and looked Van straight in the eye, something he rarely did. "Well, they didn't bring her back, did they?" And he stood up and went to bed. Two months later he was killed by a hit and run driver. He had stopped by the side of the highway to help a motorist change a flat tire. As he was working on a stubborn lug nut a car swerved onto the shoulder and that was the end of Dennis Ryan.

That was the end of Dennis Ryan, but it wasn't the last of him. It wasn't the last of the witches' brew of emotion Van felt whenever thoughts of his father lumbered through his mind. The love and hate boys often feel for *that* man in their lives. That first, huge man. It took half a lifetime for Van to tease out the roots of the anger he felt for his father. He realized he had grown up blaming Dennis for his mother's disappearance. *He killed her!* Young Van devised dozens of horrible scenarios detailing how his father had murdered his wife and disposed of her body. That charge was weak, though, even in the court of a young child's mind. There was far too much eye-witness evidence of Dennis' devotion to his wife, his unequivocal love for her.

He drove her out of the house! That was the next silent accusation Van held in his heart. His father had made her leave, by making her hate him. It was a fault in his father's character that had made her run. It had been preventable, and the blame for her disappearance lay entirely on his father.

Many years later, when the piranha who lived in his mind stopped eating for a time, Van fell upon the third source of his anger, the true, defining source. *It was my fault she left.* He had blamed himself for his mother leaving, and the guilt he felt was impossible for a little big heart to live with. So, he turned it into anger and directed it straight at his poor father, whose only crime had been to love two people more than the entire world of people put together. Van never spoke to his father about his anger. He just kept in his belly, undigested, letting just enough escape from time to time to help fill the tub of Dennis Ryan's sadness. Van knew later what had always been obvious: his mother was sick, and her sickness had destroyed their world. It wasn't Dennis's fault, nor Van's, nor hers. The most tragic of tragedies are those that are blameless.

After the State Troopers left on the night of Dennis Ryan's death, Van went out onto the back deck. The very first gnome house his father had made still stood where it had first appeared. The wood was so rotten it was practically fused to the old wooden railing which ran around the deck. More than half of the small shingles were gone, and something was growing out of the crooked window. The tiny hinges were completely rusted, but Van managed to get the door of the house open. Inside was the stuffed bunny Van had placed in there many years before, his very first, and his favorite stuffed animal. His name was Mr. Flumps, although he had gone through numerous name changes since his mother had first set him in Van's crib. She had called him Mister Snugs, Admiral Snugsly, Floppy, Mister Flopsy and eventually Van had started calling him Mr. Flumps. He was the only thing Van had of his mother, and it had only seemed right that he should reside in the original gnome house.

His father had been right, though. It didn't bring her back.

8

convalescence

"... UP ... WAKE up ... wake up ... wake up ..." Van came to in a small, white room, inclined in a hi-tech hospital bed. A rhythmic, low-register female voice was punctuated over and over by a small annoying pinch on the lower part of his right arm, near the elbow. "... wake up ... wake up ..."

"Ouch! Fuck! Okay, I'm awake, goddamn it. I'm awake!" Van leaned up in his bed and felt pain wash over him before he saw the bandages on his left arm. His skull hurt, and he ran his hand over what felt like stitches near the front right side of his head. The muscles in his neck were yelling at him. And his left ankle. A nurse stood at his side, middle-age, short and heavy-set. She looked like she wanted to pinch him some more. "No! I'm awake, for fuck's sake."

"It is time to go, Van Ryan." Van's shoulders slumped in his mind.

"Fuck. Is that ... is it you? The thing?" Van knew the answer before he asked the question. The nurse stood perfectly still, her eyes pointing straight at him, but she looked vacant, hollow. A wax replica of a hospital nurse. Her name badge read 'Gina.' Van frowned.

"It is time to go, Van Ryan. You must get up now." Without the slightest change of expression, the nurse grabbed Van's unbandaged arm with one hand, and yanked the intravenous needle out of his arm with the other. She placed a piece of gauze in Van's left hand and had him press down on the welling blood. "Hold that."

"Ow! Motherf...!" A strong hand covered Van's mouth.

"Silence, Van Ryan. We must go, and we must not draw attention to ourselves." The nurse produced a wheelchair and Van found himself muscled into it. She pulled Van's duffel bag from somewhere and put it in his lap.

They wheeled recklessly through the hallways of the hospital at what Van was sure was an unsafe speed. Gina wasn't as talented at wheelchair driving as she was at abusing her patients. Each jostle, bump and sudden stop brought some pain awake resentfully in Van's body. "Goddamn it! Settle down!" As they rounded a corner, the wheelchair crashed into a young intern with an armload of files, sending them flying across the hallway.

"Please excuse us." Gena said in a strained voice, and she pushed past the young man before he could answer. They sped down long, brightly lit hallways, slowing briefly now and again to bang through sets of double-swinging doors. Signs for different rooms and clinics hung from the ceiling and were pasted on walls next to framed pictures of generic landscapes and plaques celebrating unknown people.

After the nurse slammed the wheelchair through the last set of doors, they were in the hospital lobby. Van gathered his courage and leapt out of the chair. He limped around and faced the nurse/entity, clutching his bag to his chest. "That's enough! Stop slamming me into shit! I'm not going any further with you!" The nurse looked at Van curiously, without rancor. There was a pause, and Van wondered if he had made a mistake.

"Get back in the chair, Van Ryan." The same empty, blank look Van was growing used to sat on the nurse's face.

"No. I'm leaving now. By myself. You can't stop me." Van felt weak and his body hurt in a dozen places, but he slowly backed away from the chair and the nurse, toward the sliding door of the hospital's entrance. The nurse said nothing. Over the loud beating of his heart, Van heard the buzz of patients and doctors, administrators and family members, milling and rushing and conducting business around the hospital lobby. For every step he took away from the wheelchair, that ambient noise grew louder, now with an edge that seemed to grow sharper. The nurse just stared her dead fisheye gaze at Van. There were harsh words and arguing around him now, yelling. He didn't want to take his eyes from Nurse Gena's, but he glanced around at the dozens of people in the lobby and saw faces of people already under stress begin to get angry. Everyone suddenly seemed to be yelling at someone else. There was a crash behind him, and Van spun around to see a young lady sprawled awkwardly on the floor next to a decorative planter which was smashed to bits. Over her was a thin man with long, shiny hair and wild eyes. He was sweating, and his hands were clenched into tight fists. Slowly, and then instantly, there was motion all around Van. Everywhere he looked people were grabbing and pushing each other, and the uncomfortable sound of things breaking mixed with the yelling to provide a frightening score to a bad, impromptu performance.

Van was aware that his right hand was growing hot. He lifted it to his face and saw the slightest hint of purple whisps course across his palm. He spun and looked at the nurse. "Gina" held the same steady, unrevealing look, and she stood oblivious to the chaos growing exponentially around them both. "You!" Van yelled. "This is you! Stop this right now! Stop it!" A man careened into Van, spinning. His head was bleeding, and his shirt was torn. "Stop it!" Van yelled again. The nurse gestured toward the wheelchair in front of her. "Fine! Fine." Van fell back into the chair reluctantly. "Damn you."

Around them the violence and turmoil didn't stop all at once. Instead, it unwound; it slowed itself like a carousel when the ride is over. People holding onto other people let go of them and stepped away. The yelling quieted and then stopped, and people stared at each other in confusion, wondering why they were sweating and shaking. Those who worked in the hospital instinctively responded to fresh blood and injuries.

The post-riot chaos extended outside the hospital, and the nurse navigated the wheelchair through the front door and off to one side, away from the crowd. "Sit there, Van Ryan." She indicated a metal bench off to the side of the entrance. "Stay here." Van did as he was instructed. As he removed himself from the wheelchair and sat on the bench, a sudden change came over the nurse's face. She seemed suddenly aware, like someone who is woken in the middle of sleepwalking. Her eyes darted all around her, trying to understand the activity happening in and around the lobby as policemen, security guards, doctors and nurses moved hurriedly around her. The nurse realized at last that she was holding the handles of the wheelchair and let go, as though they were burning her hands. She was growing more confused, and as her gaze swept the crowd, she noticed Van staring at her.

"It's okay," Van mouthed to her, nodding his head. But she shook him off and, leaving the wheelchair, made her way dazedly back into the hospital.

Almost immediately, a late-model black Mercedes sedan pulled up to the curb in front of where Van sat. The passenger window slid down smoothly, and the driver, a man with a thick mustache, leaned over and yelled something to Van. Van stood up and walked closer to the car to hear the man. "Van Ryan, get in the car," he said, and Van's heart sunk again. He knew there was no point in arguing, so he opened the door. A sample case with the name of some obscure medication on it and some brochures lay on the passenger seat. Van threw these and his bag into the back seat and eased into the custom-contoured leather passenger seat. "Put on your seatbelt, please, Van Ryan. This is not a safe form of transportation." The man looked at Van directly, and Van couldn't tell if the entity was being ironic.

Van was quiet as they pulled away from the hospital. He closed his eyes and breathed for a few minutes. Eventually he asked, "Where are we going?"

"To the bus station, Van Ryan. You must board a bus and continue your journey. Too much time has been wasted."

"What about my truck? Where is it?"

"These things don't matter anymore, Van Ryan."

"What? Don't matter? That's my goddamn truck! I still owe money on it. Where is it?"

"We were able to salvage your possessions, but the truck was destroyed in the collision. It will do you no good now. We will ensure you have transportation for your mission."

"You caused that crash, didn't you? Wasn't that you - the driver of the car that drifted into me and started that little fender-bender? Trying to teach me a lesson or something? And you were the ambulance driver that took me to the hospital, right? And the doctor that stitched me up?"

"No, Van Ryan." The driver of the car focused on the road in front of him while he spoke. "Your accident was an arbitrary event. Our kind cannot control everything. It was unplanned and it has impacted your task negatively."

"Sorry about that, then." Van held up his bandaged arm. "'Impacted' me negatively too."

"We can stimulate and motivate you, and suggest an objective, but no one controls the world around you, Van Ryan. We do not have control over the weather, for instance. We cannot account for chaos, and neither can you."

"You can control the hell out of a mob of people in a hospital, though, huh? What was that? I thought you were a one-human-at-a-time kind of puppet master."

"It is true that our kind can typically only "inhabit," or manipulate one of your weaker-willed species at a time. It is possible, however, to stimulate certain general feelings or emotions in a small group of your kind, depending on how far we are from the subjects."

"I could feel something in my hand while you were doing that. I thought whatever you put in there was supposed to be 'inert.'"

"It is, for the most part, but it may react slightly if one of our kind emits energy in its presence."

"Can you use it to control me? Are you controlling me now?"

"No, Van Ryan. What we told you before is true. We cannot control you directly. But we can compel you indirectly, as you have seen."

Van looked out the window. "How long can you maintain your influence on someone?"

The man turned his left blinker on and made a smooth turn, observing traffic laws and guidelines perfectly. "As long as necessary, Van Ryan."

"Why don't you just send one of your zombies to save your pal, or whatever, then? Why me?"

"Our ability to directly influence your kind's behavior weakens with distance. If we were to send this man, for example," the driver pointed this thumb at himself, "we would lose control over him before he reached the objective. It must be you, Van Ryan."

"Lucky me," Van said, and looked out the window. They rode in silence through the busy city streets.

9

Jazz Man's Hands

THE BIRMINGHAM GREYHOUND BUS Station stood where it had for more than sixty years, directly across from the old City Hall. The squared-off, tiered, shoebox lines told of the building's mid-century origin, and the patched and faded, cream-colored brick dared pedestrians to tease out tales of protest and violence from its sturdy bones. Faint hints of pigment and paint from the building's original construction still showed through in places. From certain angles, one could almost see the smallest flecks of red showing beneath newer coats, blood shed by freedom fighters. A tall, dark, contemporary plastic sign mocked the steady old, proud predecessor that had hung there before.

Van got out of the car, leaving a very confused pharmaceutical salesman wondering why he was idling in the taxi lane with taxi drivers lined up behind him, honking. It was a small station to serve such a large city. The inside was a semi-circle of ticket windows, eight or ten small iron benches designed to be too uncomfortable to lie down on, and a pair of restrooms of questionable hygiene. It was a typical bus-station snapshot, populated by a carefully crafted cross-section of working class and lower-income Americans. Young and old folks. All races, sex, sizes and genders. Aside from hitchhiking, the bus was the cheapest way to travel. For that reason, riding the bus meant riding with fellow marginalized members of the great American Dream. Some riders were homeless. Some suffered from mental illness. Some were on the run. People minded their own business, for the most part. They were headed up the road, to a better place. They were meeting family or friends or had a job opportunity somewhere. Or they were just headed to another shitty bus stop in an inescapable line of them. On this day, one passenger found himself boarding because an alien dressed in a mustachioed salesman skin had dropped him off at the taxi stand and sent him along unwillingly, toward what could only be some fucked up final destination.

Van bought his $20 ticket to Memphis. He had no idea how much blood was left in his plastic card-shaped bank account, but that didn't seem to matter now. The world of things which "mattered" seemed to have sunk in upon itself until the dense mass of Van's mission and the things attracted by its gravity could be measured along a few long highways and a dingy old bus station. Van grabbed his bag and climbed aboard the filling bus.

He had purchased his ticket late, and the bus was mostly full. He made his way down the aisle and the folks he passed either turned their gaze away or stared scarily at him. Van's ticket was for a window seat at the rear of the bus, and as he approached, he could see someone else was already seated there. Van drew up to his row, stowed his bag in the bin above with his good arm and stood with his ticket in his hand. The man in Van's seat gazed out the window at the weathered bus station with a look like fondness, as he might have looked at an old companion. "Excuse me," Van said. The man turned slowly in his seat. He looked at Van with a close-mouthed, condescending frown.

"Excuse me?" The man said.

"I'm sorry ... um ... excuse me ..." Van felt flustered by the man's gaze.

"Oh, excuse *you*, you mean." He shook his head scornfully.

"Uh ..."

The man laughed and slapped his leg. "Ha! Got you! I'm messing with you, son." He extended a gnarled, half-clenched hand to Van. A hint of pain crossed his face as he and Van shook. "Clifford Merritt Jr. Friends call me 'Riff.'" He patted the aisle seat and scooted closer to the window.

"Hey there. Nice to meet you." Van started to wave his ticket toward the window seat the man was stealing from him, but he was tired and let it go. He sat down next to the aisle and settled in as the bus lurched off toward Memphis.

Clifford Merritt Jr, whose friends called him "Riff," was also on his way to Memphis. He was an elderly fellow. Van put him in his early to mid-70's. His smile shined through a face that was dark and weary. He was a half-dozen days out of his last shave, and the grey scrub growing from his cheeks and chin looked ill and angry. The whites of his eyes wore a yellowish hue, the overt kindness in them clad in age and ill-health. He wore an off-white, button-down shirt with many missed washings around the collar, and a dark green jacket with soiled and frayed cuffs. Sensing Van's appraisal of him, Riff Merritt hitched the jacket up by the lapels as though about to give a speech, and he pulled on his shirt cuffs until they poked out of the worn jacket sleeves. He patted himself proudly on the chest. "Man's got to have a jacket, son. Pride in one's appearance and all." Van nodded his head and smiled. The man eyed up Van's perpetual t-shirt and jeans. "You could use one yourself, I think."

"Not unless it's a funeral, I'm afraid. Or court. One suit, black. That's about it." The man gave a barking laugh, which brought about a coughing fit. He pulled a ragged handkerchief from his breast pocket and hacked into it. When he was done coughing, the handkerchief disappeared back into his pocket, and a bemused smile returned to his face.

"Don't know when men stopped wearing jackets. And hats! Hats, too. Man never left the doggone house without a jacket and a hat in my day. That's one of the reasons this world's all cocked up, you hear me? People don't give a god damn how they look anymore. Respect! Starts with yourself." He tapped his chest and looked at Van. "Now I ain't ragging on you, though. Ain't your fault this world's gone to hell. What was your name again, there?"

"Van Ryan, sir. You're probably right though. My wardrobe could probably use an upgrade." The man laughed.

"Now you're talking! Make a man out of you before we pull into the next station. Ha! And don't you go on with the 'sir' and whatnot. Riff Merritt done worked for a damn living. Know what I mean? Never put myself above others. You hear me?" Van nodded. "Well, except for maybe telling young fellas to put on a jacket once in a bit, I guess. Ha! Yeah, never trust a man wants you to call him 'sir.'" His eyes shined. He glanced out the window at the road running by, and gave a few more coughs into his hanky. His chest made a rumbling sound, like something was loose inside. It reminded Van of a rock tumbler he had as a kid. Riff hitched up his lapels again. "Yessir. A man needs a jacket." He chuckled to himself. "So, where you headed, son?"

"I honestly don't know for sure." Van pointed down the aisle and out the front windshield of the bus. "That way. Memphis. Farther, maybe." He shrugged.

"Mmhmm." Riff eyed the bruise on Van's forehead, and the bandages on his arm. "Looks like you run into some trouble, huh? How's the other fella look?"

"Ha. No, just a little fender-bender."

"Wasn't no trouble with the law, was it?"

"No. Just with cars."

Riff smiled a big, white smile. "Ha! Good, good. You don't need trouble with the law." The fine condition of his teeth shone in bright contrast to the rest of his poorly worn profile. He saw Van's attention drawn to his grin and it grew only wider. "I see you looking!" Riff tapped his front tooth with a ragged, dirty fingernail. "All real. Serious biz. Seventy-three years old and only one cavity my entire life." He beamed with pride like he was an Olympic athlete showing off his collection of medals. "I've traveled round the world, known folks, loved some ladies, played music for a whole lotta ears, you know? But fun and fame, all those songs and stories all fade away down the road, you hear me? Come and gone." He tapped his tooth again to show Van the durability. "My "immortal ivories," though! How you like that? One day they'll be all's left of me, underground. Forever." He chuckled and coughed something wet into his hanky. "Some scientists will dig 'em up a thousand years from now."

The size of the world had shrunk to just their two seats. The other passengers were just scenery. "What about you, Mr. Merritt? Mind if I ask where you're off to?"

"Man, you just won't quit with that stuff, huh? Just call me Riff, son. Riff. Hell, I'm headed same place as you." He pointed to the windshield of the bus. "We're all headed *that* way, to the next station, right? When we get there, maybe some of us will roll on together to another one, maybe not. It's like this here bus. You pick a route, point this sucker in one direction, and we'll roll on until we run out of gas. Or she breaks down. Who knows? But that's where the trip ends. And we should be grateful we made it that far. None of us know where we're headed, really. Just trying to make it to the end."

"I hear you. We don't have much control over it anyway, I guess."

"Well, I wouldn't say that, now. Life's going to sweep you along some, it's true. Like a big river. But we make an awful lot of choices along the way that paddle us in one direction or another."

"Yeah, maybe so."

"'Maybe so' my ass, son! Ha! Everyone has dreams and goals. Plans and whatnot. Destinations!" He waved at the windshield. "But about the one thing in life we can count on is that nothing, *nothing* at all turns out the way you pictured it." Van nodded his head. "Yeah, you partner up with life to cock it all up in the end." He laughed and coughed into his hanky, and Van thought he caught a glimpse of something red there. "Don't sweat it, son. We're all just memories, is all, anyways." Some of Riff's memories surfaced, and Van saw them chase each other around in the space behind his tired eyes. "Yeah. I was a drummer, in the day. A jazz man. That was me. Played with some of the greats for a set or two." He smiled to himself as his hands came out in front of him, playing arthritic beats with invisible sticks. He winced as his hands moved, while he pictured himself playing the big halls and the dark, smoky clubs.

"No kidding? That's awesome!" Van was impressed.

"Yeah, man." Coughing. "You play music?"

Van shook his head regretfully. "Only on the radio. I took a few guitar lessons once, but I never really had the knack."

"The knack? What in the hell is that? You mean you didn't have the heart, son!" He punctuated the assertion with a sharp poke in Van's chest. Van looked at him doubtfully. "Hell yeah. I know people talk about 'natural talent' and whatnot. You probably thought you didn't have long enough fingers, or good enough concentration or whatever. Shit. Man, I played with a guy for a while only had eight fingers. Eight. And he could wail on the piano like I've never heard, you know? He had heart, though. He *wanted* it. You get bit for real and it's all over, man. I'm not busting your chops, though. You just didn't want it. We all got something different."

"Yeah," Van looked at his lap. "Maybe so." They swayed along for a few miles more and Van turned again to his seat mate. "How about you? When did you figure that's what you wanted?"

"Ha! Now you're talking, man. Shit, I always knew I wanted to play drums. I played for years before I ever even saw a real drum. True story. When I was a boy, I used to hear the rhythm everywhere I went. Everything had its tempo. You put two things together and soon they're talking together, you know? Sharing a beat. Sitting in class and the teacher's writing on the chalkboard, and kid's chewing gum in the seat behind me. Other folks are walking up and down the halls. Didn't take much before I was teasing out my part, tapping out my own part of this big-ass rhythm going on around me, right?" Some coughing worked into air-drumming, the right hand banging an old school-desk memory with an over-used handkerchief. Before it disappeared into Riff's jacket, Van was sure he spotted a bright red stain. Riff's voice got quieter. There was a wheeze behind the words now.

"You alright, man?" Riff did his thing and kept the narrative rolling like Van wasn't even there.

"Music was my life. Which was good. I was lucky, for sure. You don't want just *life* to be your life. No sir. Shit will get tied up and twisted like that. No sir, better to have a purpose, you know? A distraction. Hell, an obsession even. Ha. Music. I listened to it nonstop and played it every chance I got. Wrote it, recorded it. Spoke it. Ha. Loved to it, too. Oh yeah." He was sweating, and coughing overtook him for a bit. When it subsided, he rocked back and forth slowly, and quietly watched himself dance in the window. "You do at least *listen* to music, I hope?"

"Oh yeah," Van replied. "All the time." Riff smiled again.

"What kind?"

"All kinds. Guitar music, mostly. Rock and roll. I do like some R&B, though. Funk."

"Jazz? You like jazz at all?" Riff asked hopefully.

"Some, I guess. I don't know much about it, to be honest. I have a Thelonious Monk album and some Charlie Parker, I think." Riff shook his head in mock disappointment.

"Well, I won't hold it against you none, I suppose. I'll tell you what though, none of those other kinds of music you mentioned can hold a single damn candle to jazz. Rock and roll? Ha. That's like a Sunday funny paper artist compared to Picasso, that is." He took a deep breath. "Both of them can draw, sure, and the cartoon guy might be fine at what he does. And more folks read the funny papers than go to museums, so he's more popular too. But anyone who knows anything about painting, about the work and skill and damn genius in someone like Picasso's work, couldn't possibly compare them in the first place, you know? Rock and jazz are like that."

"I hear you," Van said. "In the end, though, doesn't it just matter what people want to hear?" Riff rounded on him suddenly, with a furious, huge-eyed glare. Van shrank a bit.

"How dare you!" Riff bellowed, but his anger ran out of fuel and he sank back with a full-bellied laugh. He was coughing up fair-sized wads of phlegm now, and the color white in his handkerchief was disappearing quickly. He wheezed at Van. "Ha. You should see your face, man. Ha. True story, though. You're right, you are right. True story. Here we are talking about classes of music, and you go and cut right to the heart of the goddamn thing. What's popular." He chuckled and wheezed and coughed and spit and chuckled a bit more. He shrank back into his seat and didn't sit up straight again.

"Hey, are you okay, Riff? You don't look so good, man." Van said. He reached in, trying to touch Riff somehow. To help him, to find the sickness. Riff waved him off.

"I'm fine. I'm fine." Van noticed that the noise of the bus tires had faded away. The bus was hurtling down the highway as it had been, but it wasn't rocking anymore, and it seemed the only noise was this lonesome conversation between himself and a sick, old, gregarious jazz man. Riff's cough was slow and low now. The coagulated rumble of a lifetime's congestion deep in the caverns of the man. "I'm fine." He managed a stretched smile, lit more from memory than from events of the moment. He patted Van's hand with his own, and a vision struck Van of a dreamlike life of pride and joy, loneliness and profound wonder. And the last pat was for years of regret, passed on in a random bus, on a random night, to an insignificant stranger by one bony, leathery hand with knuckles the size of walnuts. "You know, man? You remind me of my son. Yup."

"Oh yeah?"

"Yes indeed. You look about his age. He would've been twenty-seven, twenty-eight about now." Riff drifted somewhere in the bus window. "You got kids? Family?"

"No. They're all gone."

"You're awful young for that. Sorry to hear it."

"What happened to your boy?" Van asked.

"Prison. Died in prison." He was staring into his lap.

"I'm sorry."

"Yeah, he was always no good. Ran the streets his whole life. Gangs and whatnot. He wasn't right. Thought he was some kind of outlaw or something. Kept telling me, 'I'm the hero, pop! I'm the hero! That cop out there, *he's* the villain. Not me!' In the end though, it was the villain inside that got him, you know?"

"Hell, I wasn't much better," Riff said. "After my glory years I spent a lot of time on the same streets, strung out on this or that. I had sticky fingers, back then, too. You gotta steal to feed a habit like I had. When I finally got sober, and got myself right with the law, I told myself I was going to pass on my experiences to my kid, so he wouldn't make the same mistakes as me. He was still just a boy, then. I was going to sit him down and tell him my stories about being on the streets and all, so he would make better decisions than I did. It was like ... it would give all the shit I went through a purpose, you know? Give it some meaning, instead of me just being another animal in the gutter."

"I'm sure it wasn't like that."

"Yeah. It was like that. You never do know who you're sitting next to, son. Not really. Don't forget that. Yeah, I done some dirt over the years, believe me. Done some folks real wrong. Tried to make it right, but ..."

"Did you manage to? Make it right?"

"No. I tried. I did try. But no, I never did balance the scales, you know? I tried. And I couldn't do anything for my kids, either. I tried to tell them my stories, but kids don't want to hear that mess. They don't want to listen to *anyone*, least of all their dirty, old, junky jazz drummer daddy." He coughed violently until it seemed as though something came loose inside of him. He sat back, sweating, and just looked out the window quietly for a while.

"You believe in God, son?" His voice was barely more than a whisper, now. He had stopped sweating and his skin was grey and waxy. Van was sure Riff was dying, and he knew he should yell for the bus driver to stop the bus and get help, but he was afraid that if he looked away, Riff would disappear before he looked back. Besides, he couldn't say for certain there *was* a driver anymore, and the rest of the passengers had long since faded behind the bright light shining on Van and Riff from the overhead console.

"No," Van spoke softly. "I don't think I do." Riff nodded his head knowingly, gazing in the distance through the seatback in front of him.

"Me neither, son. Me neither." He was quiet for a moment. "But I sure in the hell tried, you know?" He managed a chuckle through the disease in his chest. "Yes sir." His breath was fast and raspy now. Short and painful. "When I was getting off the dope. Sitting in a cell. When I was living on the streets. All those times. I tried so hard. I went to church. I said the words, waved my hands around, tried to get someone's attention. Anyone, you know? People yelling and praising and testifying ..." He paused and tried to breathe, "... and me standing in the middle, trying to see what they were all looking at. Got on my knees and I begged for help, and when I stood up and raised my eyes, all I saw was some storefront church drop-ceiling." Cough. Wheeze. Rattle. "As many tiles missing as there was holes in my soul." His eyes searched the bus ceiling for that missing salvation and returned to match the seriousness on Van's face. "I wanted to blame shit on someone. 'It was all God's plan!' You know? Shit. Can't nobody save you but *you*, man. That ..." The coughing took on a new personality now. Gone were the cute little fits. The light skirmishes his lungs had been engaging in were through and the battle became pitched and heavy. He stood up suddenly, precariously, and motioned toward the aisle as his chest dislodged more and more bits of himself into his bright red handkerchief.

"Riff! Shit, man!" The old man pushed past where Van sat in his seat and made for the narrow aisle. He looked determined, as though a reservoir of tasty oxygen was waiting for him there. "Fuck! Help!" Van yelled. Riff took two steps in the aisle toward the front and slowly dropped to one knee.

Other people entered the scene now. Bit players, forgotten passengers. Heads turning, noticing an opportunity to appropriate someone else's pain, make it about themselves. "Oh my god!"

"Look out! Driver! Driver!"

"Oh lord, someone get that man a doctor!"

"I can't watch this!"

The interior lights came up, and Van could feel the bus leave the comforting flow of the highway and slow its way to the rough scattered gravel of the shoulder. Riff had made it now as far as he was going, and the coughing folded him in half like laughter. He rolled on his back, gasping for breath. Van reached for him, wanting to touch him, to make him better. The need drew Van to his own knees and somehow, he managed to clumsily cradle Riff's head on his legs. Slowly the spasms passed, the bus was quiet, and they were all left with a thick, slow, ragged breathing. Riff's body unwound and relaxed some in Van's arms. He leaned down and stared into the dying man's eyes. They were fading. Van stretched out a wan smile. "It's going to be okay, man."

Riff's features relaxed, like his body, and in doing so seemed to reveal an underlying grin that had been there all along. "I know ..." he whispered, and his eyes glistened. He reached his right arm up and touched Van's wrist. He smiled with joy into Van's eyes, like a child. A quiet voice sighed, like a soft rustle of spring leaves, "*I made it.*" One more cough and two torturous breaths and Clifford Merritt Jr.'s life was over.

The space on the bus got louder and brighter and larger, and Van just sat looking into the face that was Riff's, trying to make sense of his last comment. "*I made it.*" The bus was nowhere, tens of miles of straight, dark highway in both directions. It was the middle of the night, in the middle of nowhere. Made it where, Riff?

Eventually, flashing lights broke up the night and people with the authority to pull dead bodies off buses took Riff away. Everyone sat back in their seats and the bus driver turned off the interior light and merged his way right back into the slipstream. People were loud and the road was loud. Van placed his hand flat on the seat that had been Riff's. It was still warm.

"I made it."

10

YIP'S ATTENTION

VAN'S LEG WAS STARTING to cramp. He was thirteen years old, and his class was on a field trip to the Fernbank Museum of Natural History in Atlanta. He had been one of the first on the school bus and had grabbed a choice seat toward the back. He knew it was an hour-long trip to get there, and he had brought a beat-up Stephen King paperback to help pass the time. He pulled it out of his jacket pocket and started leafing through, trying to find his place as the other kids laughed and yelled, pushing and insulting each other as they boarded. Van just put his head down, tuned out all the noise and dug into the book.

He was lost with Danny Torrance in the halls of the Overlook hotel, and he didn't look up at first when she spoke to him. "Excuse me. Is this seat taken?"

"Nope. Help yourself."

"Great, thanks. Whatcha' reading?"

Van turned the cover of the paperback so that she could see it, and that was the first time he looked at her. She had the most piercing, light blue eyes he had ever seen. Her hair was long and brown and well brushed and feathered. The smell of hairspray put its arm around his shoulder and settled in with them. "Ooh, I love Stephen King! I haven't read that one, though. Is it scary?" Van admitted that it was. "So, what's your name?" She asked him.

"Van."

"Pleased to meet you, Van. My name is Ypsilanti Day, but you can call me Yip for short." And she turned back toward the front and began talking about her home, her parents, her saxophone. Van had a hard time focusing on the conversation. When Yip turned around, her leg came to rest touching Van's leg ever so slightly, and he spent the rest of the bus ride trying to maintain that subtle contact without drawing attention to it. It was electric.

When they got to the museum, they both filed off the bus and Yip found a group of her friends and waved to Van as she took off with them.

The next time Van saw Ypsilanti Day she was bathed in the bright, hot stage lights at John E. Tuppen Middle School. She was Alice, in *Alice in Wonderland*, and to Van she was magnificent. She wasn't a good actor, but that wasn't her fault. She hit her marks, said her lines. It was just impossible for her to disappear into the role. She wasn't Alice, she was Yip. She was dazzling.

Will was playing the Mad Hatter in the play, and he was fine when Yip wasn't on stage. When he shared a scene with her, though, Will disappeared. She ate him up; ate him, the other kids, the scenery, the narrative, all of it. Gone. Just her on stage, long and thin, hair tinted a strange orange-ish color from over-the-counter bleaching products. Eyes on fire from the lights. When Yip took her bows, the crowd stood and cheered, and she looked both happy for the attention and embarrassed by it. When the cast all took the stage for their final bow together, Will held Yip's hand and they laughed and smiled at each other, and Van experienced jealousy for the first time in his life. It was hard and fast, and it cheated when it struck him. No warning, no time to throw up defenses. Just a hammer to the heart and a fleeting feeling of hatred for his best friend.

"So, what did you think?" Will asked him later.

"It was awesome, man. You were really good."

"No, dumbass. About Yip? Alice?"

"Oh. Yeah, she was great too."

Will looked off into the distance. "Yeah, she's amazing."

And that's just how it went. It all leaned toward Will. He had classes with Yip that Van wasn't in. When Van found her at lunch, Will was already there. Fate seemed to conspire somehow to always put them together. Van wanted to talk to her. Wanted to be alone with her. But it was already too late. There was no point in trying.

Yip's parents loved Will. That's what Yip said, anyway. Will told Van he had met her parents a dozen times, and each time they gave him a distant look and vague greeting. "I swear, man, I don't think they even recognize me. It's the exact same thing every time I 'meet' them." The Days were nice people, Will said. They just had absolutely no interest in Yip, her friends, her life, or anything about her. They treated her as though she were invisible at home, and when she spoke to them, they seemed surprised that she still lived there.

Mr. Day was a lawyer and he specialized in corporate law. His firm had formerly been retained by a major cereal company, whose headquarters was in Michigan. Once, during his commute between the cereal company's major plant and the Detroit Metropolitan Airport, Mr. Day passed through the city of Ypsilanti, population 20,000 Michiganders. The city of Ypsilanti made no significant impression on Mr. Day; in fact, his commute on Interstate 94 took him well to the south of the city, so he never really got much of a look at it, but the name "Ypsilanti" was tantalizing to Mr. Day. Fanciful. When Mrs. Day somehow became pregnant years later, it was the first word that came to Mr. Day's mind when they discussed a name for the baby, and as Mrs. Day had nothing better to offer, Ypsilanti Day it was. It was the most creativity and imagination either of the adult Days ever put into raising their child, but a name is a powerful thing, and Mr. Day's one-time whimsy gifted his daughter all she needed to overcome the void in her identity that life in a hollow home engendered.

For her part, Mrs. Day was too busy for family. There were meetings and appointments and speeches and lunches. Thankfully, Mr. Day's income allowed her the opportunity to hire an assistant to do things like shop, drop things off and pick things up, like Yip when she missed the bus from school. Mrs. Day was the President of the local School Board, and as such she had to maintain membership and an active presence in every civic association in town. Thus, the meetings, appointments, speeches, and lunches. Everyone in town knew Mrs. Day, even if very few people liked her much. "God, what a busybody," is what most people said about her, but the truth is that no one else really wanted to be President of the School Board, so they smiled and ate her dry coffee cake (made by her assistant) and tried to remember what policies she had advocated for in her last speech in case they had to talk to her.

Mrs. Day loved being President of the School Board, but she loved even more the idea of being a member of City Council. In her mind she already was a member of City Council, she just hadn't assumed her seat yet. She had only to officially "launch her campaign," and the rest was a formality. "I really won't have time for this, you know, once I launch my campaign," she would say to the girl who lived in her house whenever she asked a question. Mrs. Day had been preparing to "launch her campaign" for years. The truth, though, is that she was far too busy being President of the School Board, and maintaining an active membership at every civic association in town to run for City Council, which was for the best because in addition to "God, what a busybody," the other thing people said about Mrs. Day was, "Who the hell does she think she is? I remember when she used to ... on the ...with ..." That kind of reputation might cut it on the School Board, but not so much on City Council.

Other kids placed on involuntary autopilot by their parents would have handled it differently than Ypsilanti Day. Other kids might have cut school, drank, experimented with drugs, gotten pregnant, shoplifted, huffed paint and so on, but not Yip. It's true she didn't mind a little extra attention in her world. The occasional school plays and pageants helped a lot in that regard, but she never let the applause or the popularity go to her head. She soaked it in until she was full and then turned it off.

On those days Van's father forgot to make dinner Van would head over to Will's. He had a standing invitation from Will's mom, and she was an awesome cook. At one point, Yip started showing up for dinner as well, and soon she also had a standing invite. Over pot roast, ham, or meatloaf the conversation was always lively, and the attention was always on Yip. After dinner, when Van and Will used to play video games or shoot hoops in Will's driveway, now Van rode his bike home, alone, while Will and Yip settled onto the old couch in the den and watch HBO.

Van would have liked to invite Yip to dinner at his house just once, but the atmosphere in the Ryan household was similar to that in the small lounge or office in a hospital used to inform folks that a loved one was terminally ill. Out in front of the house it may be a beautiful spring day, but once one passed the threshold into the Ryan residence, color deflated, and air ceased circulating. If you didn't proceed directly through the house and onto the back deck, where the colorful appeal of fantastical gnome houses breathed life back into life, there was the sense that one might remain lost in the Ryan house, wandering through the dry, grey, commonsense floor plan forever. Van couldn't bring himself to invite Yip there.

So, Yip ate at Will's house, and sat at his table at lunch, and they worked on homework together, and ran lines together when there was a theater production at school. Will's mom would drop the three of them off at the roller rink, but during couple's skate it was Will skating backward, holding Yip's waist. They were a couple in high school, walking awkwardly down the halls with their arms wrapped around each other, getting in trouble making out by Will's locker.

Van dated some girls. Girls liked Van. He was tall and handsome, and a childhood around sadness had taught him how to tell jokes and laugh about things which tended to drag other people down. But the relationships never lasted, they never stuck. Intimacy, to Van, was like cheap chewing gum, a burst of pleasant flavor and then senseless, flavorless monotony. Or it was like starving and trying to satiate the hunger with the same fucking gum, while an endless, sustainable cornucopia of fresh nourishment laughed at your best friend's stupid jokes in front of you.

One day Van went to war, and Yip and Will got married while he was gone. He got a letter one day telling him, and a creased photo of them as a couple. Van was happy for them, and he wrote a letter back telling them so. He was happy. Van got sand and bullets and Will got Yip, and Yip got all the attention and stability that she needed. It was meant to be that way, Van thought. He never really had a chance with her. Everyone got what they deserved in the end.

11

LOST Days

VAN LISTENED TO YIP'S message three times before he got out of bed. The missed call alert had been flashing on his phone as soon as he opened his eyes. He sat up and leaned against the rickety headboard and the crappy hotel pillows and listened to her voice over and over. "Van? Van, it's Yip. Um ... what's going on? Will still hasn't come home. Yeah ...it's been three days and he hasn't been home. I called his phone and ... nothing, you know? I've tried you a few times too. Where the hell are you guys? I went to your apartment, but you weren't there, either." Quiet for a moment. Just her soft breathing. "Please, Van. Call me. I feel like something's really wrong."

Van turned the shower water as hot as he could handle it and let it burn Riff's death, the top layers of his skin and the last hundred miles off his body. The wounds from his accident ached less this morning. He dug his nails into his scalp and let the complimentary thimble-full of hotel shampoo do its job. Yip's call spooked him. He had checked his phone and sure enough, she had called him twice before this morning. Why hadn't he heard her call? How long ago had he checked in? He got out of the shower, looked at the date on his phone and sat back down on the bed.

After they had taken Riff's body away, the bus had stopped and unloaded everyone at the nearest station, in Tupelo, Mississippi. The passengers were all loaded onto a new bus, one free of the last moments and memories of Mr. Clifford Merritt, and they all dropped as one back into the paved slipstream toward Memphis. Van couldn't bring himself to get on the bus. It felt like a betrayal. He just grabbed his bag and walked away. He hopped in a cab outside of the station and had them drop him off at the nearest budget chain hotel.

That apparently had been the day before yesterday, two days ago. Van stared at the date on his phone, trying to make sense of it. He checked, and sure enough, Yip had called him the day before. Why hadn't he answered? Why couldn't he remember anything? Leaving the bus station and checking in to the hotel were clear in his mind. Where did the time go between going to sleep the night before last and waking up this morning?

So, there was a day lost. A day of his life gone. Absent. AWOL. Where does a day like that go? Does it just fall into the past, into the box of memories that fade organically over time? Or would he get a do-over? Maybe it would get shuffled into his future, and forgotten events would just be overwritten, like a video game save file.

He had to call Yip. He had to tell her somehow that Will would not be coming home. Will. What about Will? Van realized that he hadn't given Will much thought since he left Georgia. Fleeting memories of Will's death and the afternoon violence in the mountain meadow rang his doorbell and then ran away before he could answer, like neighborhood kids playing "ding-dong ditch." The memories had no emotion attached to them. Van felt more sorrow at the contented passing of a man he knew on a bus for a few short hours than for the man he had called his best friend for most of his life.

At least he was clean again. He felt awake and charged, even if he was confused. He could do this. He could sort everything out. He sat on the edge of the bed and listened to Yip's message again, "... Please, Van. Call me ..."

Riff, though. What about Riff? Van thought about the men carrying Riff's lifeless body from the bus. It didn't sound like the old man had anyone who was going to look for him, or care for his remains. The least Van could do was call someone and see if he could be of any assistance. Van picked up the room phone. "Front desk. Can I help you?" A male voice, pleasant and cheerful.

"Yes, hello. This is Van Ryan. I'm in one of your rooms upstairs. I was wondering if you could find a phone number for me? I need to call the local hospital."

"Van Ryan."

"Yes. That's right."

"Van Ryan." Van heard it. He heard it, but he didn't want to admit what he was hearing. The pleasant and cheerful voice had dropped half an octave and achieved a perfect monotone. He could see the front desk clerk in his mind, see the man's dull, vapid stare. "We already went through all of this yesterday."

"What?"

"We had this conversation yesterday. We told you it was useless to involve yourself in the affairs of that man any further. Your path and his have parted ways."

"Goddamn it ...seriously? Are you ..."

"You were very agitated yesterday. Your thoughts were not linear. You were useless to us in that condition, so we helped you rest."

"Helped me rest? What the hell does that mean?"

"You were exhausted and confused. We helped you achieve sleep earlier than you might have on your own."

"What? You put me to sleep? I thought you couldn't control me?"

"We *helped* you fall asleep, Van Ryan. It is a different process."

"What ...?"

"Enough, Van Ryan. There has been enough time wasted. Get your things and go to the front of the hotel."

"Fuck you. I'm not leaving yet. I'm starving and I need a cup of coffee, and then we'll talk about the next step." Van hung up the phone.

He got dressed, walked out of his room, and turned down the hall toward the elevators. Halfway down the hall, there was a young, attractive housekeeper with an armload of clean, folded sheets. The door of the room behind her was open, and she was obviously in the middle of re-making the bed. Van caught her eye as he drew close to her, and they shared a spontaneous smile. "Morning," Van said, and tipped his head to her without breaking his stride, or his smile. She held his gaze.

"Hello," she replied pleasantly, and as the last syllable left her mouth, Van saw her features change before him. The muscles in her face went slack, and the smile evaporated. Her dark, full eyes, which had struck Van just a moment before turned blank and unfocused. The pupils grew large as she looked at nothing. She stepped out into the middle of the hallway, blocking his path. "Van Ryan!" Van stood tall and thrust his chest out. He was out of patience.

"Get out of my way, goddamn it!"

"Go back to your room and retrieve your things."

"No. I'm going to get something to eat and make a phone call," Van said. The housekeeper turned and picked up a ring of keys that had been lying on her cart. She leafed through them until she found one that was longer than the rest. She raised it up until it was pointing directly at her right eye.

"No! Wait! Wait! Alright, goddamn it. I'll get my stuff. Let her go!"

"We will wait here until you return with your belongings, Van Ryan." The woman was completely still. She held the key inches from her eye. Van headed back toward his room and grabbed his things. When he returned, she was still in the exact same position.

"Okay. Let her go!" As he had seen with the entity's victims before, the woman resumed her demeanor as though she was waking from sleepwalking. She dropped her arm and looked around her in confusion. She saw Van and smiled warmly.

"Hello."

"Morning," Van nodded to her, and headed to the elevator.

When Van emerged from the hotel the Tupelo sun was high in the late morning sky, and the heat was already sticking around his arms and legs like cling-wrap. As soon as the double automatic doors slid closed behind him Van was approached by a thin young man wearing khaki pants and a dark-red golf shirt with the logo of a national car rental business. "Mr. Ryan, sir?" He held a set of keys out at arm's length.

"Yes?"

"These are for you." He gestured with the keys and Van took them. "All I need is a signature, please." He offered Van a clipboard and a pen and indicated where he needed Van to sign. It was a rental contract, and Van began slowly perusing it from the beginning. "It's been approved, Mr. Ryan. If you would just sign right there, please sir? Everything has been taken care of by your uncle."

"My uncle." Van raised an eyebrow and frowned at the document.

"Yes, sir."

"Ah. Well then." He signed the contract. The rental agent took the clipboard from Van, stepped aside, and gestured toward a shiny, new-ish grey SUV parked at the curb. "I see."

"The agreement is open-ended. When you are finished with the vehicle, just return it to any one of our rental offices."

"And the charges are billed to ..." Van asked.

"Your uncle, sir."

"My uncle. I see."

"Very good then. Enjoy the vehicle! Safe driving!" The agent got into his own vehicle, with the company logo plastered along the side. Before he pulled away the driver's side window slid down. "Oh, Mr. Ryan?"

"Yes?"

"Please be sure to return it with a full tank. Okay? Thanks! Bye now!"

It was a nice vehicle, better than the demolished truck Van had been pulled out of days ago. Van put the car in gear and turned out of the hotel. One of the first things he saw was a drive-through coffee place, so he pulled through and found a spot in the shade to drink his caffeine and eat an overpriced, synthetic muffin. When he was done eating, he held his phone in his hands and went over in his mind what he would say to Yip when he called her.

He was going to tell her everything, he decided. Everything that happened in the clearing on the mountain, and everything since then. She had a right to know. There was just no other way around it. He was dialing her number when suddenly the passenger door of the car opened and a young man wearing an apron from the coffee shop climbed in. Van couldn't believe he had left the door unlocked. It was a shameful security violation. He reflexively drew his knife from its sheath, holding the handle in a reverse grip, and in two movements he extended his arm in front of himself and brought it back again, burying the blade to the hilt in the throat of the man sitting in the seat next to him. The sharp blade went in smoothly, making a wet, tearing sound.

Except that it didn't. Van opened his fingers and looked at his empty hand. He wasn't carrying his knife. That was in his bag, in the back of the SUV. Van's right hand was empty. *How strange*, Van thought.

Van knew immediately that the man in his car wasn't a man at all, but merely a costume, another shell being worn by the entity. The guy had the same false, vacuous gaze that Van had seen less than an hour before, in the hotel.

"Van Ryan," the man said. The timbre and the pitch of the man's voice were his own, but the character and monotonous cadence were too familiar by now.

"Yes! Hello. My uncle, I presume. You look wonderful. I love the new you."

"Your attempt to employ humor will only impede conversation. There is no time for that."

"Of course. Are you here to scold me for stopping for coffee? It really is essential if you expect me to complete our "mission."

"Again, your use of sarcasm is unnecessary, and can only serve to impede the success of your "task," if you prefer that word. Now, you have consumed your beverage and eaten your food. You must be going."

"I'd be on the road right now, if you hadn't stopped in for a visit," Van said, trying to conceal his irritation. "Also, how have you managed this?" Van was referring to the SUV. "I hope you know I can't afford this kind of thing for very long."

"There are many people, Van Ryan, who can be convinced to do a variety of things. Managers and owners of various businesses may decide that they want to gift or loan people things or provide services without the usual paperwork. Bank account owners may decide to transfer or withdraw certain moneys and find their memories hard to trust concerning those transactions. You will find your resources adequate to fulfill your role. All you need to concern yourself with is achieving your first destination, which right now lies in Memphis."

"Right," Van said. "First destination? There's more than one?"

"Of course. Your final destination is Harrison, Arkansas. That is the location of our missing component. You will meet an individual in Memphis who will guide you there." The coffee shop employee's eyes stared at Van dully.

"So that's it? Memphis to ... Harrison? Then I'm done? That doesn't sound too bad."

"There will be trials along the way, Van Ryan."

"Trials?"

"Challenges, of a sort. It will not be easy."

"Yeah, of course not."

"It is time to go, Van Ryan."

Van nodded his head and pointed to the man in the passenger seat. "Uh ... is he coming? Won't he be missed? You did snatch him in the middle of his shift, I'm guessing."

"Yes. That is true." The man opened the door. "We will look for you ahead." The man turned to jump out of the car.

"Wait! I have to ask: in any of these hypothetical scenarios, where contracts are signed or money is moved from one place to another, will my name be found on any of these "transactions" when accountability time comes around?"

"That is not important, Van Ryan." The coffee guy stepped out of the car and went back to serving coffee, with no idea how he had spent his break. For the first time, as Van was pulling onto the highway, it occurred to him that he may be on a one-way trip.

12

MIDDLE LANE

US INTERSTATE 22, OUTSIDE of the Mississippi / Tennessee border was a parking lot. The trip from Tupelo had been quiet and pleasant. The traffic had flowed like a self-assured river, constant and steady. Part of the drive was through the Holly Springs National Forest, which consisted of a few two-blink towns and some small lakes serving as weekend getaways for cub scout camping trips, afternoon fishermen and jet-ski aficionados. The trees were thin and short, and the brush and new growth found plenty of sun to thrive through holes in the low, sparse canopy. The terrain was painfully flat, the diametrical opposite of the north Georgia mountains. Mountain trails existed to take one away from places like this.

As Van passed one of many unmarked dirt roads in the forest, with its deep ruts dug out by four-wheelers and baked in the sun, he saw a small creek running parallel to the road. It was about 50 yards into the woods, and he pulled off the road and got out of his car. Something drew him to the water: thoughts of the mountains, thoughts of Will, thoughts of home. There had been a creek like this one behind his house in Canton, growing up. Van would spend hours there during the summer months, building things to race on the current and flipping rocks to watch salamanders wriggle away to find new hideouts. When he and Will got older, they would hang out by the creek and smoke weed and talk about how the Braves were doing, and Will would inevitably talk about Yip, and Van would stare at the trickling water and listen.

Van had just turned eighteen when his father died. He had no other family to help him sort out his father's estate, no one to help sell the house. No one to help him figure out what the hell he was supposed to do next. He could barely stand to be in the house anymore; it smelled of sadness and regret. Van found himself spending more time sitting by the creek, getting high, trying to make a plan. He would sit for hours with his feet in the running water, talking to himself, the mosquitos, the salamanders and the skinks.

There was a community of American five-lined skinks living in a rotten log set back a few yards from the water who could be found on any sunny day resting their plump bellies on a warm rock or patch of baked dirt. Other times, Van would see them rustling around through the dead leaves on the ground, their bright blue, whip-like tails darting around as they tried to find a nice juicy beetle or moth larvae to snack on. From time to time, after they had had their meal, one or more of the skinks would be kind enough to stretch out luxuriously and offer their attention to Van as he ruminated about his future. As the weeks of that lonely summer dragged on, and Van grew steadily more anxious and disconsolate, he held court regularly with the creatures inhabiting the creek. And those tadpoles and snakes and lizard friends offered him their advice about his situation. Slowly that advice seeped into Van's thoughts, and those thoughts became ideas, ideas became plans, and Van's past and present now led to a future. A future in the military.

The rest of the drive through the Holly Springs Forest was quick and unsatisfying. He was grateful when the trees were behind him and all that stood between him and Memphis was fifty or so miles of federal highway. He leaned back, turned the air-conditioning a click cooler and listened to the road. No sooner had he zoned himself into driving mode, however, than brake lights lit up on the cars in front of him. First once, then again, then a dramatic slowing and eventually everyone was at a dead stop. The red taillights of frustrated cars stretched off into the distance ahead, the lanes astride him had filled, and behind Van's car a stationary parade took shape quickly. A parking lot.

Van waited, his go-foot at the ready, but nothing moved. He sat back and took a deep breath. He was comfortable enough, and cool, and the car's soft upholstery was soothing. He turned the radio on, and loud static filled the cab of the SUV. He twisted the tuning knob, and it occurred to him that he hadn't listened to an actual radio station for years. The car's stereo system was equipped to handle CD's, but those had all been in Van's truck and were ... where now? Where was Van's truck? The entity had said it was "destroyed," right? But where was it? He had been hustled out of the hospital and sent on his way so quickly he had never really asked. Somehow his duffel bag had shown up on his lap, in the wheelchair, but his poor broken truck and the various possessions rattling around inside it were lost.

The first non-static sound to emerge from the radio was a loud, sonorous voice, bloviating with conviction. It was a man's voice, deep, hollow, and relentless. A preacher's voice.

Van had heard his share of preachers. He listened now as this one ranted rhythmically across the ether, manipulating scared and gullible folks within his station's bandwidth with the timeless language of fear and guilt. Van turned the dial again before the big reveal – that the preacher needed donations to keep spreading the word. "The opiate of the masses," Marx called religion. That was only partly accurate, though. Religion lulled its followers into docility and subservience, yes. But religion could also be used to work the same masses into a fervor, to foment hatred. To incite violence. Maybe it was both the 'opiate' and the 'crystal meth' of the masses, Van thought. Either way, that shit was more potent than any other dope. With some 200-some million Americans strung out on Christianity alone, not to mention all the other strains and hybrid religions, it should be surprising that there weren't shelters and clinics for helping cross-junkies kick *that* habit.

The next station on the radio was playing country music, and Van could hear the small crinkles of static around the edges of the station's signal deaden and grow listless and grey. The airways themselves were bored. Van had grown up in the south, and country music had followed him around, crashed parties and school dances, and wormed its way into the background in stores and restaurants his entire life. Will liked country music. *Had* liked, Van remembered. But then, Will's well of creativity and critical thinking hadn't been very deep. Songs about trucks, beer, girls, football and hayfields sung with a contrived accent, accompanied by musicians pretending an electric guitar could mix with a fiddle, all that suited Will just fine. He would sing the dumbest songs at the top of his voice while Van grimaced, and Yip would smile gamely and shake her head at Van.

Van turned the knob past another preacher soliciting life savings for salvation. Finally, an old tune from a one-hit wonder, 80's German synth-pop band danced out of the radio.

Sometimes the love that lovers feel
Sometimes the nights that strangers steal
Springs of passion, winter regrets
Sometimes "friends" is as good as it gets

Love it but know, not all love is sex
Trust isn't born by just sharing sweat
Give away secrets but they're not kept
Sometimes "friends" is as good as it gets

You can't build on ashes
When the flame's gone cold
A good home needs stone
Or you'll age alone

Sometimes "friends" is as good as it gets

The song used to play a hundred times a day for eighteen months on the radio, and then Van had never heard it again, until now. He found himself singing along, and the nostalgia made him smile.

Alone, in the car, no arbitrarily possessed people with dead eyes were accosting him, telling him to "hurry up, Van Ryan," "get on your way," or "go now," which was a good thing. He couldn't go anywhere right now. People were standing by their vehicles and along the side of the road, straining to look ahead, trying to determine what was holding them up. The heat outside mixed with angry exhaust fumes and danced along the outlines of the cars, giving them the impression of being underwater.

It was a perfect time to try to reach Yip. "Please, Van. Call me ..." Van pulled out his phone and dialed her number. In his mind's eye he could see her sitting on her sunporch, reading a book about Gaelic history or Celtic mythology, prepping herself for the day she could finally get Will to take her to Ireland. It was the only thing Van had ever heard her wish for. Her phone was ringing, and in Van's fantasy she had left it in the kitchen and was annoyed with herself as she went inside to find it. Their screen door stuck at the bottom when the weather was humid, and she had to wiggle and shake it a bit to get it open. She finally made her way to the kitchen and was reaching across the counter for her phone when it stopped ringing and went to voicemail. *No, no, no,* Van thought, as he dialed her number again. *Pick up, pick up*! But she didn't pick up. Instead, a soft voice that was Yip's asked him to leave a message. Van hung up and threw his phone on the floor of the car. After a few minutes, he realized that he was yelling. He was gripping the steering wheel with both hands, his knuckles cold white, and he was pressing and yanking on the wheel with all his strength. It took some time after he had uncurled his fingers for feeling to return to his hands.

Looking at his trembling hands, Van happened to notice beyond them, on the instrument panel, that the fuel gage was tilting toward empty. He tapped the plastic panel in vain, hoping the vehicle would admit it was wrong. Instead, an indicator lit up, telling him a gas station had better be soon on the itinerary. Van looked around at the river of stationary cars and a tightness clenched his chest. He rolled both front windows down and turned off the engine to conserve fuel. The waiting heat leapt into the cab of the SUV, sucking every ounce of cold air away in an instant, leaving just a sad memory of comfort. Van turned the radio up louder, to distract himself from the heat. Something angry from the '90's northwest was playing. He leaned his head out the window, but the only breeze was the circulation of carbon monoxide from fellow captive cars' exhaust.

More people were around now, ambulatory, quitting their vehicles in anger or boredom.

Two cars ahead of Van, in the same lane, a man stood on the roof of his Honda Accord, shielding his eyes with one hand and stretching forward, trying to look ahead. A woman leaned out of the front passenger window, talking to him animatedly, but the man just shrugged his shoulders. Two lanes over, on the left-hand shoulder, two women were standing just off the road, having an argument. One woman appeared to be in her early thirties. She had long, dyed-blond hair with dark roots, pulled back into a harsh ponytail. She wore mirrored sunglasses and a white tennis visor, neither of which hid the rage welling up in her face. She pointed a long-nailed, painted finger inches from the face of the other woman. The second woman was younger. She was wearing a swimsuit top under a torn t-shirt, and bad tattoos congregated haphazardly along her arms like strangers. She was gesticulating wildly, one hand holding a cigarette and the other clutching a canned beverage in a foam beer cooler. Van could hear their voices competing, and he turned the radio up to try to tune the argument out. A screeching bellow drew his attention back, and he saw that the older woman had grabbed two handful of the other's hair and was yanking her back and forth, trying to get her off her feet. The younger woman hit her in the face with her drink, and her bad-art arms were windmill compatriots, trying desperately to connect with a face or head. Others surrounded the violence, some to try and mitigate, but more to enjoy the show.

"Hey there. Y'alright?" Van jumped a little and his right hand searched in vain for something to strike with. A man stood outside his open window.

"What ...? Yeah, I'm good."

"Sorry to startle you, friend. Just out trying to get the blood moving, you know? Couldn't just set there anymore. My truck's back there a ways. Saw your window was open. Thought I'd say 'hey.'" The man was in his late twenties, tall and unhealthy, with thin, sparse, reddish-blonde hair combed forward and trimmed high and straight across his forehead. His eyes were dark brown and blood-shot, and his freckled skin was sunburned and hung loosely from his bones. He wore a thin gold chain around his neck, and a lime-green t-shirt with the sleeves torn off that read: "I Got Worms – At Billy's Bait Shop."

"Yeah, no worries," Van said.

"Boy, wouldn't want to get into it with either of them ladies! Right?" He hooked his thumb in the direction of the fight on the other side of the highway. "Damn."

Van smiled. "Yeah, you got that right. Nothing like a little senseless violence to top off a traffic jam."

"Yeah, this jam's a mother, ain't it? I ain't been stuck this far out of Memphis before. Usually, they wait 'til you're in the city until they get you. Damn."

"You from Memphis, then?"

"Well, right outside a bit. Yeah, seems to be more traffic every year around here. Guess it makes sense. More people more traffic, right?" Van nodded. "I do hate a traffic jam, though. People start getting real itchy in a jam, you know? Like that." He looked in the direction of the fight, which seemed to have cooled off. The older woman was sitting on the guard rail, crying, while the younger one was pacing back and forth a few car lengths away, smoking a cigarette furiously. "Folks don't like being held up. Trapped. Made to set still, right?"

"That is true," Van said. He was waiting to hear what the man was selling. The guy could have been a preacher or a drug dealer, although Van couldn't help liking him a bit. At least he was wearing his own skin and didn't yell "Van Ryan!" at him every five minutes.

"Problem is, they don't know none of us are setting still! Damn! We're all running around the earth as she spins. A thousand miles an hour, give or take some. Right? They don't know that though. Or they learned it once and forgot it. While they hurry up to get to the mall, or the beauty salon or wherever."

"Yeah, you got a point there," Van said.

"Damn straight. I don't forget though. You know, while we're spinning ..."

And suddenly the man's words stopped making sense. He kept talking without a change of expression, punctuating his conversation with gestures and facial expressions, but his words were completely unintelligible to Van. They didn't sound like any language Van had heard before. He had seen a documentary once about certain Pentecostal Christians "speaking in tongues," but this didn't sound like that either. The man kept on talking. Van maintained a passive demeanor, offering a nod or two during pauses. He kept his gaze on the man's face, searching for any clue as to what the hell was going on. The noise was a series of guttural consonants and rounded, wet vowel tones, mixed intermittently with a staccato, choking sound. Then, as he watched, the man's face lost all features, all contours. It became flat and blank, with no cavity even for the sound of his talking to escape. A spark of fear grew to irrational panic in Van's stomach. *He's here for me! It's me! He wants me!* The man's face was amorphous. Suddenly a mouth opened in the face, a mouth full of perfect, straight, bright white teeth. Riff Merritt's teeth. As Van watched the teeth became smaller and worn. They faded to a dull, dark yellow, the only shine glinting off one gold tooth on the top, on the left side. The mouth opened wide on the otherwise blank face, and a booming voice yelled, "WHO SENT YOU HERE, VAN RYAN?!" Van flinched in terror.

"... course the thing is we can't see up ahead what the problem is. They's no hill around here, so you can't see but a few cars ahead. What you think it is? A wreck?" Everything snapped back into place. The man was talking as he had been, and his freckled face and red-rimmed eyes hadn't changed at all. "You okay, man? You look a little pale. You alright?"

"Yeah, I ...I'm good."

"So, what do you think? A wreck?" He asked Van again.

"Probably," Van said. "That's what it is. Yeah."

"Mmhmm. Although I was in a jam once outside of St. Louis for a couple hours, and we found out later that a woman had laid down in the middle of the road to commit suicide, and nobody could get her to move. The state troopers come and tried to get her up, and soon as they loosened their hold on her she went and laid back down again. So they done it again and this time she managed to get ahold of one of the troopers' guns, and she stood in the middle of the road threatening to do herself in, holding the gun up under her chin, you know?"

"What?" Van asked, trying to maintain his part of the conversation while his mind scrambled to figure out what had happened a moment ago.

"Damn cops shot her dead. Right there. Found out later she had been arrested for shooting dope and the court done took her child away from her. Turns out she was just laying on the highway trying to get someone to talk to her about getting her kid back, you know? Wasn't right for those damn cops to gun her down like that."

"Damn."

"Damn right. They didn't have to do that. Bastards." The man kicked a stone under Van's car. "This one's probably just a wreck though."

"Yeah, probably a wreck." As Van spoke, a cool, strong breeze blew from behind them down the length of the highway. At the same time, a large flock of birds passed above the stalled cars in a twisting, undulating mass. The flock turned and folded on itself like smoke caught in a corner. It turned and swelled and flowed west, toward Memphis. The breeze followed behind, teasing and tickling the drops of sweat on Van's face and arms. Van saw the two ladies sitting on the guard rail pick up their heads, and further up the road the other, younger lady stopped pacing. A ripple of hope, barely perceptible, flowed back to front up the long line of hot cars. Then, a moment later, red brake lights started to blink off ahead in the distance, and then closer, and closer. Finally, the cars around Van started to shudder and inch forward.

"Well, sorry to chew your ear off, pal," the man said. "I best get back."

"Not at all, not at all. Helped pass the time. All the best to you."

"You too. Hope you find what you're looking for in Memphis!" And he was gone.

Had Van mentioned that he was looking for something in Memphis? He couldn't remember. The cars lurched and sputtered, stopped two more times and then climbed back up to cruising speed. A few miles up the road, he passed two police cars and an ambulance by the side of the road. He didn't see any sign of an accident, however. No twisted metal or broken glass. No crumpled chasses on fire or people standing around crying and dazed. Just two state troopers standing by their cars, one talking on his radio, and an ambulance parked quietly, no lights flashing.

Traffic jam. Side of the road. Fella turns into a fucking demon. What the shit was that all about? Was this something to do with the alien? Were there thin walls in the space the alien was renting in his head? Had it woken something else up, something that lived there already? Were the wolves not the only thing to be afraid of?

What was the name of the place Van was headed? Hamilton, Arkansas? Harrisburg? He could probably just ask any person by the side of the road, and they would turn into an alien zombie and tell him where it was, and that he needed to be on his way. Harrison. That was it. Harrison, Arkansas. Now that he remembered it, that name sounded familiar. He had never been to Arkansas, but the name "Harrison, Arkansas" sounded familiar.

The traffic was up to speed and the miles to Memphis ticked down quickly. There were dozens of choices on the radio now, and Van tried a few before he turned it off. He needed the quiet to pull himself together. He watched the road in front and the signs flying by and avoided turning his head far enough to lock eyes with any other drivers. If he saw them, he would have to acknowledge them. And if he acknowledged that they were there, driving in their cars, he would have to know, have to verify for himself whether or not they all had faces.

Part 2

The Music

13

MEMPHIS

IF SMOKE HAD A home, it would live in Memphis. The smell of burning woodfire mingles and moves in and out of rib joints, packed clubs and holes-in-the wall, down busy tourist-thick sidewalks and wet back-alleys. Everywhere, the delicious aroma of burning meat covered barely by sweet, charred sugar, smoked tomatoes, and a kiss of aerosolized vinegar. Moments after landing downtown, one's hair and clothing smells of cigarette smoke and barbeque, and all that's left to complete the ensemble is blues music and a sweet glass of bourbon.

Van rode the flow of traffic into the city and ended up down by the river. *Memphis, Tennessee,* the entity had said. *There you will meet someone who will guide you to the silent component's location.* So Van was here, looking for "someone." Or they were looking for him. Either way, Memphis was a big place, and Van thought the chance of just bumping into someone willing to "guide" him to some unknown location housing dead or dying aliens was pretty slim. He found a parking space on Front Street and started walking.

A sign for the Orpheum Theater grabbed his attention, so he turned left onto Beale Street. Early evening walked with him, dimming the sunlight and dialing the neons brighter. The street was thick with tourists, revelers, and an industry skilled at making money off both. Guitar music stomped and cried out the doors of the bars and restaurants. Passersby held their plastic cups high and happily spilled beer on each other. Van's forward momentum slowed as he was jostled and blocked by the crowd. Feeling closed in, he peeled off onto the sidewalk and sat down at a metal picnic table to watch. The table belonged to a restaurant called Rascal's. Their front window glowed with neon beer signs and was papered with playbills advertising upcoming musical acts.

Seated on top of another table close to Van's, a boy about twelve or thirteen sat looking at him. He wore dirty jeans and no shirt, and his hair was thick and long. He stared unflinchingly at Van, without interest or curiosity. It was unnerving, and Van was about to speak to him when suddenly the boy pointed at Van and signaled that Van should follow him. He stood up and took a few steps up the street before turning and looking at Van again. Van hesitated, unsure what the kid wanted with him. His mind ran through a handful of CSI scenarios involving stabbings or beatings and being robbed in a back Memphis alley. The boy made the gesture again, urging Van to follow. Van shook his head slowly and got up to leave when the boy opened his mouth and yelled, "Van Ryan" in a pubescent voice so loud and clear it cut right through the murmur and chatter of the crowd on the street. Folks stopped in amazement at the sound of the boy's voice and laughed at Van's reaction.

The boy's call was like a solid kick in the kidney for Van. It was so unexpected, Van's chest seized up and his knees literally buckled. He reached out for the table he had been sitting on and doubled over, trying not to vomit. Van had heard his name droned at him from soulless, empty automatons for days now, but to hear the entity's command come from a child's mouth had a startling effect on him. He felt the anger rising. Helplessness. Injustice. He saw images of coming violence from behind the glass of his own eyes.

The boy was still staring. Van caught his breath and walked over to him. He had to obey. He knew that if he didn't follow where this child led him, the entity would cause the boy harm somehow, or hurt the people around him. As Van crossed the sidewalk toward where the boy was sitting, he heard the clatter of horseshoes, and suddenly a medium-sized brown horse drew up along the curb next to Van. It had a black mane and wore black tackle and a black fabric sign along its flank which read "Memphis Carriage Tours" in white cursive lettering. The horse tossed its mane and turned its head to look at Van expectantly. A bright white blaze stood out on its forehead, like a starburst viewed through a cloud. Van looked around, and saw people had stopped in their tracks and were staring in wonder at Van and the horse. He felt a poke in his side and looked down at the boy, who poked him again and then pointed at the horse. "Get on, Van Ryan," the entity said in the child's voice.

"What? I ... I don't know how to ride a horse." But Van again knew arguing was hopeless. He felt another poke in his ribs and without looking again at the empty-eyed child, he stepped up to the horse. There was no saddle or stirrups. Van had never been on a horse or near a ranch in his life. All he had as a resource was every western, every cowboy movie he had ever seen. It wouldn't be the first time he had pulled off something stupid guided only by the dim memory of an old television show. Another real moment based firmly in fiction.

The horse was more stout than tall, and it stood in the street, below a high curb. Van twisted his right hand into the horse's mane and grabbed hold while he leapt clumsily, stomach-first onto the beast's quivering back. He rotated himself and sat cautiously upright, hugging the horse's flanks with his legs. The horse immediately started walking, slowly at first. Van clenched handfuls of horsehair desperately with both hands to keep from falling off. People moved and stumbled out of the way as the horse trotted through them. Folks reached a tentative hand up as they went by, touching the animal's strong hindquarters in wonder.

The horse ever-so-slowly gained speed as it headed east on Beale Street. Tourists and wanderers moved clumsily aside, some with surprise on their faces, and some without noticing Van and his mount at all. Bars and restaurants passed by. Neon signs in a dozen different fonts, all spelling the word "Blues," adorned newly renovated, tired old buildings. The horse turned on a side street, and then again on Union Avenue. Now they passed music museums and shrines once inhabited by legends when the shrines were just places, and the legends were real people. Structures of wood and stone fed by real sweat and pain before magic and mythology turned every doorway into an altar.

Van rode the horse for as long as it wanted him. It could have been ten minutes or an hour. After the first few awkward blocks, he just leaned into it and enjoyed the breeze and the noise of the city. The horse's shoes on the pavement were loud and jarring, but soon became hypnotic as horse and rider flew around cars and bicycles, flowing smoothly between the lanes of traffic, the road's shoulder, bike paths and, occasionally, the sidewalk. Only once did they pass the law; a police car parked along the same side of the street as Van and the horse. One of the cops was standing next to the car, and he looked surprised when the horse flew by.

"Hey!" He yelled. The other cop leaned out of the driver side window and started talking into his radio while his partner got in the other side. Just as they were about to pull out and follow, a Memphis city street sweeper stopped right in front of them, blocking them in. Van laughed out loud and turned back into the wind as the horse slowed only slightly to take another turn.

Somewhere in the Pinch District the horse slowed suddenly and clip-clopped its way to a stop along the corner of two quiet but well-worn streets. The horse stomped its iron shoes a few times and appeared to gesture with its head toward the building in front of them. The horse turned around to face Van and its lips appeared to move, as though it was about to say something.

"No!" Van yelled, and he launched himself off the horse in sort of a controlled fall. "None of that shit! No! I get it. You want me to go in here, yes?" The horse moved its heavy head up and down. "Great. Here I go. Shhh! Don't!" Van looked the beast in the eye and tried to see through to the unpossessed animal. He placed a gentle hand on the horse's face. "Thank you," Van whispered, and then louder, "Beat it, now. Get out of here." The horse sauntered down the block, turned a corner, and was gone.

The building was short, one low story, but it ran along most of a city block. Grey cinderblock climbed up from scrub weeds, broken glass, and gravel to meet weathered plywood, painted primer white. No windows at all, just patches of bad graffiti and a thousand staples, each holding a torn corner of a forgotten band's playbill. Van would have written the place off as just another abandoned building except for the yellowed, poorly lit plastic sign over the entrance reading "Elle's Belles."

A young man in an old Army jacket, sporting a scruffy goatee, stood by the door, smoking a cigarette. He looked at Van curiously as Van walked up to the entrance. "Yo! That your horse?"

"Nope," Van answered. "Loaner."

The man laughed and took a long pull on his smoke. "Right!"

"Cover?"

"Nah man. You're good." Van climbed the two concrete steps, opened the door, and went inside.

14

ELLE'S BELLES

A GOOD BAR SHUNS three things: police, violence, and sunlight. A good bar is a dark bar. If you enter in the afternoon, it should be dusk inside, no matter how many windows there are. And if you show up at night, it should look like your standard home lighting if two-thirds of your lightbulbs had just blown out. The bar itself can be lit up some; lit enough to make sure the bartender is pouring a good drink and bright enough to be sure everyone tips. But there need to be dark places in a bar, places for people and phenomena to hide. Corners and tables the light just can't seem to reach. Some folks want to be the center of attention. That's easy enough for a drinking establishment to accommodate. Other people aren't as comfortable with their regrets, their appearance, with their magnificent *deviance* on display. The perfect bar must provide a comfortable place to those who want to dance on the bar as well as those who want to disappear while they drink. Those who want to be invisible in the crowd. Or those who just want to conduct themselves indecently. There should be shadows available for everyone who wants one.

The sign on the door said it was always Happy Hour at Elle's Belles, but if anyone was happy when Van walked in, they were keeping it to themselves. It took a moment for his eyes to adjust to the dim lighting. There were a handful of people at the bar and a few girls playing pool at one of the tables. It was quiet, no one was talking or laughing much. A short girl with a head full of curly, dark black hair was lost in thought at the juke box, tapping the glass with a quarter in time with the music in her head. Behind the bar an older, corpulent woman stood smoking a cigarette, wearing a faded shirt with the bar's name. She nodded when Van walked in.

"Ah! There he is!" She said, as Van approached the bar and sat on one of the crooked stools. The leather seat was dark and cracked, and it leaned so that Van felt like he was going to slide off.

"Me?"

"Yeah, you, honey." The bartender opened a bottle of Beck's beer, threw down a cheap coaster and set the beer in front of Van. "That's yours."

"How ...? Do you know me?" The bartender smiled and called out to the girl at the jukebox.

"Hey Spot, sweetheart!" She gestured, pointing at Van.

The girl leapt to the bar in two clunky strides and landed on the stool next to Van. She spun around completely once before leaning in close. "So, who the hell are you, huh?" She asked expectantly, her eyes squinty and her curly bangs falling all over half of her face. She had a mountainous mess of thick, dark curls on the top of her head and the sides were cut close, with a clutch of racing stripes shaved on one side. Large and small freckles sprinkled her nose and spread east and west underneath her dark eyes. Her lips were chapped, and there was the lightest sketch of a shadow on her upper lip. She leaned in closer and raised her eyebrows. "So?"

"No one, why?" The girl and the woman behind the bar both stared at him. Van continued uncomfortably. "Van Ryan." Silence. "My name." More silence. "What kind of place is this?" He asked the woman behind the bar.

The glass front entrance opened, and the guy who had been outside smoking came in. "Yo' man! That your horse?" He laughed. "'A loaner,' the guy says! That was crazy! Yo, Mama, that dude's crazy!" He saluted Van before disappearing through a door with a sign reading 'Fuck Off!' A smell of grease and meat and moldy mop water eased out as the door closed.

Both ladies stared at Van even harder. He shook his head and took a long pull on his beer. When he set it down the condensation dripped happily from his hand onto the bar. The cheap paper coaster started disintegrating immediately.

"What, already?" He asked, a little louder.

"Tell him 'what,' Mama," the girl said. The bartender nodded.

"Well, Mister Van Ryan, about ten or fifteen minutes before you apparently rode into town, a fine-looking lady officer of the law made her way in here and told us to be on the lookout for you. She gave a description ..."

"Exactly like you!" The girl interjected.

"Yup," the older lady continued, "exactly. She said that when you got here, we should give you a beer. A Beck's, specifically. She gestured grandly at Van's sweaty beer. Van sat, waiting for the story to continue. He wondered how a "fine-looking lady officer of the law" knew his favorite beer.

"So? That's it?" He said after a wait.

"Not exactly," Mama said. "She said to tell you that Spot here was 'your guide,' whatever that means."

"Ah," Van said."

"You gonna tell us what that all means, or you just want us staring at you all night? Not that I mind too much. You are pretty easy on the eyes." A mock wink from Mama and an endearing genuine cackle. Van didn't know what to tell them, what he *should* tell them.

"HEY!" The girl on the next stool smelled like cigarette smoke, vodka, and something artificially fruity. She had a malicious, gleeful gleam in the corner of her eyes. "Mama asked you a QUESTION, Mister STAN Ryan!" It was impossible such a big voice could come out of such a small frame.

He couldn't tell them the truth, could he? He really didn't know what the truth was. "Um," he started, "it's ... a treasure hunt ..." Both faces half-squinting, half wincing as he said it. The young girl lit a cigarette and held it as though she wanted to throw it in his face.

"Okay. Here it is. Ready? My best friend was eaten by wolves a few days ago. Some sort of alien lives on the mountain where we were hiking, and it ... I don't know ... made us join it in this clearing where it spoke to me through a deer and ordered these fucking wolves to eat Will, and then it said I had to listen to it, or it would kill other people. So, it tells me I have to go somewhere and do something for it, and I need to go to Memphis and find a guide. Then I was driving and there was a car wreck, and I woke up in the hospital in Birmingham and took the bus and met a guy who died on the way to Tupelo. The alien thing got me a truck and I drove to Memphis and got on a horse and here I am." Both women were silent and looked at Van with very wide eyes. "The cop? I don't know. 'Welcome to fucking Memphis?'"

Both women burst into laughter, along with the outdoor-cigarette guy, who was wearing a dirty kitchen apron now. "I

TOLD you that dude was crazy, Mama!" He poured something in a foam cup from the bar soda gun and made his way through the Fuck Off door again, chuckling. The woman behind the bar, 'Mama,' was wiping tears from the corners of her eyes, while her stout frame shook with laughter.

"Okay then, sweetie! You keep your secrets then ... that's fine. That was a good one though." She turned around to take care of some girls at the other end of the bar. Van took another long pull on his beer and glanced at the curly-haired girl on the stool next to him. He could swear she had been laughing a moment ago, but now she was staring laser beams through his eyes and brain and into the dark cave at the back of his mind where he kept his secret files.

"Sorry about your friend," she said, her dark eyes diamond-tipped.

"Thanks."

"How'd he die?"

"Wolves."

"Wolves."

"Wolves. Fur. Sharp fucking teeth chewing on his insides. My best friend." Van turned to get Mama's attention for another beer. He could feel the girl's curiosity now through the side of his head, traversing his ear canal in search of answers.

"Why a deer?" She asked in a steady voice.

"What's your name?"

"Why a deer? Why was a deer talking to you?"

"Tell me your name. No more questions until I know your name."

"Spot." Van was dubious. "Spot, alright? That's my goddamn name!"

"Okay."

"Fucking problem with that?"

"Nope. First person I ever met with that name, but it's fine. I mean, it's a fine name. Whatever." Van finally caught Mama's attention, and she brought him another beer. "What do you drink, Spot?" He asked.

"Fucking tequila! Although sometimes vodka. Or wine too."

"Two fucking tequilas, please." And they drank those tequilas, and then *mas* tequilas. A half-dozen shot glasses clanked, and salt and lime wedges danced when Spot slammed her last one on the bar. Her eyes blazed with pride and malice, and she thumped herself in the chest with her fist.

"You smoke, stranger?" She asked Van. He shook his head. "Good! That shit's disgusting." She lit a cigarette and grabbed a handful of hair on the top of Van's head and held his head still while she leaned in close. "I'll be right back. Gotta piss!" She jumped off the stool and clumped off into a dark unknown on the other side of the room. Her feet were small, but her boots were big enough to kick holes in people.

Belle's was bigger inside than out, narrow but long. The bar was u-shaped, in the middle of the space. Van sat at the bottom of the "u," with his back facing the door. For many years he could only sit where he could see people coming and going. It didn't seem to matter anymore. Life seemed more interesting if you didn't see threats coming, if you gave chaos a starting chance.

To the right of the bar, as Van sat, were two handfuls of scarred-up tables and a scattering of mismatched chairs of all sorts. At the far end of the room there was what appeared to be, to Van's eyes at least, the world's smallest stage. Some musicians were there now setting up, jostling each other to place a mic stand and a small amp. When Van and Will were in high school, Will's parents used to go out of town and Will would throw parties in his basement. This place had the same feel, but it was smaller. Running along the left side of the bar were a couple of tired pool tables, the worn felt trying desperately to hold together. Beyond that were bathrooms and a storeroom and dark spaces where mysteries happened.

"You doing okay, sweetie?" Mama was checking in on Van's beer situation and decided he needed another. "There you go, now." She had short, white hair, and a face owned by hard times, but still renting space to kindness.

"Thank you," Van replied. "So ... are you Elle?"

"No, sugar. Elle was my sister. She died going on five years now. We bought this place together some twenty-seven years ago." She stared at the scratches, stains and cigarette burns in the surface of the bar. "Just me now though! The girls call me Mama. You hungry, sweetie? We got burgers if you're hungry." Two women caught her attention, and she expertly peeled her attention away from Van with a practiced smile and turned to them. They laughed with Mama as they ordered. They were locals, and they teased each other while they waited for their drinks. They kissed each other, and then blew a kiss to Mama when she brought their order. Looking at them, the couple playing pool, and the small groups of friends sitting at the tables and laughing at the bar, it dawned on Van at last that Elle's was obviously a gay bar. Van shook his head at himself, embarrassed at how ignorant and blind he stumbled through most of his days.

"Yo." Spot was back. She moved like a rough-hewn stone rolling down a hill, in fits and starts, fast and unpredictable. "What, no more shots? Mama!" So, they did more shots, and Van started to feel them. "Yo! There's my girl Shelly!" And she was off again. She jumped on a tall, dark-skinned girl with a shaved head and tattoos around her neck and shoulder who had just walked in the door. They laughed and hugged, and the tall girl went into a story.

And then there was music. The trio had situated themselves and led in with a deep walking riff from the obviously well-traveled stand-up bass, plucked by a man who seemed far too young to make his instrument speak so frankly. Another guy straddled a wooden box covered in cardboard and wrapped in black felt. He started tapping and stroking the box, coaxing out a soft, hesitant rhythm. The third instrument was dressed as a plus-sized woman in a tight, red, knee-length dress. Her long, platinum hair was done in curls. She drifted into her opening lines, quiet whisper warnings of restrained bellows, hiding.

Rumor ... said ...

A voice like silk smoke drifting quietly across the room ...

If I never left you in that dream

Settling ... infusing ... filling your clothes, your hair.

Maybe life would still make sense,
Not doing this every daydream dance,

The singer built tension and breathed despair, backed by bass lines more felt than heard.

Maybe not wasting every chance.

And now the sultry growl grew into an accusation. The band picked up the tempo just enough to wake the pulse, enough to force the audience to attend.

Spent too much time in the passing lane
Smiles, the spin and slide, pouring rain.
Memories of strawberries and cream;
You took the real world,
I'm left in the dream.

The pipes were wide open. Her voice was strong without being loud. Van glanced around and saw more folks had made their way to the tables, as though the music had floated out and plucked them right off the street.

"Yo." Spot was back. "Pretty good, right?" She gestured toward the stage, toward the singer. Van nodded. "Yeah," she said. "I hit that. A couple of times, actually." She nodded her head proudly.

"Impressive."

"Damn straight! Oh, hey. Open your mouth." With his attention still half on the music act, Van did as he was told. "Now stick out your tongue." She reached over and put a very small, white square of paper on his tongue. Van raised his eyebrows as she put another piece of paper on her own tongue and swallowed it. "You want me to guide you somewhere, yeah? Well, something's crazy about the way that cop came in here like that. Didn't seem right. And your story is all fucked up. I had a friend tell me once a long time ago, 'Never trust anyone unless you've tripped with them.' So, let's see what you're about, Mister Stan Ryan."

"It's Van ..."

"Whatever, shitbird."

Will was gone. Eaten by wolves. And Van was dosing with a sketchy girl he just met, in a city he didn't know. He was sitting with his back to the door and why not? Is this why the entity wanted him to come to Memphis? Why the asshole alien had Van ride in at sunset like a schizophrenic cowboy? And the cop? What about her? Well, the Beck's was cold, and the music kicked ass, and why not just settle in and let this trip lead him where it may. His life was a goddamn hallucinogenic nightmare now anyway. Why not double down? Can you take acid while you're already knee-deep into a nightmare? Would it be the same dream you'd have if you somehow fell asleep while you were tripping? Both possibilities were exciting and terrifying, and Van took a deep gulp of his beer to wash the dose down. One thing was as true this night as it had been every other night of Van's life: he had absolutely nothing to lose.

15

THE DOSE

TAKING LSD IS A commitment. When you drink or smoke weed you can count on the fact that after a couple of hours, you'll be more or less yourself again. Once you've dropped acid though, you have voluntarily surrendered the next eight-plus hours of your life to another reality. You're out. Not home. There's a reason they call it a "trip." You might as well get someone to pick up your mail and feed your cats, because you're going to be gone for the day. There are things to see and learn, pit stops to make.

There's a time between swallowing that little piece of paper and first feeling its effects that's tense and nervous. For thirty or forty-five minutes you think about what's to come, maybe worry a little, but you have no idea what to expect. You can't predict what's coming because you will not be you. You can't foresee what reality will look like when everything kicks into high gear, because you'll be seeing it all with a different set of eyes. The brain that thinks *"maybe I've made a mistake"* will soon be relieved of duty, to be replaced with something far more imaginative and adventurous. A radio receiver with infinitely broader bandwidth.

Van was waiting. People normally drop acid at concerts, shows, parties, maybe spiritual retreats, events of that nature. Smart people don't take acid with odd strangers they meet at dive-bars in unfamiliar cities. Normal people don't willingly surrender control of themselves in circumstances like these, but Van had lost control of his life days ago, when he first stumbled into a cursed meadow on a mountain and lost his best friend.

He had had quite a bit to drink and he was feeling it, but he knew that soon it wouldn't matter. Depending on how much speed was in this acid, the alcohol would soon be singing backup in the hallucinogenic band setting up in his head. Spot had run off to play and climb all over her friends by the pool tables as soon as she had dosed Van. He got up and moved across the room to a small table against the wall, where he could see the band, the bar, and the whole room. He smiled a personal smile and sipped his beer while he listened to the band.

Maybe I am the things I've done,
Or maybe I'm just another one.

He could feel the chemicals working their way through his system. A lightness in his chest, a tightness in his stomach. A chalky sensation at the back of his throat and, between sips of his beer, a burnt battery, synthetic taste in his mouth that wasn't going away any time soon.

"Yo." Spot had found him. "What you doing over here, Stan?" Van shrugged.

"Van."

"Right. Who cares? Check it out, yo. My girl Angela thinks you're cute." Van could see bright red hair waving to him from the pool tables on the far side of the bar. "What d'ya say?"

"What?" Van gave a cursory wave and turned back toward the stage.

"I thought maybe later we could both ... you know?" Van laughed. "What's funny, asshole?"

"Nothing," he said. "I'm good. I'm just laying low until the fun starts. No telling where we'll be later."

"True. I'll tell her to stand by. Fuck you, loser." She smacked him in the forehead and ran off.

Sleep, yesterday's lover.

Dream of tomorrow's

Walk of shame.

The singer's voice was a buttery growl now, and it pulled the lighting sideways around Van. The thick light enveloped him on both sides, the form of it shaped by the singer's words. Elle's had filled up nicely by now, and every table was occupied. There was a clamor at the bar and a rise and fall of laughing and yelling, and the clacking of pool balls on the far side. The folks at the tables were drawn in by the music, and their quiet murmurs and comments rumbled a low rhythm that filled out the three-piece. The air was hot and damp now. The building's old a/c unit fought a losing battle against hot bodies and the Tennessee summer evening, and the humid air served up songwriting as it caressed and hugged its way around the crowd. A smile showed up on Van's face again, and it was comfortable there. It wanted to sit there for a while.

Several tables in front of Van, he noticed a woman sitting, swaying gently to the music. Her back was facing him, and she wore a soft blue and white sundress, and her hair was cut short and dyed blonde. While Van watched she ran her fingers through her hair, from front to back, which always made Van breathe deeply. She must be here for him, Van thought. She had found him! He got up and made his way clumsily through the narrow space between tables and smiled down at her. She cocked her head up at an angle to look at him, and he could see right away it wasn't her. It wasn't Yip. Or was it? He stared at the woman, willing it to be Yip. She turned her face up, looked at Van, and said in a clear voice, "Harrison, Arkansas, Van Ryan." Then she turned back to enjoy the music and Van knew it wasn't Yip. He mumbled away, kicking chairs unintentionally as he went.

Suddenly Spot was there again. She pulled him out of the tables and off to the side, against a wall. She grabbed his shirt and pulled his face down toward her. "Do you feel it? Do you feel anything? Are you coming on yet? Yes? Fucking say something!" She shook the front of his shirt. She was pale and sweating and her irises had been eaten by her pupils, which were now working away at the whites of her eyes.

"Yeah," Van replied. "I think so. Yeah." He turned his head to look around the bar, and the people and the fixtures moved a bit slower than his gaze. When he held his head still and his gaze steady everything looked fine. But when he turned or looked away it seemed like time had taken another track and he had missed the train. "Yeah, no, It's definitely on."

"Ha! Yeah boy! Boom! Now wait! Listen." She got serious. "Do NOT leave without me! Got it?"

"Roger that," Van said, the smile settling back on his face.

"Do NOT leave me! Under any circumstances, loser! I gotta piss again." She was gone.

Van had to go too, so he ambled his way around the bar and past the pool tables to where the rest rooms lived. He glanced around as he went, trying to discern exactly who did and who didn't know he was tripping. It was important that they didn't know. He felt like an alien hiding among them all, and if they found him out they would mob him and crush him and dissect him on one of the pool tables, the one with the least amount of felt. The bathroom door was painted shiny black, and the sign read, in lower-case letters: "boys." The door swung inward on its own and, stepping in, Van stood facing a dirty sink and a mirror. The toilet was off to the right, but it was too late. The mirror. He saw his image in the mirror. The drugs in his system helped him to see his *actual* image in the mirror. His eyes, his own enormous pupils, two galaxies swirling in concert with each other. In perfect synch. The image in the mirror was someone he had never seen before. The Van in the mirror looked out at a stranger. He saw creases and old acne scars, odd bumps and gaping pores he had never seen before in a lifetime of looking at himself. His face wasn't symmetrical. One eye seemed a little lower than the other, and although he had never broken his nose, it leaned a bit to one side. The hair on one eyebrow looked thicker than the other. It was overwhelming to see himself as strangers must see him. Was he attractive? Would he find himself attractive? This must be how Yip saw him. Van felt caught in the mirror, trapped, and he struggled to look away. Instead, he looked into The Van's eyes and was drawn in and lost. He grew small and was pulled into the optic nerve behind the eye and he followed the path like a log flume ride to the occipital lobe. From there he climbed atop the spongy surface of his brain and jumped and climbed across its twisted surface. From this vantage he peered up into the layers of tissue separating the brain from his skull, and he could see blood vessels pulsing and flashes of different colored light as electrical impulses performed their perfect, mysterious symphony in the operation of *him.* He thought of the trip through the universe he had taken with the entity only days before. *This* was the universe of his *mind*, however, and it was glorious.

The bathroom door crashed open and a young, sweaty man with his shirt tails hanging out rushed in, already working to undo his fly. He wore a sticker on his shirt that said *"Hi, my name is Harrison!"*

"Oh, sweet Jesus, I've gotta go! Sorry to bust in on you like that," he said.

Van snapped away from the mirror and wiped his eyes on the backs of his hands. "Oh my god," he said, pulling himself from the draw of the mirror. "Thank you so much, man! Thank you! I would have been there forever!"

"Uh, sure thing." The man said.

Van looked at him closer, looked at the sticker on his shirt. His mind flashed back to a news article he had read in his apartment a few lifetimes ago.

"Harrison? Arkansas? *The Most Racist City in America?*"

"Uh, sure, man." He shrunk away from the vastness of Van's pupils. Van staggered out the door. He hadn't peed.

He stepped out of the bathroom into a room of Wills. Every person playing pool, and everyone sitting and standing around the pool tables was Will. The all stared at him silently, motionless. The only sound was the music carrying over from the other side of the bar. Van was terrified. He knew that Will could tell he was tripping. He slowly inched his way around the room with his back against first the wall, then the bar. The Will's eyes followed him, all moving together. When he was at the bottom of the bar's "U," where he had been seated earlier, he looked away, looked for Spot, and when he looked back, the Wills were gone. They had been transformed back to people drinking and playing pool.

He made his way to the bar and Mama brought him another beer. "Put that on MY tab, Mama Bear," the man sitting next to Van said. "And hello to you, Sugar," he said to Van. "Someone looks like they're having fun tonight!"

"Thanks," Van. He wiped his face with a handful of cocktail napkins. "Yeah, tonight is ... strange. Let's say that."

"I bet! Well, my name's Thomas."

Van smiled. "Mine's Van. Thanks again for the beer."

"My pleasure, handsome! My, you really do look like you're having a good time!" He was looking at Van's eyes. "Would you like to dance?"

"That's flattering, really. Thank you, but I'm here with my girlfriend."

"Oh really?" He placed his well-manicured hand on top of Van's. "Are you sure?" A big smile. "Is it serious? What's his name?"

"Spot." The man dissolved into crystalline laughter.

"Hell, honey. Spot's *everyone's* girlfriend!" This tickled him, and Van joined in with a knowing chuckle. "When she's done with you, you come see me now, honey. You hear? We'll get you all sorted out." He patted Van's cheek and laughed himself off to another part of the bar.

Time had become a spec-ops warrior, camouflaged, unannounced, operating in the wilderness on its own, self-reliant. There was a mission, but it was classified. All that mattered now was for Van to *be*. To wait. And watch. Where was Spot?

Van was sitting in his original seat at the bar when Spot showed up again. She had her arm around a long, leggy blond girl's shoulder and when they stopped in front of Van, Spot grabbed the girl's face and gave her a long, wet, noisy kiss. "Yo, Stan!" She yelled when they came up for air.

"Van."

"Whatever, dude. This is Misty. She's from Arkansas too, like me. Where'd you say you were headed?"

"Harrison? Harrison, Arkansas. That's it." Van said. Spot stopped cold.

"What did you say?"

It was getting harder for Van to speak properly. There was a delay between hearing, thought and speech which was growing exponentially. His brain was functioning just fine. Better than fine. But the thoughts weren't making their way out of his mouth very well. "Harrison. Arkansas. I'm pretty sure. Why? You're supposed to g..." Spot dropped her arm from the blond girl's shoulder and slapped the half-full beer bottle out of Van's hand. It spun around sideways, splashing delicious German beer on a half-dozen of Elle's patrons before hitting the floor in an explosion of foam and green glass.

"Spot! Goddamn it, girl!" Mama called.

"What the fuck?" But Spot grabbed the front of his stretched-out shirt again and pulled Van down to her level.

"I'm FROM Harrison, you ASSHOLE! How did you know that? Who the FUCK are you?" And she let go of his shirt, spit on the floor, and ran outside. Van stood still for two beats and then looked around to see that everyone was staring at him. They all definitely knew he was tripping. He ran after her.

16

ALONE TOGETHER

IT WAS NIGHT WHEN Van burst out of the front door and down the concrete steps of Elle's. Streetlights ruled the corners. He spun around, trying to figure out which direction Spot had run, but she was nowhere in sight. He felt panicky. He could feel himself losing focus around the edges, and he needed her help maintaining a border. Van looked down the two streets in front of him and chose to go to the right. He took off at a quick jog and made it all of three steps before he heard coughing along the shaded side of the building. The noise came from behind the old, rusted hulk of a car that had once been driven over the curb and sidewalk and then left there next to the bar, a perfect monument to drunk driving.

"Spot?" Van called, and suddenly a small, extremely high, curly-haired girl with clunky Doc Martin boots was hanging on his neck.

"Oh, thank god!" She cried. The pulse in her neck was running like a horse race. "Where the hell were you?" Mad. "Oh, I'm so glad you're here." Grateful. "Why the fuck did you leave me? Why did you leave me? I've been out here for hours, goddamn it! I told you not to leave me!" She punched him in the chest.

"Ow! Shit! You left me, damnit! You ran out of the bar. I followed." He grabbed her shoulders as she held his arms and they stood like that, connected for a momen as the outside world continued around them. "It's only been a couple of minutes. Everything's fine." They turned and walked aimlessly down the street, huddled together, no destination in mind. Just knowing that they would walk where they walked together.

"Fuck, Stan, I'm tripping balls!"

"Van."

"Yeah, Stan. I said that. Damn."

"Me too, though. Tripping big balls!" Van said. He was breathing deeply, feeling every bit of dark, new air that he drew into his lungs; feeling the oxygen rejuvenate his blood cells. He held the air in as long as he could with every breath, treating and rebuilding each individual cell of his body at a time. He could feel each one swell and turn from dull to bright red.

"Harrison, Stan. Why Harrison?" Spot was holding her arms out in front of her and opening and closing her hands for inspection. "Why? Why?"

"Don't know. Really. We're supposed to go." They walked in silence. Cars drove by occasionally, threateningly. Van wanted to run each time he saw headlights, but it was more important than ever no one know he was tripping. He had to keep them safe, hidden out in the open. It was hard to see inside the cars as they passed, so he couldn't tell if they were being watched or not. He *knew* they were being watched, though.

After a badly dented, faded yellow, late 1970's Ford LTD passed them, Van turned around and noticed Spot wasn't next to him. She'd dropped off half a block or so ago, and she was squatting down, examining an old fire hydrant. It was rusty and filthy, and it had been painted over and over through the years, most recently a school bus yellow color. Spot was staring intently while she chipped off yellow paint flakes, large and small, into a pile at the base of the hydrant. Van didn't want to disturb her, so he sat on the bit of gravel and dirt between the street and the sidewalk. He leaned back on his hands and looked up at the streetlight above them. It burned down from the darkness above like a Klieg light, spotlighting Van in his debut stage performance as "The Van" in *What the Fuck Have you Done Now? The Musical.* He felt the light pressing down on him, persuading him to stand and recite his lines. Coughing and a rustling of feet, a murmur of discontent told him that the audience was growing restless as they waited. He turned his back to the imagined crowd and crawled his way ever so slowly out of the spotlight. An eternity later he had finally reached the edge of the circle of light and as he pulled himself into the dark, he felt a cool relief. From his new perspective, a halo glowed around the head of the lamp, and colors that had no business being in the sky in this neighborhood radiated beyond that halo. Beautiful purples and greens and dark oranges rippled through the city sky, so happy to be seen.

"New," Spot said. Van sat up and noticed that he had cut the heel of his palm on a small piece of glass. It was bleeding, and he saw some blood had gotten on his jeans. Spot was standing, pointing at the hydrant.

"Okay," Van said.

"New, Stan!" She pointed more determinedly.

"Van! Yes, it looks new." She had plucked off most of an entire layer of paint. "At least different," he offered.

"Asshole," she said, and set off down the street again. Speaking was getting trickier. Van's mind was running like a super-collider, much faster than the mechanics of his speech machines were capable.

Time trembled. Streets became taciturn, preferring to keep to themselves. Van and Spot walked along in a tunnel of their own awareness, everything fresh and new and only theirs. In the less-traveled neighborhoods of this old, thriving city it seemed, for a moment, like a quiet tour, a stroll through an amusement park in the off hours. People appeared occasionally, but, like animatronic characters along a park ride, they weren't meant to be interactive. The world was most interesting away from the sidewalks, but leaving the ride came with a risk of getting lost behind the scenes.

And then Spot *was* lost. She was lost and Van didn't know when he had last seen her. Looking and calling her name didn't help find her, and he didn't know in which direction he should be walking. He yelled and echoes of his own voice made him nervous. It didn't sound like him. Each time he yelled it caught him off guard and he thought it was someone behind him also looking for a lost friend. Finally, he picked a sidewalk which seemed less familiar than the others, and hoped it brought him to her, wherever she was.

After four whole blocks Van saw a bus stop under a flickering streetlight, with a figure sitting on a metal bench. "Spot!" He yelled and ran toward the bench. It felt like he was running through thick, knee-deep mud, and when he got there, he was sweating and tired. He sat down on the bench, breathing deeply, and noticed the other person was not Spot.

"Hey Van."

"Hey Will." It was Will, as real as Van had ever known him. He was dressed, not in jeans and vest and pack as Van had last seen him, but in their high-school baseball uniform, and Van could tell it was the day they had won the state championship. "Congratulations," Van said to him. And the streetlight flickered, and it was the flickering light on the school bus, driving back home from Macon. Everyone else on the bus was laughing and singing, but Will and Van sat apart from the team, in the back of the bus.

"I never even touched that girl. You know that." Will was grinding his teeth and staring at the back of the bus seat in front of them. "Now she says she doesn't want to see me anymore. What am I supposed to do, Van?" Van remembered this conversation. And Will had, in fact, touched "that girl," and other girls before her. Yip had found out, and she was ready to dump Will right before graduation.

"You know ..." Van tried.

"I mean, I don't want to lose her. You know, man? I can't lose her. I mean, I'm lucky to have her, she's lucky to have me. We fit, right?"

"Well dude, call me crazy, but maybe if you stopped fucking other girls ..."

Will laughed. "That's good, man. You're right, though. I'm done, I swear. I'm a one-woman man, from now on." He crossed his heart. "So, she'll take me back, right? You think?"

"Pretty sure," Van had said. "We all get what we deserve, I guess."

"Let's hope not!" Will said, and he was smiling again.

The bus was a bench again, and Van jumped off it. "What the shit?"

Will was older, married Will. Will from now. He wore jeans and a t-shirt under a beat-up flannel shirt, and he sat with his elbows on his knees and his hands clasped. His head hung low, and his face looked as sad as Van had ever seen him. He turned his head to look at Van and opened his mouth to speak, but as the words came out, his face became Spot's face as she walked toward Van from behind the bench. "WHY?" She yelled at Van, through Will's mouth. "WHY WHY WHY WHY?!!" And she slapped Van, hard, so that he stepped backward a few paces and would have fallen if she had not snatched his stretched-out shirt with both hands. She leaned back to strike him again, but he grabbed her wrist and she folded into sobbing, and he sat them on the bench and held her close until she stopped. Will was gone.

They sat still on the bench, not talking. Alone together. Van could hear her breathing. Her breaths were thick and short. The air was neither cool nor warm. It seemed the temperature of the air around Van was the same as the temperature within, creating a perfect equilibrium. Oxygen and carbon dioxide flowed back and forth freely not only through their mouths and noses, but also through the pores of their skin, their eyeballs, their hair and fingernails. Van looked at his hands and noticed that his right hand was glowing slightly. He looked closer and saw pink and violet rays of light pulse randomly beneath the skin.

"Hey," he said to Spot. She sat with her head back and her eyes closed. She was sweating furiously. He could see her eyes moving frantically behind her eyelids. "Hey!" He poked her arm.

"Hmm!" Her face turned stern, and she tried to ignore him.

"Hey! Look!" She opened her eyes reluctantly. He held his hand up in front of her. "Can you see that?"

She looked at his hand and then looked at him. She stared into his eyes for a long time.

Finally, she said, in a quiet, sad voice, "Harrison." She looked into her lap.

"Come on," Van said. He put his arm around her shoulder and began walking again.

It was darker now. Sounds didn't echo, they died where they were born. The light didn't reflect from things like it had earlier. Shadows swallowed the light. Van and Spot, hand in hand, walked past an automotive body shop in silence. A rusty chain-link fence topped with twisted barbed wire ran around the length of the shop's yard. A long, rolling gate, two car widths wide, secured a driveway leading from the repair bay to the street. Or would have, had it been closed. The yard was littered with vehicles in various states of disrepair. A group of men sat around the yard, on the cars, car parts, trash cans and two or three cheap aluminum lawn chairs. They were talking loudly and laughing, voices thick with booze or drugs. The streaking flash of lighter flames and the slow, red coal of cigarettes burned all around the yard. Van turned on his and Spot's superpower, their tunnel consciousness invisibility, to float past without being noticed. But they were on the downside of their trip now. The acid was in the early stages of wearing off, and with it their invisibility. A beam of light shot out from the shadows in the yard and fell on him, and then on Spot, and froze there.

"Yo! Check it out, homie!"

"Oh snap! Hey honey, who's that?"

"C'mere for a minute baby! Hey!" Man-sized shapes began jumping and standing and moving toward the gate. Spurred into interaction with the real world, Van didn't know what to do. Talk? Run? Fight? Again, his hand went for his absent knife. Spot's hand closed on Van's like a hydraulic vice.

"Hey sweetie! That your boyfriend? Lemme talk to you for a ..."

Suddenly police red and blues and a bright spotlight lit up the shop, and the man-shadows scattered. A lone MPD cruiser rolled up to the curb in front of Van and a woman police officer opened the door and got out. She drew her weapon and shot at the shop several times. There was a symphony of crashing glass and stray ricochets. Spot fell to the ground and covered her ears, her mouth wide open. All Van could do was stare.

"Van Ryan!" He looked up into the dark, lifeless eyes of a female Memphis Police Department officer. "Can you understand us, Van Ryan?" Van nodded. "Help us with her." The officer bent down and grabbed Spot under one arm. Van held her under the other and together they were able to get Spot into the patrol car and shut the door.

"Who? Are you ...?" The cop was female, and she was black, and she had probably bought Van a Beck's earlier in the evening. "I don't know what's happening."

"You found your guide, as intended. Now it's time to go, Van Ryan. Take this car now and find somewhere to sleep. Tomorrow you and the girl must continue on to Arkansas."

"Harrison."

"Yes."

"Where ... what do I do then? What am I looking for?"

The MPD officer pointed at Spot, curled up in the back seat of the car. "She'll know," she said, and walked away. Van got into the car, found the switch to turn the flashing lights off, and drove very, very carefully, searching for a safe place to land. Things were getting soft around the edges, and Van could smell his own sweat, mixed with beer and dirt and fear. Spot fell asleep in the back of the patrol car. The speed component of the LSD was spent, and so were they. The dream needed sleep.

17

Daisy Chains

"HOUSEKEEPING!" KNOCKING, WAKING YOU up way too early in the morning is as much a part of a hard night's "morning after" ritual as drinking Gatorade and eating something greasy for breakfast. Mumbling something at the hotel door from behind your hangover and scrambling to find a clock or your watch while you try to remember what time checkout was, this is all absolutely part of the routine. If the housekeeper, who only wants to clean your room so she can check it off his or her list, decides to open your door to see if you are dead or gone, don't get mad. Just jump out of bed and yell something incoherently with a hotel bedspread around your waist while you gently slam the door back into place and lock it. "Not yet! Not yet!"

The water coming from the bathroom sink tasted like shit, but Van couldn't stop himself from drinking it, tiny plastic cup after tiny plastic cup. His mouth tasted like a dentist had done a cast of his teeth and forgot to remove the plaster. His toothbrush was in the rental car, parked somewhere down by the Mississippi River. He was tempted to go down and get one from the front desk of the hotel, but he wasn't sure he would make it back. The room was dark and still when he came out of the bathroom. He walked over to the heavy curtains and opened them just a bit, and a blazing beam of morning light stabbed its way viciously into the room.

"Don't look at me!" A small, dry voice called from the bed. Slow rustling and movement and a dash to the bathroom. "Oh god damn," Spot whispered. And the sound of water and washing and spitting and drying. A few minutes later Spot opened the bathroom door. "Fuck," she said.

"Yeah," Van agreed.

"Ouch."

"Good morning."

"Fuck you." She tried to lay back on the bed, but the sun shone right on her pillow. "Fuck this sun too, goddamn!" She hid her face and scrambled to a faded chair in a dark corner of the room. "Where are we?"

"A shitty hotel by the Interstate, I think." Van looked at the writing on the room's phone. "Yup."

"How did we get here last night? Wait, hold on," she looked at the sole king-size bed in the room, "did we ...?"

"No," Van said with a chuckle. "At least, I don't think so."

"How did we get here? Hold on, did we get arrested?"

"No. It's a long story."

"Wait ... what the hell? Were we in a cop car? Are you a fucking cop?" She put her hand on her head. "I'm so confused! Oh well. Man, I'm thirsty. Let's roll Stan! You can buy me some juice before you take me to jail."

Van laughed. "*Not* a cop. Don't worry about that. Like I said, long story." He put his shoes on and they headed out the door. As they walked down the hall to the hotel elevator, Spot stopped and looked at him intently.

"You're going to Harrison," she said.

He nodded. "*We're* going to Harrison." She turned and strode down the hall. She didn't speak for a long time.

As Van had assumed, the police car was gone when they got outside. Parked in its place, however, directly in front of the entrance, was his grey SUV rental. A young man in a golf shirt tagged with a dealership logo approached him with a clipboard in his hand. Van realized this was not, in fact, the same car he had been driving, but one that looked just like it.

"Mr. Ryan?" The man asked.

"Yeah, hi." Van took the set of keys the man was offering and signed the contract. "My uncle?" he asked.

"Yes, sir, that's right. Um ... Mr. Ryan, as I was parking this vehicle just now, I noticed a duffel bag in the back. When I called back to my office about it, they said that it was brought to the dealership by an MPD officer early this morning, and that the understanding was you would want it dropped off with the car. Do we have that right?"

Van glanced into the back of the car and recognized his bag. "Perfect. Thank you." He nodded to Spot and opened the passenger door for her. The SUV sat high, and she had to leap onto the step. Van walked around to the driver's side and waved to the dealership man as they drove away.

"Thank you, Mr. Ryan!" The man yelled after them. "Please don't forget to fill the tank up before your return the vehicle!"

As Van turned out of the hotel parking lot onto the main street, he noticed Spot staring at him. "Who the fuck are you, Stan?" She asked. Van just shrugged.

"No one."

"Bullshit," she said. He nodded his head at her. "Who the hell has unsolicited rental car drop off when they get up?"

Van just shrugged. They drove around until they found a gas station and picked up water, Gatorade and shitty road snacks. Neither of them had the patience or stomach to sit in a restaurant, so it was honey buns and chocolate for breakfast, and a drive thru coffee for the road.

"So," Van asked her, "Harrison?"

Her jaws clenched and a sneer involuntarily crossed her face. If they had been in a cowboy film, she would have spat on the floor of the stagecoach. "Fucking Harrison," she said. "Ass-end of the hillbilly universe. Alright then. We'll have to go by way of Little Rock, though. If I'm going back, I need to pick something up there."

"In Little Rock? You know folks there?"

"Turn here. Left! Left goddamn it! You want 40 West. Yeah, I live there, genius."

"Ah." Van found the entrance ramp. As soon as he was on the freeway he saw a sign, "Little Rock - 135 miles." They drove in silence. The rhythm did its thing, droning them on, blurring the time and distance. He thought she was asleep for thirty miles or so, but then suddenly she sat up and took a long hit from her Gatorade bottle and settled back to watch out the window.

"Hey," he said.

"Hmm." She didn't turn her head.

"I was wondering." Pause. "You haven't asked me why I need to get to Harrison."

"Nope."

"But you're taking me there. And you obviously don't want to." She shook her head.

"Fucking right about that."

"Why? Why are you coming?"

"My momma." She turned around in her seat and pulled her legs up in front of her. "She told me I should help you. Last night. I saw her."

"While we were high?"

"Yeah. She was sitting there, in the grass in someone's yard or something. She had bunches of flowers, and she was making daisy chains. Like we used to when I was a little girl. I was pretty good at it, making bracelets back then. You slit the stem with your thumbnail, you know? Push the stem of the next flower through. Slit that stem ... just keep on doing that until it's the right length. And momma would take the flowers with the longer stems and braid them together and make crowns for us both. So, she was there last night, and I sat with her, and I made one, but I fucking lost it." She rubbed her wrist. "But it was her, and I know I was tripping, but it was *her*, man. And she told me you were going to Harrison and said that I should help you. And that I would know when the time came what I was supposed to do."

Van nodded. "Where is she now? Is she in Harrison?"

"Yeah. She's in Valley Springs Cemetery. Off Elm Street. It's real pretty there in the fall."

"I'm sorry."

"Don't be. She died when I was thirteen." She looked out the window again. "Left me there."

"Your dad still around?" Van asked.

"Nope. He started drinking pretty hard after momma passed. Spent some time in prison. Got out and went right back to drinking again. I heard he died of a heart attack a couple years ago."

"I'm sorry," Van said. She looked at him.

"I haven't been back there since I left, five years ago. I don't know what you are, man, but you better be the real deal."

"Right."

"Who the fuck are you, then? Where're you from?" She asked him.

"Georgia. North of Atlanta. I own a shitty little bar. That's it. Nothing special."

"Yeah. How about before that?" She looked at him sharply.

"What?"

"Fuck that. Before that. The real shit." Van didn't say anything. "The real shit, dickhead! You were either military, or a cop, I can tell." Van shrugged. "Yeah, I keep messing with you, but you weren't a cop. I know cops. You were military, right? A soldier?"

On the word "soldier" the world canted 30 degrees or so and at 70 mph all that held them to the world was the tenuous contact between the car's tires and the asphalt of the freeway. Thoughts of missions past threatened to turn them further on the axis of time, or erode the friction that held them to the road. The right missions recalled might flip them upside down altogether, and all things not firmly anchored could go flying through that space between above and below. Back toward the beginning. Reality itself depended on how well secrets were kept, and Van took that responsibility very seriously. Anything less and all of Van's world could release and blow to the four winds, like fluff from a dandelion.

He nodded. "Yeah. A soldier. A marine."

"Yes! You were a soldier in some shitty desert somewhere, and you didn't stay in 'cuz you weren't the lifer type."

Van just nodded his head and kept his attention on the road in front of them. Signs flashed by for Little Rock, but the city didn't seem to be getting any closer. "How long were you in?" she asked.

"Three and a half years. They politely asked me to leave."

"Trouble?"

He nodded. "An "Other Than Honorable" discharge. 'You're a good marine, Ryan, but fuck off.' Like that."

"*Were* you a good Marine?" Van paused for a while before he answered.

"Yeah. I was. I guess."

"Hmm ..." She looked at Van. Her features had softened some. Van leaned over to turn on the radio. "No!" She said and slapped his hand. "Sorry. Just leave it for now." They both breathed and listened to the road.

"Tell me a story, Stan Ryan," Spot said after a while. "Tell me about your girlfriend. Is she tall? Redhead? Huge boobs? Tight ass?"

"Who said I had a girlfriend?"

"C'mon. You got them puppy eyes like your owner took you to the kennel while she went on vacation, and you're waiting on her to come pick you up."

"Yeah ..." And he brought Yip forth from the space she owned in his mind's eye. "She has these large, easy blue eyes, the first thing you notice about her, you know? They turn down just a bit around the outside edges. And they know you when they look at you. You can't keep secrets from eyes like that. Her skin is pale white, and freckles everywhere. And it's soft, her skin, and always warm. She told me once that she runs hot, like always above 99 degrees, and any time I've touched her, it felt like she had a fever."

"Ooh."

"She has an incredible sense of humor. She's always smiling. And she loves music."

"Everyone loves music, Stan."

"That's not true. Not true. My friend Will's parents never listened to music. Didn't own a single record, never listened to music on the radio, nothing. Weirdest thing."

"Yeah, something's wrong with someone who doesn't like music," she said. "And animals. You don't like animals, you suck, right? You like animals, Stan?"

"More than people."

"There you go. So anyway, all that stuff about your girl ..." She pantomimed snoring. "All I want to know is what's up in the bedroom? Nice? Good stuff?"

Van smiled grimly and didn't answer right away. "No sex." He drove a mile while she waited. "She's not mine. I've known her since we were teenagers, but she's not mine. Never has been."

"What? Shut up!"

"It's true."

"That is some fucked up shit, Stan." Van just nodded his head and drove on. She was going to say something else, but she saw the look on his face, and decided against it.

The car was silent as they both went away into their own worlds. The tires hummed and the air rushed over the car and collected noisily behind it, and Van and Spot both climbed around thoughts they could more easily avoid when things were noisy. The car cruised on, and the city got a mile closer every minute.

As the numbers counted down on the road signs leading to Little Rock, the freeway got more crowded, bunched up some, slowed down a lot. Spot rousted herself and let him know they were almost there. "Just about four more exits," she said. While Van was stopped in the far-right lane, waiting for traffic to move, a Greyhound bus inched slowly by them on the left. The driver was playing a game, trying to keep the bus moving as slowly as possible in what was essentially stopped traffic. Van looked up and it crawled past, and there, smiling a big, huge, bright white smile, with teeth that would last forever, was his good friend Clifford Merritt Jr. Riff winked at Van as he slapped a rhythm on the seatback in front of him. Then traffic in the bus's lane picked up and it disappeared into the crowd of cars ahead. Van merged the SUV onto an exit ramp, and he and Spot made their way into the city.

18

Plastic Bricks

VAN WAS NEVER SUPPOSED to be in the infantry. He never saw himself as a tough guy. He had been in a few fights in high school and had held his own well enough, but he didn't like it much. He never bullied anyone, or yelled, or bragged. He played sports, but never really excelled at any of them. No one would have called him "competitive" in any sense. He was more a Navy sort of guy, he thought. He had grown up listening to his father's exploits on the high seas and thought that ropes and life vests and storms were a better fit for him than bullets, body armor, and forced marches.

Toward the end of Van's senior year, his high school held a "Career Day" in the school gym where businesses set up tables and booths and talked to students about their futures. Businesses would try to screen promising kids and sign them up for job interviews or internships. The less-promising kids they shooed back toward the rear of the gym, which was broken into four sections: Army, Navy, Air Force and Marines. The Coast Guard had a table as well, but it had been chased off by the other four military branches into a lonely corner by itself. Each branch had their own banners, their own small television set running enticing promotional videos. Each booth was manned by a team of impeccably dressed, highly trained recruiters prepared to gobble up the poor, the working class, and the disillusioned youth who strayed past their lairs.

Van went straight to the Navy booth. He had consulted the day before with the denizens of the creek behind his house, and all agreed that was the best plan of action. Van approached the Navy's table and was immediately confronted by a Chief Petty Officer in brilliant dress whites. He wore a name tag on his uniform that read "Hollis."

"Hey there, bud!" He somehow compelled Van's hand into his own, pumping it in a merciless handshake. "Interested in joining the Navy? Want to see the world? Have some adventures? Make some friends for life?" He nodded his head as he peppered Van with questions, answering them himself.

"Well ..." Van began.

"Damn right you do! Damn right. I can see it right off. Let me tell you, buddy, I've been a sailor for thirteen years, and I've loved every minute of it. Every minute. So, tell me, bud, what made you consider joining the Navy? Here, wait, do me a favor and sign this while we're talking. Just your contact info, you know?" He slid a clipboard and a pen toward Van. There were half dozen entries before Van, other wayward souls about to be shanghaied. "So, why the Navy ... what was your name?"

"Van. Van Ryan. My old man was a sailor. Merchant marines."

"No shit? Oops!" He hunched down and looked around. "I'm not supposed to use that language here. No kidding? So, it's in your blood, huh? The sea? Adventure? The wide open horizon?"

"Maybe. Something like that."

"Of course it is!" Other people were gathering around the table, picking up brochures and literature stacked there. "Listen, Van, here's what I'm going to do. I'm going to call you, alright? I've got your info right here, yes?" He looked at the clipboard. "Yup. There you are. Now, I'm Chief Petty Officer James Hollis, but I want you to call me Jim, okay?"

"Sure."

"Great. I'm going to give you a call tomorrow, and we'll set up a meeting. I'll come to your house, pick you up, whatever. Then we can sit down and talk about your future without all this ..." he waved around at the crowd in the gym "going on. Sound good?"

"Sounds good."

"Outstanding! Great meeting you, Van!" Another commanding handshake and Van was dismissed. CPO Hollis pounced on the next kid at the table. "Hey there, bud! Interested in joining the Navy? Want to see the world? Have some adventures? Make some friends for life?"

Sure enough, CPO Jim Hollis phoned the following day, and came to Van's house to pick him up. "Nice place," he said to Van, with a dubious look. "Your parents around, Van? I could introduce myself to them if you want."

"No. No parents. Just me."

"I see. Sorry to hear that." He looked at Van soberly. "You eighteen, by chance?"

"Just turned."

"Ah. Okay then." He looked at the house and then into Van's eyes. "I think we need to get you the fuck out of here pronto, yes?"

"Yeah," Van said. "That's the idea."

"Roger that. Tell you what, let's go get a bite, and we'll talk." So, CPO Hollis drove them downtown to Pointer's Pizza and told Van about his own career in the Navy, as a submariner. He asked Van about his high school grades and told him about the Navy's Nuclear Power School. "Right, first you go through boot camp. Then you go to your "A" school, for your job rating. Then it's six months at Nuclear Power School in South Carolina, and six months at a Nuclear Power Training Unit and you're in. Bam! A little under two years of training and you're set for life. You can get stationed on shore, on an aircraft carrier, or on a submarine, like I did." Van nodded along, trying to follow. "Here's the killer thing. Let's say you don't love the Navy, right? You can get out after only six years and get a job the next day at any power plant in the world. That's how good the training is. A good paying job too."

Then he started throwing dollar signs around. The Navy could offer Van a fat chunk of money to sign up, more when it came time to re-enlist. There was duty pay and hazard pay and another chunk of cash to put toward college after his first enlistment. For someone who had only ever made a few hundred dollars working part time here and there, it was a fortune. Van felt like it was all too good to be true.

"Okay, Van, how's it sound? You still interested?" Van just nodded, speechless. "Great, great!" He pulled out a well-worn binder full of forms and brochures. "Let me get you to just sign right here if you don't mind. This isn't committing you to anything yet. We'll need you to take the Armed Services Vocational Aptitude Test, to make sure you're not an idiot. You're not an idiot, are you? Then a Physical Fitness Test. Can you run around the block and touch your toes?" Van nodded. "Yeah, I figured. Good, no problem then." He wrote notes and filled in forms. "Ah, wait. One more thing. It's kind of stupid, but they're strict about this shit. Have you ever done any drugs?"

Van winced. "I mean ... I smoke some weed once in a while."

"Okay, okay. No big deal. You're young. I get it. I used to spark a doobie now and again myself before I joined, you know?" Van cringed inside. "Look, here's what we do. When was the last time you smoked? Honestly."

"Umm. The day before yesterday?"

"Right. Okay. Let's see. It'll take thirty days or so to get it out of your system before processing. We've got the ASVAB and PFT and I'll stretch it a little. No big deal. Okay, check it out. I'm going to put the date that you smoked down here. See it?" Van nodded. "Okay, and when they ask you, just say that you tried it once at a party, and you didn't like it. Right? That way if it does somehow show up on the piss test you're covered. Make sense?"

"Got it," Van said.

"Sweet. And no more! Don't smoke any more, okay?" Van gave him a thumbs up. And that was that. His name was on the forms, he was in the system, and the mill wheel started turning. Van had officially joined with countless other men and women throughout history in the most noble, the most inevitable, the most idiotic of institutions. He felt as though he had become a part of something, and he had. He was now a locking plastic brick, thrown into a huge pile of other plastic bricks. He would be pulled from the pile by costumed children with stars on their shoulders and joined with other bricks to fashion hammers or walls. The children would smash the hammers against the walls, and the walls would fall or hold, and the bricks would break, and the costumed children would lie and brag and go home until the time came to play again.

Once Van signed the paper, time seemed to align more with something large and incomprehensible than with his small life in Eastern Standard Time. Van took his test and did well enough. He did his run and touched his toes. And one day, CPO Jim Hollis picked Van up at 0600 to take him to the Military Entrance Processing Station in Atlanta. He was to spend the day being poked and prodded and tested and interviewed and at the end of the day he would be sworn in, and his term of duty would begin. He would be shipping out for boot camp a week later.

"Alright man, here you go," CPO Hollis said when he pulled up in front of the MEPS building. "Just do what they tell you and everything will be great." Van got out of the car and the recruiter rolled down the window. "Oh, and don't forget! You smoked once and didn't like it, right?" Van gave him a thumbs up and Hollis pulled away.

There are dozens of M.E.P.S. stations around the United States, all different shapes and sizes, but they all serve the same function. They take the raw detritus scooped up en masse by legions of military recruiters across the country and shake it and poke it and sift it until workable, usable raw material rises to the top. Candidates are formed into lines and moved from one spot to another, from one room into another. They're given a complete physical examination, a mental evaluation and a handful of interviews. Discerning eyes question and examine.

Van went through the routine. He stood in the lines with other tired, excited boys and girls who, like him, were too hopeful, too optimistic to resent their voluntary commodification. Finally, late in the afternoon, when it seemed like he must be getting near the end of the ordeal, Van's name was called, and he was pulled out of the herd and directed to a less crowded part of the building. An aide knocked on a nondescript, unlabeled door and Van was admitted to a small room populated only by a Petty Officer Second Class seated behind a metal desk. There were no other chairs in the room, no decorations, or pictures on the walls. On his desk was a stack of files, and there was an open file in front of him.

"Are you Van Ryan?" He looked up briefly from the file.

"Yes, sir." The man looked through the file.

"It says here that you smoke marijuana, Mr. Ryan."

"Well sir ... I tried it once, at a party. Didn't like it much, though."

"I see. Can you tell me when that was? That you "tried" it?" He glanced at Van, skeptically.

"Um, yes sir. It was ... it was about a month ago."

"The date, please?" Van's mind raced. He tried to remember what date he and CPO Hollis had come up with. He blurted out his best guess. The man at the desk took closer look at the file. "That's not what it says here, I'm afraid."

"Well, maybe ..."

"I'm afraid the Navy doesn't need you, Mr. Ryan." He closed the file with purpose.

"Wait, what?"

The man reached into the bottom drawer of the desk and pulled out a ticket, a bus ticket, and slapped in on the desk in front of Van. "Thank you for coming in, Mr. Ryan."

"Now wait, I ..."

"You are dismissed, Mr. Ryan." Van picked up the ticket and stumbled out of the M.E.P.S. station into the dismal afternoon.

Van had no idea where he was. No idea where the M.E.P.S. was, where the bus station was. He was walking, wandering the city streets not seeing the stores and businesses he passed. People traveled the same sidewalks, and more than once he bumped into them without noticing. He crossed streets haphazardly, twisted up in a storm in his mind. Sometimes he crossed with the traffic light, other times cars swerved to avoid him. No matter how fast he walked, or where he turned, there was no path in front of him.

What the hell would he do now? How could that have happened? He felt betrayed. By the Navy. By CPO Hollis. By his father. By his friends down at the creek. He was *sure* there was unanimous consent regarding his decision. It was what they all wanted. It was what he was supposed to do. How could they have been wrong? Van felt this was just another example of life kicking him along where it wanted him. Taking control of *his* path. Just when he was beginning to shape his own future he had been sidelined. T-boned. Blown off course by an off-season wind.

Van tripped over a crack in the sidewalk, and he stopped walking. A tree grew between the sidewalk and the street. It was an old and smug tree, and its roots grew under the sidewalk and made it crack and peak like a pubescent mountain range. He felt nauseous and he had to pee. He looked up and watched a Marine Corps Staff Sergeant in his resplendent dress blue uniform walk through a glass-fronted, strip mall office door onto the street in front of Van. The sign and posters on the front of the office read *"Marine Corps Recruiting,"* and the Staff Sergeant stared steadily at Van, sizing him up. "You want to talk to a Marine recruiter, son?" Van had wandered halfway around the city of Atlanta with a crumpled bus ticket in his hand only to trip on that particular bit of broken sidewalk, at that exact moment. Was that fate? Van's head hurt, and he had to pee.

"Don't have much of a choice, I guess," he said. "Do you have a bathroom in there?"

And so, it was to be the bullets after all.

19

A SHINY .38

SPOT LIVED IN AN old, renovated warehouse off a side street in downtown Little Rock. They entered through a sketchy back alleyway entrance and climbed two flights of stairs before she fumbled with her keys to unlock a heavy, dented, metal door. It swung open to reveal a huge, open space that had been converted into an apartment. Two of the walls were exposed brick, one long wall was wood, and one was newer sheetrock, where dividing walls had been added to section off part of the space into several small rooms. Light streamed in from a bank of high windows along an outside wall on the far side of the apartment. Exposed pipes and ductwork ran above their heads, and the floor was unfinished concrete, painted mottled brown with some sort of acid stain.

"Wow. This is amazing!" Van said.

"Yeah, thanks. It's subsidized. The city had a drive to grow this area into an arts community. I was lucky to snag this. It's a good space for ..." She waved her hand at the most prominent feature of the space: an overwhelming number of paintings and art tools and supplies, strewn and hung and leaning all around the apartment. On one side of the room was an easel with a work in progress, and several tables were covered with paint and brushes, solvents, knives and rags.

"God damn it!" Old metal kitchen cabinets, a stove and refrigerator ran along the most inside wall, across from a sink and a butcher-block island. It was a decent-sized open kitchen arrangement. Empty beer cans, paper plates and a giant pizza box lay on the island. Next to the kitchen, along the long wall topped with windows, there were second-hand pieces of furniture, arranged around a worn braided rug. There were two well-used couches, a rattan chair, several beanbag chairs, a wooden coffee table that looked hand-carved from the stump of a large tree, and several crates and boxes serving as end tables. Practically every surface was covered in beer cans, cheap vodka bottles, food remnants and cigarette butts. "I swear to FUCKING god!" She stormed past the kitchen to the other side of the space, where the rooms had been constructed. He heard Spot yelling, and soon a second voice rose to meet hers.

Van walked back over to the painting on the easel. It was stunning. The artist had used a variety of media: paint, yes, and bits of fabric and paper. The image was a female form, a young woman, at a slight angle from the viewer. She had her hand out, and she was blowing something, some dark, particulate substance off-frame: smoke, dust? At the center of her body there were small colored pieces of glass, stone and tile affixed to the canvas, which reflected the light so that the subject was glowing from within. The outlines of the woman's form were drawn somehow opaque, ethereal, the boundaries barely defined. The background of the painting was white, except the bottom right, where a murky mass seemed to be forming, with bits of newspaper and textiles giving it substance.

The sounds of two people arguing became less muffled as a young woman burst into the studio space, tears on her face and a backpack over her shoulder. "Fine," she yelled over her shoulder, "see if you can find anyone *else* to put up with your bullshit!"

"Just get the fuck out!" Spot followed behind her. "I'm sure she'll take you back!" Spot's face was red, and her cheeks were also wet. "Don't worry, I'll clean up after you, little baby!" The girl ran out the door, and Spot slammed it shut after her. She stood, leaning her forehead against the closed door for a minute, breathing heavily.

"Sorry about that, Stan," she said to the door.

"No worries," Van said. "Sorry for ..." He gestured toward the door.

"Yeah. Whatever," she said. "It was coming. We both see other people, you know? It's all good. But this place is sacred." She gestured around the apartment, at the mess. "Look at this shit!" She pulled a trash bag out from below the sink and started throwing things into it.

"So ..." Van said. "These are yours, then?" He indicated the art around the studio.

She nodded. "Mmmhm. Goddamn cigarettes, you know? I told her over and over about smoking in here. It gets in the canvas." She mumbled to herself as she cleaned up. "She had quite a party as soon as I was gone, huh?"

"Spot?"

"Jesus Fucking Christ! Will you look at this shit?" She closed the lid of a greasy pizza box and revealed a shiny .38 caliber revolver on the kitchen counter underneath. "What the hell do you think they were doing with this? Fuck! What a bunch of idiots!"

"Is that yours?" Van asked.

"Damn straight! You don't see any bullet holes anywhere, do you? God damn bunch of children, I swear." She took the gun with her into the bedroom and emerged shaking her head.

"Hey Spot?"

"Hm?"

"These are amazing." He walked around looking at the other pieces. A lot of them were variations of the same technique and style. Most incorporated the female form, but there were some male nudes, and some portrayed birds or landscapes. Some of the canvasses were just black, solid color or gradations. "Where did you study? Seriously, these are incredible."

"Oh, thanks. I've always scribbled stuff. I was studying with a woman here in Little Rock for a while, but she OD'd last year so ..." She wrapped up the full trash bag and set it by the front door. "You hungry? I'm goddamn starving."

"Yeah, I could eat."

"Chinese?"

"Sure. That'll work."

"Sweet. You're paying though. There's a number on the fridge. I'm gonna catch a quick shower."

"Wait ... what's the address here?" Van asked, but she was already gone.

"Shrimp fried rice for meeeee ..." She yelled from the bathroom, and Van heard the bathroom door close, and the shower start to run. He found the restaurant menu hanging on the fridge under a magnet in the shape of a bunch of grapes. The magnet read "Italia!" He got the address to the apartment from some unopened mail on the kitchen counter.

The food showed up right before Spot finished with her shower. Van heard the knock and opened the door. An Asian man wearing jeans, a button-down dress shirt and an Arkansas Razorbacks baseball cap stood outside, holding a plastic shopping bag heavy with to-go containers. "Van Ryan!" The man barked.

"Goddamn it!" Van yelled back at him, impulsively.

"This is most likely the last time we will be able to communicate with you, Van Ryan. As we told you, the farther away you travel, the harder it is for us to maintain contact with you."

"Oh no!" Van said, sarcastically.

"You have fulfilled your task well up until this point, Van Ryan. However, now comes the difficult part."

"More 'trials?' Challenges?"

"Indeed. You must accompany the girl, and you must do what needs to be done."

"And what it that?"

"When you are near the silent component of our self, the bit of our form which was absorbed into your skin will separate itself from your hand and become whole again. You must put it in direct contact with the component. Do you understand?"

"Yeah, I guess so. What's going to happen then?"

"We are not entirely sure. As we told you, this has never happened before. This action should bring us back in contact, however, and bring that component back into the collective."

"And what happens to me then?"

"That will depend on you, Van Ryan." The fog lifted from the man's eyes. He shook his head and looked around him, at the bags in his hands. He handed them to Van and looked at the ticket stapled to the bag. "All set!" He smiled and walked slowly away, shaking his head.

Van closed the door and set the bags on the counter just as Spot got out of the shower. She came out in a fresh pair of torn jeans and a loose, black, sleeveless t-shirt. Her huge, tousled bale of hair was damped down and hanging around her face in thick, wet curls. "Sweet! Grub's here!" She walked by him in a warm, soapy breeze and started pulling take-out containers out of the bags.

He pointed at the magnet on the fridge. "You been to Italy?"

"Not yet, but I will. I'm going to Rome someday. Eat good food, look at good art. Maybe swim in the Mediterranean. Maybe fuck some Italians. I think Rome must be the exact opposite of shitty Arkansas, or anywhere here in the South, culturally."

"Maybe so."

"I mean, don't get me wrong, women my age in Harrison can come up with thirty-eight different ways to cook Deer Meat Cornbread Fritters in possum fat. That's creative, sure, but that ain't the same thing as composing a poem. Or drawing a picture. Or even creating a swan statue out of a block of ice with a chainsaw, you know? You ever seen that shit? It's amazing!"

"They do that in Rome? Ice sculptures of pond birds?"

"I would think so, wouldn't you? But it is hard to come by good, fresh possum fat there, I hear. At least in the winter. So, there's that."

The food was hot and messy, and they ate it right out of the cartons, Spot with chopsticks and Van with a plastic fork. Spot dug out two bottles of cheap champagne from the crisper drawer in the fridge, and they drank out of mismatched wine glasses. "Why not? I've been saving this for too long. This seems pretty 'special occasion' to me." They looked at each other and Van could see she was thinking this might be her last chance to drink it.

After the food was gone and things put away, Van sat on a worn, comfortable sofa and allowed the last few days of exhaustion to sink into the cushions with him. Spot curled up in a wicker papasan chair next to him, and they both sat quietly, sipping champagne, and looking at the three-quarter full moon through the row of windows high on the wall in front of them.

"I don't want to go to Harrison, Stan. Harrison is a bad place. It's a very bad place." Spot said after a while. "Lauren doesn't want to go to Harrison."

"Lauren?"

"Yeah, Lauren. Think I was born with assholes calling me 'Spot?' Lauren was a happy little girl in Harrison until her mother got sick and died. Fucking left her there. Left at home with a broken daddy and an older brother who promised to take care of her." Quiet. Sips. Moon. "But he didn't take care of her. He didn't."

"What happened?"

"After their daddy went to jail the first time ... he decided that "taking care of her" meant *taking* her. Taking possession of her. Treating her like a girlfriend." She breathed a long breath in and out. "But on the down low, right? Like, no one can know it. That's what he tells her." Van looked at the floor and shook his head. "He treats her like a man treats a woman, you know?" She poured some more wine in her glass. "Lauren loved her brother. She didn't know any better."

"Where's that piece of shit, now?"

"Oh, he's still in Harrison. People love him. He has a whole bunch of redneck mouth-breathers working for him. They're into all kinds of stuff. Growing weed. Selling pills. Straight-up jacking trucks and stealing shit. They do it all. They love him in Harrison. Even the cops love him." Sip. "There's no fucking justice in this world."

"Sometimes," Van said softly. "Sometimes, there is."

"If there is, I haven't seen it. So I'm damaged goods, Stan. What do you think about that?"

"Whatever." He shrugged his shoulders. "Aren't we all damaged? Doesn't life shit on all of us? Our first scar's after birth, right?" He pointed at his belly button. Spot laughed. "People say our memories define us, or our 'deeds,' but that's bullshit. It's the damage we've suffered. The scars that are left after. That's what defines us. Fucking scars are badass. Tough-ass skin grows over a wound, protects it while it heals."

"What about the damage we do? To others?"

"Yeah. That too. That's definitely part of who we are."

"That's deep, Stan. I think that's the most you've said since I met you."

"Yeah, well you do enough talking for both of us." Spot threw a bottle cap at him. "Seriously, though, I don't know. I've been doing a whole lot of thinking the last few days. I feel like maybe I'm starting to figure some shit out. Stuff that's been rattling around in my head since I was a kid. Your scars suck. Mine suck. But what would the world look like without them?"

"You going to tell me damage 'builds character?' Isn't that a military thing?"

Van smiled. "Yeah, 'pain clears the brain.'"

"That's it."

"Onions, right? Aren't we supposed to be like onions? Layers and whatever? What if it's more like scar tissue? Layers of scars, one on top of another."

"If we're onions, what is the core supposed to be?" She asked. "When you're born? And you just grow these slimy, stinky layers from there?"

"Right? And what's the onion skin supposed to be?"

"Skin, you dumbass. Your skin, wrapped around all your stinky layers." They laughed. "So, let's see your scars, Stan." Van didn't answer at first. "Come on man, I told you about mine."

"Scars heal ... They heal. They just look like hell? I don't know."

"Tell me. Soldier shit, right? War shit?"

"War shit. Yeah, something like that." He took a long sip and he stared at the candle burning on the table between them. It danced and dodged in his eyes, but his gaze was steady and distant. "My scars have dead people in them. Same for a lot of folks, probably." Another long sip, and another refill. "I killed over there. A lot of us did. Some guys it sticks with, others not as much, you know? I was good at it. Killing. But I wasn't made to kill. I like to think that."

"Are there people who are made to kill?

Van thought about it. "Maybe not, I don't know. People sure can learn to kill, though. That's a fact. I had a Staff Sergeant who used to say that the more people you killed, the less it mattered who it was. I don't know ..."

"Why'd they kick you out then? Because you didn't like killing?"

"I don't know ...they like it when you kill the right people, but they don't care so much what happens to anyone else. I know guys killed women and kids, still got medals. Brass doesn't give a fuck. No one finds about that shit. They control the narrative, you know? I suppose citizens of every country are told their soldiers are special. Noble. Their soldiers obey the 'rules,' whatever they are. We're no different than any other invading army, though; rape, murder, whatever."

Van stood up and wandered around the room. He walked over to the exposed brick wall and stood facing it, tracing an uneven line of mortar with a finger. "Guy in my unit liked to kill kids, you know? Fucking sniper. Picked them off like they were little targets at a fairground shooting game." Van breathed. He had started. There was no stopping now. "I was his spotter. We were a two-man team. I was there. I fucking saw him do it. He kept saying he was doing it to 'win the war.' Said every kid he killed there was one less terrorist down the road. 'They all say it's their *destiny* to martyr themselves fighting us,' he used to say. 'Well, it's my destiny to waste them before they get the chance.' I tried to get him to stop. I went to our platoon commander about it, but he didn't want to hear anything. He just wanted the mission accomplished. So, he blew me off, and more kids died."

"Fuck," Spot said, quietly.

"Yeah. So, one day we had orders to clear this village. We were told there were insurgents in the area. You know, "insurgents." Van made quotation marks in the air. "Guys who were just protecting their homes from us. We were supposed to go in and flush them out. Fucking psycho and I, we were sent in first, to try and secure a high point for him to provide sniper cover for the rest of the platoon. We went in quiet, employed every stealth tactic we knew. We found a house taller than the others, with a nice, commanding view of the whole village. We almost made it there."

Van was pacing now. "Someone behind us tripped a booby trap or a mine or something because he fucking blew up, and all of a sudden everything went to shit. They must have been waiting for us because the whole place lit up with bullets and debris and ricochets and shit bouncing around and dinging off everything around us. I turned and saw my partner get picked up and slammed against a wall by something, a grenade or RPG or whatever. I couldn't hear anything at that point, and I had no idea what the fuck was even going on. I grabbed him by the front of his body armor and shoved him toward the nearest house, kicked the door in and dragged him inside. I propped him up against an inside wall and tried to see how bad he was hit. He had some burns, and his face was fucked up and something had burrowed into his stomach pretty good. The bleeding was the bad kind. 'Aw fuck, Ryan ... get me a corpsman, man. I'm hit.' Over and over and over. He was in a lot of pain. I grabbed the radio to call it in, you know?" He looked at Spot for the first time. "But I couldn't do it. I couldn't make the call. I looked at his face, at the pain, and I thought about the kids he had killed. Who fucking knows how many? So, I crouched down next to him, and I watched. I watched him cry and beg and shit himself. I watched him die."

The air in the apartment was thick with Van's confession. It was out. He had told it. A siren sounding somewhere in the city broke the heavy silence. "The discharge, then." Spot said.

Van nodded. "There were those, like my Lieutenant, who thought I did it. I killed him. They knew I had tried to report him. They said the explosion could have been caused by one of our grenades, and some of the wounds could have been caused by my knife. Whatever."

"Did you? Do it?" Spot asked quietly. Van shrugged and shook his head.

"No. It doesn't matter. Whether I stabbed him myself or watched while he died, fewer kids died in that war. They couldn't prove anything one way or another, so they put me on the next plane back to the states and just like that, I was a civilian again."

"And you became a big businessman." She smiled.

"Oh yeah. Slinging drinks, now." He nodded his head. Spot poured out the last of the bottle into Van's glass and they clicked glasses in a hopeless toast. "To onions." Van said.

"*Two* onions." She pointed at each of them.

"To swimming in Rome!"

"To Rome!" They drained their glasses and Spot stood up. "Let's hit it." Van stood and

she held out her hand. He took it and she guided him into the only bedroom. She undressed quickly with her back to him, and dove under the covers. He did the same, and they both lay with their heads on their pillows, their faces inches apart. Van placed his hand gently on her face, and kissed her, tasting the wine on her breath. They both opened their eyes at the same time and Van smiled. Spot burst out giggling. "Get the fuck out of here, Stan!" Van was laughing too. They both realized, at the same time, that the affection they were feeling for each other wasn't physical. It wasn't romantic. It was better than that. Van rolled on to his back, content and relieved of the tension and pressure. The warmth of another body next to his, though, was a welcome pleasure itself, missing for too long. Spot snuggled up to him. Van saw a wall come down in her eyes. It was replaced with vulnerability. She laid her head on Van's chest, which was soon wet and warm from her tears.

20

Ten Feet Down

HE KNEW HE WAS dreaming. He knew he was asleep and living a memory, sketched with a dull pencil and rubbed around the edges. Will and Van and Jimmy Russo, all in their junior year of high school, stood at the edge of a dirty neighborhood swimming pool. It was a September evening, and there was a chill in the air. Shell Wave Community Swim Club had closed early that year. The Pool Manager had died in a tragic fire at his home the week before. When the authorities investigating the fire looked at the pool's financial records, they discovered that the Shell Wave Board of Directors had been diverting funds meant for pool upkeep into their own pockets. So, without draining the pool or removing anything, a padlock had been placed on the pool gate. Will, Van and Jimmy Russo had been drinking, and they decided to sneak into the pool to take a look around.

Jimmy Russo was notorious for having a weak bladder, and he had to pee every five minutes when he was drinking. So, when he went off into a corner behind the snack bar to relieve himself, Will & Van came up with a prank. When Russo returned, trying to button his pants while he was walking, Will yelled at him, "Yo, Jimmy! Look at that fucking water, man!" It was dirty and still, and an off-color residue floated on the surface.

"Yeah, that's nasty!" Russo offered.

"Right? I'll bet you won't jump in there! Ha! He won't, will he Van?"

Van walked over to the side of the pool and leaned over. There were indeterminate shadows along the bottom, which may or may not have been items of pool furniture, thrown in by fellow delinquents. "Naw, he won't do it. Jimmy don't have the balls to jump in there."

"Fuck you!" Russo yelled. He walked unsteadily over to where Van stood. "I ain't scared!"

"Ha!" Will laughed. "Let's see you do it, then!"

"I'll do it if y'all do it!" He looked at the water. "I ain't goin' in there alone, though."

Will joined the others at the side of the pool. "Alright then," he said. "Line 'em up, boys! Let's do this." Will stripped down to his boxer shorts and moved up until his toes were hanging over the edge of the pool.

"We really ...?" Russo asked. Then he shrugged and undressed. Van caught Will's eye and winked as he shed his shirt and pants and joined the line.

"Alright, kids!" Will said. "On the count of three, right?"

"Like, on three?" Russo asked. "Or three and then jump?"

"On three, man. What else? One! Two! Three - we jump, got it? Damn!"

"Alright, alright ..."

"Okay then, ready?" Will started the count. "ONE!" Van and Will bent their knees and stood again, preparing for the jump. "TWO!" Russo saw them and joined in on the warm-up. They all bent down, waiting for the last count, ready to spring. "THREE!" Will yelled and leapt up, but he caught himself before he went in, and stood at the edge with a smile on his face. Jimmy Russo jumped straight in. Van did the same move as Will, almost catching himself, but in the end he half-fell, half-jumped in and went straight to the bottom.

They were in the deep end, only ten feet down, but it felt to Van like he drifted down for hours. The quiet that lives underwater isn't just a lack of noise. Stillness surrounds your face and head, and it insulates you from sound. It keeps the sound away. The water was dark in the pool, and cloudy, and jumping in disturbed the shadows. Van felt his left foot touch bottom and something soft and strong wound loosely around his lower leg. Cold. He kicked his leg and felt whatever it was, rope or cord or tentacle, tighten. He was caught, and he couldn't see what it was that had him. He bent over and tried to free himself, tried to punch and tug at the creature that gripped him but he couldn't get it to let go. He worked at it for a minute or so, until his chest started to hurt. He looked up and could clearly see the outline of the surface of the water, only three or four feet above his head, and he realized that he was going to die. He had never considered his own death before. Apparently, he was going to drown in this dirty fucking pool, but okay. He wasn't afraid. He was running out of air, but it was quiet, and he was alone, and in a moment, his lungs would fill with water and that would be the end. He thought he could make out Yip above him, leaning over the edge of the pool ...

Suddenly there was a huge concussion and the water turned and roiled around him, and a figure ... it was Will ... tried to pull Van free. He swam down to where Van's leg was snagged and followed the rope back to where it was pinned under what looked like a soda machine lying on the bottom of the pool. Will moved the machine enough to create some slack in the rope, and Van was able to free his leg. They both broke for the surface and Van held on to the edge and filled his lungs with sweet southern, early evening fall air. He saw Jimmie Russo across the pool, half dressed, peeing on a fence. Will swam over and hung on to the pool edge next to Van. “What the fuck, man?” He asked, incredulous. He gestured toward Russo.

“I don’t know man.” Van looked at him sheepishly. “I forgot to not jump.”

Will looked at him deadpan and climbed out of the pool. “You know, Van, sometimes I don’t even know why I hang out with you. You’re so fucking helpless.” Will grabbed his clothes and walked to the car without glancing back. As she followed him, Yip turned and looked for a long minute into Van’s eyes. Then she disintegrated.

Van sat straight up in bed before he was even awake. He hadn’t thought about that evening for a long time. Thought about Will saving him. A score had been tallied that evening. A debt accrued. Will never let him forget it. Things changed between them. It was like had Will received a promotion over Van. As close as they’d been, Van had never really felt like Will’s equal. Van was always invited to Will’s house for dinner, for special occasions, or just to hang out, and the rest of their relationship always had that same feel to it. Van was invited to be friends with Will. Will allowed Van to be his friend. Can one person be in charge of a friendship? Will was in charge, and the truth was Van *was* grateful for his friendship. Will gained power over Van that night, and Van let him have it.

Spot ... Lauren was still asleep, turned away from him, curled up and wrapped in the covers she had stolen during the night. It was just past dawn, and Van got out of bed quietly and went into the bathroom for a birdbath. He wasn’t comfortable enough in her apartment to take a shower, and he didn’t have fresh clothes to change into anyway. So, a quick wash of the essentials and he felt like most of a new man. He checked himself out in the mirror. Not quite ready for a job interview, but for what was on the agenda today, he figured he looked good enough.

He made his way through the kitchen, finding coffee and a machine to brew it. He threw a few eggs in a pan and found some bread for toast. It all came together just in time for Spot to wander in, yawning and scratching her head. "What time is it? Whoa. Did we get married or something last night?" She laughed. "Thanks."

"Least I could do," Van said. "Not sure what I'm getting you into today, you know?"

"Yeah. That's the question, isn't it? What are we getting into? Do you know?" They sat down with their food at a linoleum-covered folding card table.

"Not exactly. I need to go somewhere in Harrison. You're supposed to know where." He blew on his coffee. "Do you have wolves in Arkansas?"

"No," She thought for a minute. "I don't think so, anyway. Spider would know about that. Why?"

"Spider's your brother?" Van asked. She looked at her plate and nodded.

They cleaned up the dishes and Spot went to get herself together. While he waited, Van spent the time looking at her canvases stacked up against the wall. He wasn't very educated when it came to art, but her work drew him in. It made him feel curious, excited. Confused. He looked at one spot on the canvas and he needed to see more, needed to understand what he was looking at. The last one he examined was a smaller canvas in a home-made frame. A young woman, nude, with the focus in the foreground of the picture. Behind the subject was a set of twisting railroad tracks, leading to a mountain range in the distance. The hills were a dark, cloudy red against a twilit sky, and the girl was dripping water, as though she had been swimming. On her shoulder, something small and blue. Van leaned in close. It was a blue-tailed skink, smiling at him.

21

Like a Baseball

THEY GOT ON THE road around 10:00 am. Most of the 150 miles to Harrison was spent in silence, Van and Spot each caught in their own storm of apprehension and dread. For Van, it felt like troop movement before a combat mission; the thrill and excitement of impending action coupled with the drudge of the transport, and uncertainty about the action ahead. And fear, multicolored fear. Since the moment Will died on the mountain so many days ago, Van had been set on a path he didn't understand, and now the end of that path was approaching, for better or worse. There was a feeling of relief underlying all the other emotions, a sense that one way or another, a resolution was a handful of highway exits away.

"Spot." Van had left her alone for an hour or so, after she gave him some simple directions, but it was time to talk. "Hey. Lauren."

She turned and looked at him in silence for a moment while her train of thought slowed down. "Hey," she said.

"You ready to figure out what's happening here? What's in front of us?"

"Yeah," she said. "What do you know?"

"I don't know much. I told you, some sort of being ... alien or something made wolves kill my friend Will ..."

"Are you telling me you think all that wild shit you told us at the bar was real? Really real?"

"Really real. It spoke to me dressed like a freaking deer. It told me to get on the road to Memphis. Along the way it ... interfered ... in different ways. To compel me to obey it, kind of. It like, possesses people, you know? Sometimes directly, sometimes ... like the car rental guy, you know? He was okay, but I bet someone at his office was possessed and made the shit happen for us to get this car."

"Or lady cops loaning out squad cars."

"Exactly! Exactly. So anyway, this thing told me I need to go to Harrison, and that you were going to help me get there."

"It told you to find me at Belle's?"

"Well ... not exactly. Um ... fuck, this is weird ... I was downtown and a horse showed up and took me to Belle's."

"A horse."

"A horse."

"Stan, what the actual hell?"

"I know ... I know."

"So, what does any of that have to do with Harrison?"

"The entity ... the alien told me there's another one of its kind there that's blown a fuse or something, and I'm supposed to ... fix it somehow."

"How?"

"I don't know ... you're asking me questions and this shit just sounds weirder and weirder. I swear it's all true though."

"Yeah well, you're insane Stan. No doubt about that. How are you supposed to fix it?"

"It gave me a piece of itself. I'm supposed to touch the broken part with the part I have. Boom. All fixed. There.

That's it. Now you know the whole thing. I swear, every single thing I've told you is the truth."

"Where's the piece? Show me?"

"I can't. It ... it got sucked into my hand, like. It'll come back out when I get where we're going."

"Dude ... you're really pushing it with this shit."

"I know, I know."

"If this is all true," she said. "why don't you just take off? Let this thing deal with its own crap."

"It can hurt people, you know?" Van said. "I've seen it. He can make people hurt themselves ... or other people. People I care about."

She was quiet then for a few miles. Van watched her chewing everything over in her head. She was trying to decide exactly how crazy he was. "Alright. Momma said I should help you, so I'll help you. But you're going to help me, too."

"What do you need?"

"Later. Right now ... this has something to do with my brother," she said. "It must."

"I'm listening," Van said.

"Everyone always liked Spider, you know? One of those people, could fit into any crowd. Played football, dated hot chicks, partied, all that. Then momma died and he took it pretty hard. He started fighting with my daddy when he was around and wouldn't go to see the old man in prison when he was locked up. Spider still smiled and joked around, but it felt like something had dried up behind his eyes. That's when he started coming after me." She was quiet for a bit. Her face was stone, but warm, the heat rising from somewhere deep inside.

"What ..." Van started.

"I'm getting there," she said. "He started spending a lot of time up in the hills, by himself at first. He took his rifle and fishing pole and an axe our daddy gave him, and he disappeared for days at a time. He'd be gone, and daddy wasn't worth shit, so it was up to me to keep the house up and feed myself and so on. Momma's family had left her a little money, which went to daddy when she died, and I made him tell me how to get to it to keep us paid up on all the bills. There was a lot to worry about when Spider was away, but I was okay with it, because at least he wasn't around after me, you know?" Van nodded, listening.

"Anyway, word got around that other fellas were going with him into the hills, and they were building something up there. At first, I just figured they were up there growing weed or making meth or something, 'cuz that's about all that happens around there that's interesting. So, one time he came home, and it was bad ... pretty bad. He hurt me that time. So, I had enough. My daddy had an old bayonet *his* daddy had used in World War II stashed in an old trunk in the attic, and I fished it out and followed Spider, intending to stick him with it. One thing he didn't know: I may not be very big, or strong, but I'm sneaky as fuck. I'd learned how to make myself small and blend into corners and shadows, you know? I'd learned to hide from *him* over the years, so I knew how to follow him without him knowing. I slipped into the back of his pickup and laid low, sketching the trip in my mind as we went from main roads to back roads to off-road trails. It was twilight when we came out on the bank of Cone Creek, right on a sandbar, and Spider got out of the truck and crossed. The bluffs on that part of the river are riddled with caves, and I watched from the back of the truck as the light from his flashlight disappeared into one. I jumped out and waded across the creek as quietly as I could and followed him into the cave. It led up a short climb until it exited on top of the bluff. From there, Spider turned away from the creek and followed a small path for a quarter mile or so through the forest. The trees thinned out, and there was a small clearing with an incline at the far end leading to another cave, and this second cave was where he was heading, where he had been spending his time. In the clearing, just inside of the tree line, were some shacks and shit. I couldn't make them out much in the fading light, but I saw Spider. He headed into the cave and lit a fire. I couldn't get any closer without him catching me, but he was in there for quite a while, and I could hear him talking to someone. Or himself, I don't know." She stopped to catch her breath.

"What was he saying?" Van asked.

"I don't know. I couldn't hear him well enough. I only heard the sound of his voice, and he went on for a long time. I leaned against a tree as close as I dared and froze my ass off waiting for him. After an hour or so he put out the fire and went back the way we came. He almost caught me crossing the river behind him, but there wasn't any moon out, and by the time he shined the flashlight behind him, I had slipped by him and hid by the side of the truck until he got in. Then I hopped in, and we headed back to town."

"Damn, that's some crazy, secret agent kind of shit. What would have happened if he'd caught you?"

"I would have made a fucking hole in him with my granddad's bayonet. I should have anyway, but I needed to know what he was up to, up in that cave."

"Did you ever figure it out?" Van asked.

"Not really. But I did go back up there, a couple of weeks later."

"Tailing him again?"

"No. I went by myself, early in the morning, during the middle of the week when I knew he was away. It was a nice day, and I took my time. It's beautiful country along there. I've never been a big fan of caves, though. Kids at school always went to the caves closer to town to party, you know? Fucking creep me right out. I'm not claustrophobic really, it just doesn't feel right to me to be *underground*, you know? At least not until ..."

"Agreed."

"So, I came up on that clearing again, up on top the bluff? They had all sorts of shit built there. There were a couple of living quarters it looked like. Bunks? Or barracks? I don't know. Some of it was made from regular lumber, some looked like boards they had cut themselves from trees or whatever. Anyway, there were probably four or five small buildings in all. The cave was above the clearing, reached by a short, kind of steep climb." She stopped for a moment. She was growing agitated as she told the story. "The cave was bigger than I had thought, once I was inside. It went back a couple hundred feet or so, and the walls sloped up high, so the ceiling was mostly dark. Straight ahead was ... it's hard to describe ... like a big lump coming out of the wall of the cave. It was like four feet high and maybe fifteen or twenty feet long. The rock around it had been chipped away some, so it made ... not really an altar, or a shelf, just a rounded-off mass, you know? Coming out of the wall. A big rectangular lump. And it was a different color from the rock around it. Everything above it and around it was a dark color, with patterns. When I looked around, I realized the whole cave was like that, black and dark red streaks and patches. But the lump coming out of the wall was like, kind of pinkish." She paused again for a minute or two. Van didn't say anything.

"So just about then, I heard voices, outside. By the camp or whatever it was. I just about peed my damn pants. I looked around and saw in the corner, on the left as you enter the cave, there was a dark shadow. I scurried over there like a fucking cockroach and saw it was a small opening, leading to a tunnel to who knows where. Now I told you I wasn't a fan of caves, right?" Van nodded his head. "Well, I wasn't too keen on crawling through rat tunnels underground either. But I figured anything was better than getting caught by Spider and his idiot friends in their freaking sacred cave or whatever in the middle of nowhere. So, I jumped in it and scurried my little ass along and thank god it only went a couple hundred yards before it dumped me out in the middle of the woods way back behind all their bullshit. I hauled ass and that was that. After that I sold all my shit, dropped out of school and moved to the city. Best thing I ever did. I haven't been back since."

"Has your brother tried to contact you in Little Rock?"

"Friends of his show up places 'coincidentally,' you know? Asking me questions. 'Hey, aren't you Spider's little sister? What are you doing now days? Where do you live?' That kind of thing, you know?"

"Right. Keeping an eye on you. Probably doesn't want to spook you, have you run even farther away."

She nodded her head. After a minute she asked, "So what do you think? The cave? The camp? Any of that make sense to you?"

"Yeah, it does. And no, you're not crazy. You're not. There's some weird shit going on."

They drove a bit in silence. Eventually, Van asked her, "Hey, you know what a skink is, right? Little lizard? Stripes? Bright blue tail?

"Yeah Stan, I know what a skink is. Why?"

"See any up by that cave? Or around the creek?"

"Damn, I wasn't up there on a nature walk. I don't know."

"It's important."

She looked at him seriously. "No, I didn't see any skinks, Stan. But I wasn't really looking for them."

"Okay, I just thought maybe, since you painted that one ..."

"What?"

"The smaller painting, at your place."

"You're freaking me out, Stan! I've never painted a goddamn 'skink' in my life. Why would I? Weirdo."

"Hmm," Van said, unconvinced. They drove for a while in silence.

"Hey Stan," she said, "what if, instead of an onion, we're more like a baseball? You ever open up a baseball? What if life was more like that. One super-long piece of string; all the conversations, relationships, break-ups, books you've read, movies you've seen ..."

"Bands you liked."

"Right. All spaced out and wound tight around some dark fucking center no one can see. All of it wrapped in dinged-up leather."

"Stitched together with ...?

"The scars, right? Our scars. Holding it all together. And the string ... the string winds around itself. Over and over, the string is constantly touching itself. Over and over again. Around and around. Different places, different memories, experiences. Folding together over time. Compressing, you know? Building on each other."

"Yeah. That's pretty good." Van thought about it. "I like that."

"See, I'm not just some little kid. Some stupid fucking little girl."

"I never thought that. Not even close."

Her brow was furrowed, and her eyes narrowed to angry slashes in her face. "Well, someone does, and he's about to find out what's what.

22

Home-Cooked Meal

VAN WAS ALWAYS WELCOME at Will's house, whether Will was there or not. Mr. Snowden always had a corny joke and some advice on hand, and Mrs. Snowden was sure to offer Van a hug and something to eat, no matter what time of day or night it was. They were sweet and solid, friendly to those in their immediate orbit, and Van felt indebted to them. They pitied Van, and they felt it their responsibility to care for him, to help raise him. They pitied Van's father as well, and Mrs. Snowden often gave Van food to take home for Dennis. The Snowdens cared for Van and his father because it was the Christian, charitable thing to do, and because it made them feel good about themselves.

There was a short flagpole in the front yard of Will's parent's house and from it forever flew a perfect American flag. Every stitch was strong, the colors were full and proud, and there wasn't a hole or a tear to be found anywhere in its sacred fabric. Mr. Snowden ran it up every morning and brought it down in the evening. The flag was an important symbol for Will's family, a symbol of strength, self-determination, and of a passionate refusal to question anything they had ever been taught.

Will's father owned Snowden Document Management, a mid-sized company which helped businesses and individuals scan, categorize, store, and destroy digital or paper files. It was a solid, dependable business. The Snowden's weren't rich, by any means, they just always seemed to have a little more than they needed. Will never wanted for anything: a modest car when he turned sixteen, a trip to Ft. Lauderdale for spring break, a senior management position at Snowden Document Management when he graduated high school. The Snowdens lived a comfortable life.

Their comfort was predicated on one fundamental characteristic the family shared, and each of them embraced individually: a proud lack of curiosity or critical thought. They believed what they were told, and they were all the happier for it. Believing what they were told and then embracing that knowledge as their own meant that they were always correct. Change was anathema in their world. Mr. Snowden lived the same life his father had lived, and Mrs. Snowden assumed the same role in life her mother had assumed. Will acted out a bit, as teenagers do, drinking and raising just a little hell, but everyone understood that once he graduated high school, things would settle down and he would dutifully begin transforming into his father. It was a happy, secure life.

When Van was young, he loved going to the Snowdens. Mr. Snowden always greeted Van with a firm handshake, or a friendly clap on the back. Mrs. Snowden always found everything surprising. "Really? That's, *amazing*!" She told Van when he mentioned that he was working at Taco Bell. "Oh, my *goodness*! I just can't *believe* it!" She remarked when he told her the city was repaving their street. All of this while she moved perpetually around the kitchen, cleaning up the last meal or preparing the next.

The lighting was different at the Snowden house; it was brighter somehow, warmer. Things sounded clearer. There was almost always a window open somewhere in the house, offering a fresh breeze. The change in mood Van felt when going from his dark, sad home to the Snowdens' was profound. Dinner at their table was animated and interesting. Mr. Snowden always addressed Van with respect and seemed to value his opinion when he spoke. And if Mr. or Mrs. Snowden let loose with slurs or opinions about people of other colors or nationalities which most folks would term "racist," Van just let it ride, because he knew they were good people, and they only meant it in the best possible way.

As Van grew older, his affinity with the elder Snowdens lessened. At the same time, Will was shaking off his youthful diversions and fancies and falling in line with his parents' "commonsense" way of thinking about the world. "Well, that's just the way it is" became a familiar response when he and Van were talking. "That's the way it's always been" was another. Will had never been a big thinker, but after high school he took a job at Snowden Document Management and reeled in his view of the world to an arm's length perspective. Answers to just about any question Will was presented with were right in front of him. He never had to peer very far or stretch his neck out to understand anything.

Yip was there now, at dinners at Will's house. The Snowdens loved Yip. Everyone loved Yip. Mr. and Mrs. Snowden would sit at opposite ends of the table, and Will and Yip would sit on one side and Van on the other. Mr. Snowden loved to tease Yip, and her laugh would compete with the luscious smells of Mrs. Snowden's cooking to fill every corner and crevice of the house. At times Will's father would make an off-color remark, or offer an anachronistic, socially unacceptable opinion on something, and Van would swear Yip glanced at him as if to say, "Can you believe this guy?" But she never spoke up. She just smiled and nodded and gave Mr. Snowden more credit than he deserved. As Van had done for so many years.

After his discharge, Van was invited to the Snowden home for Sunday dinner. To them, Van had only been away for a couple of years. They didn't know that he had been gone for several lifetimes. How could they know that? He'd been taken to that place *outside*, where all his assumptions and beliefs about his place in the world had been scorched, and the ashes buried deep. These people had never been to that place. The truth was, Van no longer belonged here, in their house. No longer belonged in the world that had been Van Ryan's world. Maybe no longer belonged in the world at all.

He arrived early and stood outside, watching another brand-new flag flap proudly atop the Snowden flagpole in the late afternoon breeze. Will's father saw him standing there and came out to greet him. Mr. Snowden's hair had gone completely white, and age had thinned him out. Some men put on weight as they age, as if experience has offered them more than it has taken away. Cal Snowden was the other kind, a man whose stubborn disavowal of a changing world made him an obstinate, intransigent form to be weathered and degraded by events around him. Van reached out, and the handshake he received was slighter than he remembered.

"Hey there, Van!"

"Sir."

"Good to see you!"

"You too, sir. Thanks for having me."

"Or course, of course! You're always welcome here, son. You know that." He looked Van over, took in his short hair and his tan, deep like a toxic dye which would never scrub out. "You look good, Van." He looked up at flag flying over their heads.

"You know, we're real proud of what you did over there. Real proud."

"Just did my job, sir." This had become Van's go-to response to all the trite compliments and expressions of gratitude people gave him. He had learned that people offered those kinds of statements from a place of guilt, and the comments were supposed to serve instead of real questions about Van's wartime experience. Most people didn't want to know about that - about the bullets and the blood. They just wanted to demonstrate their patriotism and move on to easier topics.

They went inside and Mrs. Snowden hugged Van and then Will did, and lastly Yip. Her hug stayed with Van. He barely touched his chest to hers and patted her on the back lightly before he pulled away, but the warmth and the softness and the smell of her hair stayed with him. He took his seat across from Will and Yip, and Mrs. Snowden served them all and the meal was good.

"Van, Will tells me you bought a tavern downtown," Mr. Snowden said.

"I did. Guy I know was trying to get out. He gave me a good price on the whole package."

"Tough business, that. Most bars go under in the first year or two, don't they? Gotta watch people don't rob you blind."

"Yes sir. That's true. I plan on being there to run it myself, though. I got plenty of time now."

"Better than getting your ass shot off by some towel-head though," Will said. "Am I right?"

"William, you watch your language," Mrs. Snowden admonished him. "We don't talk like that at the table."

"Sorry, ma. Better than getting your 'butt' shot off I meant." Everyone chuckled. Mrs. Snowden looked satisfied. "Van, tell them that story you told me last week," Will said.

"That rag-head trying to kill those privates on your base." Van shook his head and looked at his plate. "Come on, man! So, Van's at this camp over there, right? And the phones are like pay phones, and they only take local currency. So, this one rag-head goes around offering to exchange their money for American money. He sees these two privates outside one of the phone booths, digging in their pockets looking for change ..."

"Excuse me for a second." Van stood up.

"You alright, honey?" Mrs. Snowden asked.

"I'm fine. Excuse me." Van walked out of the dining room, down the hall, past the first-floor bathroom and out the front door. His head was spinning. *Rag-head. Towel-head. Camel-jockey.* Van had used those terms, yes. Shitty names for the guys on the other team. They had all talked like that, over there. But hearing Will try to get a laugh using an insult he probably picked up from a movie, or a show ... it was obscene. Absurd. It was a real-life, dramatic character in Van's war being turned into a cartoon caricature in the Snowden fucking dining room. By an asshole who wouldn't survive thirty seconds in a firefight. Who had everything, and deserved none of it.

It was his last meal at the Snowden's. As he passed the flagpole outside, a breeze picked up, and the flag stood proudly at attention.

23
COLLECT CALL

"REST AREA," the big, blue sign read. *"Last Stop before Harrison."* A white arrow pointed toward the exit ramp. The sign was a hostile warning, a label wrapped around a tourist-sized glue trap. A pair of the old red & green cardboard 3D glasses, or Roddy Piper "They Live" sunglasses would reveal the messages *"Get Out," "Turn Around." "Run for your Life"* beneath the signage. Sometimes, when a gun is pointed at you, and you're out of defensive options, your only move is to charge straight down the barrel. Foolhardy bravado might alter the trajectory of the bullet. If not, at least you'll see it coming.

"Pull in here," Spot said. "I have to pee."

"Roger." Van gave her the thumbs up and drifted off the highway into the Rest Area. He pulled into a parking spot next to a small RV which was disgorging a young family of five.

Like bus stations, highway rest areas offer excellent cross-sections of American highway travel. No matter what state, each rest area presents a school-project diorama, a swarming model of humanity on the move. A pair of brown, rustic-themed buildings with slanted roofs welcome weary travelers, offering meagerly landscaped walkways and plastic-covered boards with faded maps and outdated info about local flora and fauna. In the bathroom building, folks deposit unimaginable tons of waste day in and day out, hopefully wash their hands, and then hit up the vending machine kiosk for a Mountain Dew and a handful of Snickers bars. On the far side of the parking lot dogs crap gratefully, and two out of ten owners clean up after them. People at rest stops take naps, deal drugs, suffer medical emergencies, have sex, commit assault or murder or suicide even. But most folks are oblivious to all of that, and just stop to stretch their legs, take a leak and get something to drink before they head on their way.

While he was waiting for Spot, Van spied a pay phone, and figured he'd try calling Yip. He didn't have enough change in his pocket for a long distance call, so he decided to try calling her collect. He hadn't done that since he was a teenager. His friends would call each other collect, and while they were connected, as the operator was saying "Collect call from ... do you accept the charges?" the person making the call would yell something like "Meet us at the bowling alley!" or whatever, and then slam the phone down before anyone was charged. Now he just dialed and hoped she was home.

"Collect call for Ypsilanti Snowden from Van Ryan. Do you accept the charges?"

"What? Who ...? Yes! Yes please." After dreaming and dreading this call all week, the familiarity of her voice pushed all the confusing chaos out of his mind. "Van, is that you?" She asked.

"It's me, Yip."

"Oh, thank God! I've been calling you ..." Van realized he hadn't looked at his phone in days. He wasn't even sure if he had it anymore.

"It's been ..."

"... they found Will's body up on the mountain, Van! What happened? How did that happen?" She was sobbing and her words were coming like an avalanche.

"Yip, I'm sorry ... There were wolves ..."

"Why didn't you tell me? When you came in the other day?"

"I couldn't bring ..."

"They think you had something to do with it!"

"The wolves, Yip. I'm so sorry. I couldn't stop them."

"Van, they said he might have been stabbed with a knife! How ..."

"... I couldn't save him ..."

"How could this happen?"

"I'm sorry, Yip. I tried ..."

"You were his best friend!" She was crying now. "I know he wasn't always nice to you, but ..."

"The wolves, Yip. They were too fast. There are so many things I can't explain to you right now."

"Is this about us?"

"It's so complicated, Yip. You wouldn't believe me."

More crying. "He's gone! I can't believe he's gone. What have you done, Van?"

"I couldn't save him ..."

"What have you done?"

"Yip, you're not listening ..."

"How could you?" A pause. "Was this about us?"

"Yip ..."

"Was this about us, Van? Us? It was just a kiss! Just a kiss!"

And with those words, "Just a kiss," Van could smell her. He could smell the perfume she wore in high school, smell the shampoo, the hairspray she used. He could smell the skin in the crook of her neck, where it joined her shoulder and invited his face to rest. He could smell beer on her breath and her lips as he leaned in to kiss her. It was late at night, Will was passed out drunk, and for one rare moment they found themselves released from their normal roles as "friend" and "friend's girlfriend." For a moment, they allowed themselves to experience being together as boy and girl. To feel the heat in that moment as man and woman. Inhibitions dulled by the alcohol, they were drawn together. Then she thought she heard a noise coming from downstairs and it was over. It was just a kiss; quick, exploratory, accidental maybe, on her part. But for Van it lasted for the rest of his life.

"Things changed that night, didn't they?"

"Look Yip, I know you're upset ..."

"Didn't they? Between us. Between you and Will?"

"Will was the best friend I ever had, Yip. I would never ..."

"You resented him. After that night you resented him. I saw it. The way you looked at him. The way you looked at me. I know how you felt about me, Van. How you always felt."

"You're upset, Yip. You're upset. Of course you are. I'm so sorry about what happened."

"It wasn't his fault, Van. It wasn't his fault. I liked you too, you know. You just never tried to get close." Van was quiet then. "You never paid attention to me. He did. I just wanted someone to pay attention to me."

"I didn't ..." Van was speechless.

"They think you did it, Van."

"The wolves ..."

"There aren't any wolves on those mountains! You know that!"

"Yip ..."

"You keep talking about wolves, Van! There aren't any fucking wolves!"

"He wasn't good enough for you," he whispered into the mouthpiece.

"Bears! You should have said it was bears. There aren't any fucking wolves anywhere around here!"

"Look, Yip ..."

"They're looking for you, Van."

"I'm sorry." Van hung up the phone. He couldn't say "goodbye," couldn't admit to himself that he would never see her again.

Spot was standing outside the car, waiting for him. She offered to drive, and Van tossed her the keys without saying anything. He walked around to the passenger side and got in. She started the car. "You okay?"

He nodded. His face was hard like polished granite, but a white-hot fire burned behind his eyes she hadn't seen before. As she pulled out into traffic on the highway toward Harrison, she felt afraid of more than just her brother.

Part 3

The Dance

24

Behind Enemy Lines

LESS THAN A MILE after crossing the Harrison, Arkansas town line the billboards stood tall. There was no subtext or innuendo about who owned the city, or who was welcome and who was not.

"Welcome to Harrison!
Beautiful Town / Beautiful People!
No Wrong Exits. No Bad Neighborhoods"

The picture on the billboard was of a man and his loving wife and their two happy sons, all wearing pastel colors and wide smiles. All white. The billboard below that one was yellow with big, black lettering:

"DIVERSITY IS A CODE WORD FOR #WHITEGENOCIDE"

Spot's face was a combination of embarrassment and anger. "I told you," she said. A few miles farther along, the same family with the same *"Beautiful Town ..."* message, only with a more modern font and background. The sign above that one that read, in the same yellow and black style:

"Anti-Racist is a Code Word for Anti-White"

Then, another one:

"It's NOT Racist to LOVE Your People"

... which was an ad for the local AM radio station: "White Pride Radio." The top left quadrant of that sign was a picture of an adorable young white girl holding a puppy, and along the bottom, in a mostly illegible font, it read:

"Harrison: Love Lives Here"

"Wow," Van said. "You weren't kidding."

"Yeah. This fucking place ..."

"Is it Klan? Is there a big Klan chapter here or something?"

"Yeah, it's Klan, it's 'heritage.' All of it."

She followed the route from the highway to downtown Harrison. It was laid out like a lot of small southern towns. At the dead center of town was the County Courthouse. Three stories tall, square, and built of sturdy red brick, the courthouse had stood in that location for more than a century. It occupied a small, quiet, square park with cultivated grass and shade trees. There was a veterans memorial to one side, and a freshly-painted gazebo for public events. A small, two-lane street went around the park, and on the far side of the street, the park was enclosed by neat rows of businesses. There were café's and a drugstore, a shoe store, a hardware store, a post office, a barbershop. There was a beauty supply shop, a karate studio and an insurance broker. Van looked around, expecting to see something terrible. Bonfires and pitchforks, confederate flags flying, nooses hanging from all the trees. But all he saw were white folks going about their business; driving, shopping, walking their dogs, talking. Like countless other southern towns. It was a slow, quiet place where you could pay your taxes, have a bite to eat and get your hair cut all in the same spot. Then you could sit back on a park bench with some lemonade or sweet tea and bake in the afternoon sun while you scrutinized people driving around the square.

That's what folks were doing now. They were watching Spot and Van as they drove slowly around the town square. "What're they all looking at, goddamn it?" Van asked. It was eerie.

"Right? They know we don't belong here. Also, look at how old everyone is." Van hadn't noticed, but she was right. There wasn't one person walking or sitting around the square who was under sixty years old. Every single one of them shaded their eyes or ducked their heads so that they could look directly at Van and Spot. He felt as though they had snuck across a closed border into a foreign nation. They were spies now, behind enemy lines. Even being young and white wasn't a good enough disguise. Their white skin uniforms weren't enough. A man sat on a bench on the square, facing them as they drove by. He wore brown pants, a short-sleeved checkered shirt, suspenders, and an American Legion hat. He was eating French fries out of a Styrofoam clamshell container, and he stopped eating, holding a single fry in his greasy fingers so he could stare at them as they passed him.

Van shook his head. "Hey, we're not stopping here, are we?"

"Hell no." She turned off the square and sped up. Van knew that outside the downtown there was sure to be a supermarket, some department stores, maybe a mall. The town would have grown out from the courthouse, with newer businesses and neighborhoods lying further away from the center of town. But the town square was the heart. Where tradition lived.

After a few blocks, she took a turn, and then another, and then pulled over in front of a white, ranch-style house badly in need of some fresh paint. She took a deep breath and sat back in her seat.

"What's up?"

"That's where I grew up." She pointed at the house. It sat back about fifty yards from the street. The driveway leading to the house was cracked and broken. It looked like the roof wasn't very old, but the siding showed some mildew, and the paint was peeling. One shutter hung crooked. The yard was mostly dirt, and what grass there was lay dying. It was a nice house, small. It could have been cozy, in another world. But Van knew it had never been that for Spot. He could see in her face that there were no good memories here.

"Really?" Van asked. "Who lives there now?"

"Spider."

"What? Your folks ... your father left it to him?"

"He left it to both of us. One of Spider's dickhead friends told me when he looked me up in Little Rock."

"You didn't come home when your old man died?"

"Nope."

"Why are you letting that asshole live there? Sell it and split the dough with him!"

"No! I don't want to deal with him. Trust me, it's never that simple with him. I'd get dragged back into all kinds of shit."

"That's a good little chunk of change sitting there. You deserve your share."

"I'm telling you it's not worth it!" The fire in her eyes took on a dangerous intensity.

"Okay, okay. I get it. Let's get out of here, yeah? Fuck this place."

"Yeah. Good idea." She pulled away from the curb. "We need to head out of town a little ways."

"Yes, please," he said. "*Far* out is fine by me." She smiled. "You were right, this place sucks."

"Yup."

"How the hell did *you*, an artist, a sexually confused young woman ..."

"NOT confused!" She laughed.

"I know, I know. I'm kidding. Seriously though, a creative type like yourself, coming out of here? How did *that* happen?"

"I don't know, really," she said. "I always wanted to get away from here. I never fit in. I was always different. I don't know if it was my momma dying, or what my brother did to me, but it sure occurred to me pretty early on that the shit we're all taught is mostly fucking lies. Like we're born in someone else's story, and we just live in it unless we learn differently. Someone else wrote it, not me. It's all a movie script, you know? The bible, the law, fairy tales, "heritage," it's all the same bullshit."

"Yes."

She waved at town around them. "These assholes are just characters in someone else's story, man. Someone gives them their lines, boom! You're a person. Congratulations, asshole! Who the hell says white people should rule the universe? Well, that guy's daddy's daddy's daddy said so, so we'll just keep that one rolling on. Teach his kids, too. 'Cuz they do, you know?"

"Do what?"

"They teach this evil bullshit to their shitty little ankle-biters here like it's essential curriculum. Like if you could just take a school kid and sit him at his little desk and give him his little evil primer and teach him to conjugate hate 5,000 different ways. Do they even diagram sentences in school anymore? These little fuckers could diagram sentences by Nathan Bedford Forest. Or Andrew Jackson. Or fucking David Duke. I'll tell you that."

As they drove away from town, the roads got smaller. Dried lines of tar filled never-ending cracks in the pavement, like crazed porcelain. "Yeah, I hear you," Van said. "I bet there's some God happening here too, yeah?"

"Shit. They think God *lives* here. Religion is the worst script of all! You can't get people to let go of that one. How are they going to deal with all their fear, then? What are they going to do if they can't pretend that all this scary, horrible shit happening to them has some sort of glorious purpose behind it? No, they'll just call it God, and thank you very much. It's impossible."

They drove for thirty minutes before she slowed down and started looking around them. "Shit, this is more built up than it was last time I was here." New housing stood boxy and grey. Every house looked like it was built from one of four designs, then painted one of two colors. Older houses persevered in between new development. The older ones stood on larger lots, sparse, and far between. "There!" She said and turned into what looked like someone's driveway. It was a long, narrow, poorly paved road running along a wooden fence bordering someone's property. When the fence ended, the road kept going. Soon she found another road, this one unpaved, a county road, with a county number. "Alright," she said. "I think this is it."

25

SANDSTORM

THE DESERT IS COLD at night. Brisk, hard, pinching cold. It gets into your wide eyes as you stare at the magnificent, terrifying panoply of stars blanketing the sky. The round moon is another wide eye, mocking, revealing the cold, painfully flat landscape which stretches out, grasping for the horizon. Cold but not quiet; there are things alive in the desert at night, skittering, rustling, disturbing the sand and small shrubs that fight ferociously for their right to exist. Things moving unseen, reveling in the sun's slumber. The night cold is welcome, clung to, and grieved for as the daylight comes again.

Daytime in the desert is absence. Deprivation. Emptiness filled with heat. Water and green vegetation; resonant, eternal symbols of life and fertility, are alien in the desert. The heat is merciless, sadistic. Inescapable. Occasionally a breeze generates movement of the air, but it brings no relief. The hot wind merely picks up pinches of sand and sticks them to the sweat on your hands, your face, your neck. The sweat is the life-saving water leaching involuntarily from your body, cooling you and killing you. The heat scorches the hairs and mucus out of your nose, clearing out a charred pair of tunnels for the hot air to set fire to your lungs.

The ground beneath your feet is a lie. It shifts and slides. It exists as a tangible semi-solid one moment, the next it emulates water and flows in whatever direction the wind is blowing before, finally, it dissembles into a million sharp, tiny shards of glass as it swirls and billows, obscuring your vision and tearing at your flesh. The ground promises to be firm, and then pulls you in, threatening to encase you in sand. Desiccate and preserve you in oblivion. How many of us are buried in the sand? This thought lives in your mind as the sun mounts the sky every dawn.

The creatures of the desert reveal themselves in the daytime. They are the scorpions and the snakes, the geckos and the beetles. They have all fought from the moment of their birth to survive this cruel landscape, and it has made them mean and treacherous. The vipers sneer and the scorpions threaten. The smallest will kill you. Lizards of all types lay still in whatever shade they can manage to find, and they stare in contempt or ignore you as you pass.

Too long. Too long in this place. The preachers say Jesus fought Satan in the desert for forty years, but they don't know that the desert is Satan's *home*. Jesus didn't stand a chance. Moses and the Israelites supposedly wandered around the desert for forty years as well, and it made them so fucking insane that God didn't even want them around anymore. Forty years. In forty years, you're a shell, burned out from the inside. Gone are love and compassion and philosophy. All that lives inside is survival. And despair. Forty years. Forty days. Forty hours. Forty years. Forty years. Forty. 40 ... 40 ... 40 ...

Van longs for the creek behind his old house, where he can soak his feet in the cool water and tell stories to the only ones who love him. Who understand him. He longs for the mountain trails and trees ... yes. He would do anything to see a tree. Anything green growing above his ankles. And Yip ... if he could see Yip. But not here. Not here. She doesn't belong here. He pictures her walking toward him, out of the desert. A sandstorm approaches from behind and Van tries to warn her. *Run!* He yells into the wind. *Run! Run!* He yells until the sand fills his mouth and throat and silences him. The storm catches her and tears her cashmere sweater to shreds. She drops to one knee with her hand raised toward him and she is lost in the dark, whirling nightmare. He wakes up screaming her name, again, as the sand rustles against the outside of his tent. The sand tells him every day now to go. Go! You don't belong here! We are going to eat you! The vipers and scorpions and sandstorms and bullets! There is nothing for you to conquer here! You'll be a mummy, lost for the ages in the shifting dunes of ancient, foolish death. Van screams inside his mind against the taunts and threats the desert flings at him without pause. He beats his fists against his eyes and gives up sleeping because he is more vulnerable when he sleeps. The desert pleads with him to lay down and dream, but Van knows it only wants to murder him. No one knows. No one knows. No one knows what the desert is screaming at him. No one knows. No one hears the combat in his mind. He doesn't want anyone to find out, because they would assume he was going mad, and the madness is the only thing tethering Van to reality at that point. No one knows.

It's so cold at night.

26

THIRTY-EIGHT STEPS

THERE WAS NO ROAD anymore. Spot was driving the SUV slowly along a small, well-traveled path through the woods. White oak and hickory trees grew here, interspersed with desperate young shortleaf pines fighting for sunlight. The trees weren't very tall, but the canopy was thick above them, and brush choked off visibility on either side of the path. Spot had opened her window and leaned out occasionally to gauge how wide the path was. The air smelled fresh and humid and there was the sound of running water nearby. Even with the car's enhanced suspension, dried ruts made by other vehicles jolted and slammed Van and Spot around the cab. Van held his mouth closed tightly so he didn't chip a tooth.

"You alright?" He asked Spot. She was sweating and the veins and tendons in her hands and forearms stood out like cables. She looked ready to tear the steering wheel from its mountings.

"I got it. I got it. Almost there ..."

Ahead, another dirt trail crossed the one they were on, and she cut a sharp left. This path only ran a few hundred yards before it emptied onto a rocky riverbank. Thousands of smooth pebbles and medium-sized rocks ran along both sides of a fair-sized stream as far as they could see. Spot turned onto the bank and drove south carefully. The creek bed was shallow, and the shore was flat. On the opposite side of the creek huge sandstone bluffs towered hundreds of feet above the water. After a minute, she said, "There it is! Over there." She was pointing across the creek, at the wall of the bluff. Van only saw small yellow beech trees and shrubs, dotted by an occasional sugar maple, its leaves glowing like a campfire. Spot pulled forward and found a place she could hide the car in the woods, away from the water. It wasn't hidden exactly, but it wouldn't be the first thing someone noticed if they passed by. "I'm not sure where the rest of them have their trucks stashed, but this'll do," she said.

They got out of the car, and Van popped the back hatch and dug around in his duffle bag until he found his knife. He pulled it out of its sheath and inspected the blade, and then fixed the sheath to his belt. He turned and faced Spot. "Hey, listen," he said to her, "you don't have to do this. You can just tell me how to get there. I can manage."

"Fuck you, Stan. You're not the only one on a mission here," she said, and they headed out.

The water was late-summer warm and moving at a gentle pace. Pants rolled up to their knees, just above the water's surface, Van and Spot walked carefully to the other side of the creek, one hand holding their boots, the other waving for balance. They stepped cautiously, searching with their feet for sand and pebbles, and avoiding larger, sharper rocks. On the far side they sat on the bank and put their boots back on. "This is the perfect time of year to come out here," Spot said. "The water's a lot higher in the early spring, and it's cold as fuck in the wintertime."

They walked away from the creek, toward the bluff. Spot headed straight to a grouping of saplings and bushes at the base of the towering sandstone wall, and as they approached, Van could see it was all camouflage, a wooden screen fabricated to conceal an opening in the wall. It was obvious up close but would easily hide the cave from canoers traveling on the creek. Spot moved it aside and nodded for Van to step into the opening. She followed and pulled the screen back in place when she was through.

It was cool inside the small cave. Spot clicked on a flashlight and showed the beam around. To their right was a pool of water, the echo of its motion trickling softly off the cave's walls. The reflection from the light shimmered on the ceiling of the cave. A hundred feet or so ahead of them was an incline that rose off to the left, out of sight. "Well, that's new," she said. "That used to be just, like, a dirt ramp. It was a bitch to climb up. Someone's been busy." Steps had been chiseled into the stone, and there was a rope handrail waist high running through a handful of iron rings driven into the wall. The stairs were steep, and they were damp. Van's adrenaline was high, and he had to force himself to go slow and take care not to slip. His mind ricocheted from estimating distances around the small cavern to air quality to mineral composition of the rock. There were thirty-eight steps.

There was no cover across the opening at the top, leading out onto the bluff. It emptied into the woods, facing east, away from the creek. These weren't the tall, thick oak and birch trees of the Georgia mountains. They were red cedars, small hardwood saplings and stunted pines. A worn path led away into the woods, and Spot started off warily, quietly. Their boots and the fading rush of the creek below were the only sounds, until Van heard a rustling behind them, and turned to see two figures step onto the path from either side. They were each wearing improvised camouflage "ghillie" suits, netting with strips of fabric and random bits of foliage hanging randomly all over them. Their faces were heavily painted in black and brown, and their eyes were shadowed by the trees. It was good camouflage. Van and Spot must have walked right by them. One carried a long, thick pole with a sharp metal tip driven into the end and bound tightly by a leather cord. It was a stout, menacing-looking spear. The other man held a compound bow with an arrow notched and the string drawn tight. The steel-tipped arrow was aimed at the center of Van's chest. There was no defense, no escape option. "Go on," the man with the spear said, and his partner gestured down the path in the direction they had been heading. Spot waited for further instructions, but the two men just stood quiet and still, so she turned and started off.

There was a breeze blowing, cooling Van's legs where they had been in the creek. The trees shading them were young, but the trail felt old, ancient. Birds sang histories and creation myths and the leaves above them rattled and whispered careful warnings. Grey squirrels with huge tails leapt between trees and circled the trunks from top to bottom and back up again, keeping pace with the humans. The forest creatures chirped and chattered to each other. The path wandered back and forth for a quarter mile or so, and Van knew they were being watched by the forest as they walked. More than once, he felt the steady gaze of the one with racing stripes and the bright blue tail.

Suddenly, the path fell away, and the terrain opened into a long, rectangular glade bordered on the left by a thick tree line of red cedars and pines, and on the right by a steep embankment, encumbered with vines and roots, twenty or thirty feet high. At the far end of the meadow, a couple hundred yards away, there was a subtle rise leading to a large rock face and, Van suspected, Spider's cave. Directly in front of them, at the entrance to the glade, a signpost was driven into the ground. The sign read:

"NO TRESSPASSING – WHITES ONLY"

There was an irregular row of structures along the left side of the clearing, in front of the tree line. The first few were rectangular and were oriented with the long ends facing the tree line and the center of the clearing. They were made of hewn wood and scraps of metal. The roofs were thatched, some in more need of upkeep than others.

"Oh shit! Spot!" A short, stocky man with shaggy red hair was walking out of the first hut, and he stopped in his tracks and pointed at her in surprise. "Dudes! Check it out – it's Spot!" He trod over on stout legs, holding his arms out too far from his sides.

"Steve Penske," she said.

"Damn, it's been a long time, girl! Who's your friend?" Steve Penske kicked his head back at an angle so he could size Van up.

"Van, this is Steve Penske. Steve Penske, Van Ryan."

"Hmm." He gave Van a look that said he wasn't finished with his evaluation yet. "Yeah, me & Spot go way back. Ain't that right, Spot? Way back." He stood looking her up and down. "*He* know you're coming?"

She hooked her thumb over her shoulder without turning around. "Well, we had a welcome committee. I'm thinking 'yes.'" The two men in camouflage who had escorted them through the woods stood casually by the entrance to the clearing. One of them, the man with the spear, was laughing and talking to someone else. The man with the bow was smoking a cigarette, and through a cloud of smoke he stared intently at Van.

Others had come out of the second hut now. "No way! It *is* her!"

"Damn, girl, you look good!" There were assorted wolf whistles and catcalls.

The men gathered around Spot and Van, all wishing her well without kindness. Sizing her up. She didn't answer their questions, and they didn't notice. It was conversation and posture from a crowd of testicles. He could see in their eyes the potential for aggression. Sex and violence growing from the same drive. Malevolence toward Van was less concealed. Suspicion, jealousy, instinctive hatred simmered right at the top of the pot. Van and Spot had been in the compound less than five minutes, and Van found himself was sizing up weak points, considering potential defensive postures and avenues of escape.

Spot was trying to move her and Van forward, onward through the camp, but men kept planting themselves in front of the newcomers, insinuating themselves between the pair, all of them wearing shades of insecurity, begging openly for attention. Some had muscles, some had flashy smiles, and all wore at least one article of camouflage clothing.

"Hey Spot, check this out!"

"Yo, Spot, remember that time we ..."

"C'mere and give me a hug, girl!"

"Spot, who the fuck is this guy?"

"Sister!" This last yell came from closer to the far end of the glade. Hearing it, all the other men peeled away from her and Van and grew quiet. A figure walked toward them down the length of the compound. "Sister!" He called, with a round, full, burnished voice used to being heard and obeyed. "My darling, my sister! You're back! I told them you'd come back. I told them all you'd come back." The man walked steadily, one foot softly treading in front of the other giving him the quiet pace of a predatory cat.

Spider wasn't tall, but it didn't matter. Van immediately felt as though he was standing downhill of the man, although the terrain was level where they stood. Spider's dark hair was shaggy, cut shoulder-length and combed back on his head. He wore aviator sunglasses, green cargo pants and two days-worth of beard on a square jaw. A loose-fitting black t-shirt and commercial, imitation combat boots with comfortable rubber soles completed his militia commander costume. He walked right up to Spot and held his arms out wide. "Sister," he said. She was looking at the ground as he approached and offered him only a tentative greeting.

"Hey," she said, still looking away. He wrapped her up and she allowed herself to be absorbed into the embrace. He held her quietly for a minute while her reticence dissipated.

"It's good to see you, girl." She looked up from inside his embrace, and Van could see that her face wanted to believe him. "And you?" He turned to Van, his hand outstretched.

"Van Ryan."

"Of course you are! A pleasure to meet you, sir. Yes. We've been expecting you both. You are most welcome." Spider shook his hand firmly and winked. "Come on, both of you. Let me show you around!" He took a step, and then spun back around. "First, though, Mr. Davis? Would you please take custody of our guest's pigsticker there?" Van turned and found that the man who had held the bow on him, who had escorted them in, was standing right behind him, his weapon slung across his back. He nodded toward Van's belt and held out his hand. Van unfastened his belt, slid the sheath off and handed it over. The moment Davis grabbed it from him, Van felt a jolt pass between them. A flash of light and concussion, like a blow to the head. He looked into the man's eyes and saw nothing there, no history, no regrets, no motive. Just the promise of violence. Waiting. The man looked at Van's knife admiringly, turning it over in his hands before unbuckling his own belt and sliding the sheath on. For the first time Van heard a slight humming sound, felt it just next to his ear, where the jaw began.

"Good. So. You probably guessed that these two buildings are barracks," Spider indicated the first two structures.

"How many can you sleep?" Van asked, looking around them.

"Maybe twenty or so if we pack it in a bit."

"For campouts, Jamborees?"

Spider smiled. "Yeah, campouts." He waved them on and pointed at the next building.

"This is the chow hall. Seats about a dozen for eating, drinking. Meetings, you know?" This structure was slightly longer than the other two, and it ran parallel to the tree line, instead of perpendicular like the barracks. About thirty feet from the building was an arched oven made of stone and mortar with a solid piece of cast iron serving as a door, and a crooked chimney capped off by scrap metal. Alongside the oven was a large grill built of the same stone and mortar with a rusty grate serving as a cook top. It looked well used. Charcoal and ash colored the grill, and bits of past meals were charred and crusted to the metal. "I see you eyeing up our kitchen there, Mr. Ryan. It was no easy feat hauling that oven door up here, I'll tell you. Am I right, fellas?" He turned his head to address the handful of men following them. Gratuitous chuckling agreements. "We've hauled quite a bit up here over time, haven't we?" Murmurs. "Everything you see that we couldn't make from what's here, we had to haul across the creek, up through the cave and up the trail here to the camp ...

That iron door though ..." He laughed. "Yeah, we could have started a fitness business or something, for people who wanted to get in shape, hauling all this. I know I lost more than a couple of pounds." He slapped his stomach, and it sounded hard. His arms didn't show much muscle, and Van guessed most of the heavy lifting probably went to the other guys. He seemed fit, though. Thin and tight, like a runner, maybe. Or a thief.

"Over there is storage ..." He gestured toward a trio of smaller buildings standing away by themselves. They were all built similarly, with solid, small tree trunks standing as corner posts and crudely hewn planks serving as walls. Small windows had been cut into three sides of each one, and these were covered with a weave of small branches. Slabs of corrugated metal served as roofs, slanted to allow rain to run off. "And over here ..." Spider started to turn away, toward the other side of the camp. Van turned with him, but movement caught his attention in the tree line next to one of the storage buildings. Dead leaves and brush rattled, and bushes were disturbed three feet above the ground, and although Van only caught a fleeting glimpse, he knew what he had seen. And he knew that the term "lone wolf" was a fallacy. Where there was one wolf there were more. The humming sound near his jaw increased slightly.

"What kind of storage?" Van asked. Spider stopped and turned to face him.

"Well, there are the targets, kitchen implements, tools there. Weapons in one. Whatever. Toilet paper! Ha. You'd be surprised how valuable that can become. Anyway ..." He turned again.

"Why's that one off by itself?" One of the three sheds stood away from the others a bit. Van took a step in that direction, and suddenly Davis stood in front of him, blocking his path.

The man was a full two inches taller than Van and he moved like murder, with economy of purpose. His eyes were iron. Van's knife dangled mockingly from the man's belt.

"Meat," was Spider's answer. "We keep meat in there sometimes. We hunt deer and other game up here, and we hang it in that shed to cure." He glared at Van.

"Got it."

"And over *here* ..." Spider pulled Spot close to him with one arm and turned her toward the next item on his tour. He leaned into her, as if he were talking to her exclusively. Her eyes were on the ground, and her shoulders were hunched. She seemed to have fallen into herself, deflated. "Over *here* we have weapons training." On the east side of the glade were three archery targets on stands, stuffed with twigs and leaves. "Mr. Davis, would you do us the honor, sir?" Davis walked back the way they had come, toward the entrance to the clearing. He stopped walking after fifty yards or so and unslung his bow. He turned, notched an arrow, sighted in and hit the target dead center. It flawless execution. He walked briskly back to the target, retrieved his arrow and resumed his place by Van's side.

"Very impressive." Van said.

"He never misses." Spider rocked on his heels like a proud father.

Van turned and looked up at Davis. "Remind me never to run from you, then," he said.

Stacked near the targets were other close combat weapons: staffs, spears, wooden swords. "I don't see any guns." Van said.

"Correct! Very observant, Mr. Ryan. We do not allow firearms in the compound. Guns cheat nature, we are here to respect it."

"Well, this man's bow is as lethal as a rifle, isn't it?

"Yes it is. But the effective range is reduced. Indigenous and aboriginal people have hunted with the bow for somewhere between 40,000 and 70,000 years. A bow and arrow can be made in the wilderness, from the wild itself. The same can't be said about a gun." They had reached the center of the clearing. Ahead a path split into two; one trail led up the hill toward the cave, and the other headed to the right, toward a large cabin. "So over there you see the main lodge …" He pointed off to the right. "We'll head over there shortly, but I'd like to show you something else right now."

At the base of the hill, to the left of the path leading to the cave, two tree trunks had been driven into the ground five or six yards apart and concrete poured around the base of each one. Pulleys were attached to each of the tree trunks at the top, and thick rope was run through each pulley to create a line between the tree trunks which could be raised and lowered. The ground between the two trunks was dark and bare. "Well, that looks interesting," Van said.

"Right?" Spider said, with a strained smile. "This is where we process the deer and game after we hunt."

"Well …" Van stopped suddenly and listened. A noise had come from the "meat" shed, he was sure of it. Several of the other men had heard it as well, and they tried their best to conceal their reactions from Van. There was a banging sound. Davis started for the shed, but Spider stopped him with a light touch on the arm.

"There you go!" Spider said too loudly. "Something's at it again. Bobby, if you wouldn't mind, please sir." He waved toward the source of the noise. "See what I mean? That's why we have to keep the meat secure. Plenty of scavengers in these woods."

"Predators also." Van said.

"Of course."

As he listened for noise coming from the storage shed, Van realized he was also hearing the other sound, the humming sound, constantly now. It was the background for all other noise in the camp, like the vibration of a car's tires on a road trip. A noise incorporated into a setting, not loud enough to distract from conversation, but eventually you were going to realize you were yelling to overcome it.

"Do you hunt the predators, the wolves for example?"

"We *feed* the wolves. We feed all of this." He gestured at the woods around them. "We take what little we need, and we offer what we can." His smile was like late winter sun reflecting off the icy crust of old snow. It was preferable to a dark day maybe, but it hurt your eyes to look at it. And it warmed nothing.

27

BLOOD AND LAND

"ALRIGHT, COME ON THEN. Let's go check out the main event!" Spider led the way up the short, steep path to the cave. The grass was sparse and the stones along the path were shiny from wear. The path cut back two times, the climb in full view of the glade below. Spider led the way, with Spot and Van behind him and Davis bringing up the rear. The hum in Van's head grew from just a sound into a physical force as they made their way up the path. It went from being a vibration hiding behind his consciousness to a low frequency tremor, reaching from the soles of his boots up through his shins and knees. With each step Van felt his own control over the integrity of his movement lessen, like a piano player trying to play a concerto during an earthquake. With just another handful of shaky steps, they were at the top.

"I'll stay out here," Spot said.

"Don't be stupid," Spider held her arm. "Come with us." She jerked her arm away and sat down on a large rock near the entrance to the cave.

"I don't fucking want to go in there. I'll stay right here."

"Suit yourself," Spider said, and stepped inside.

The cave had a wide entrance, which Van had seen from the compound below. As Spot had described, it was a couple of hundred feet from the entrance to the back wall. The walls were sloped inward , and the ceiling was high enough that it was hidden from the daylight coming through the cave's entrance. It was hot inside. Stepping inside the entrance, Van took a deep breath of thick, dark air. To the right, as they entered, were shelves constructed of wood, a large metal locker and a camp bed with a decomposing wooden crate serving as a side table. To the left of the entrance the ceiling and the far wall drew together some distance away, creating a corner of dark shadow, and Van guessed that Spot's escape hole was hiding there. Van noticed all these details inadvertently, absorbing the general outline of the cave through his peripheral vision. The focus of his attention lay straight ahead, along the cave's back wall.

The entity Van had come in contact with in the Georgia mountains had been covered in earth and forest detritus, but beneath that it had been similar in size and form to the one he was looking at now. This one was much longer than tall, and it protruded several feet out of the cave wall. Sharp grooves and edges above and to the sides of the form looked like someone had tried to dig it out of the cave wall but had given up. The form, the entity, was a dark, pinkish color. It pulsed with a dark light in time with the unforgiving humming sound now reverberating through Van's entire body. His brain swelled and swirled inside of his head until his skull threatened to crack open like a thin-shelled factory-farm egg. Through the tumult in his mind, Van saw that it was time, that this was the moment. He walked toward the form and held his hand out to touch it, to accomplish his mission, to be done with the alien and its influence over him. Before he reached the back wall, however, he felt a tug on the back of his shirt. Davis had hold of him. At the same time, Spider stepped between him and the object.

"No. No, I don't think so. No touching. Not yet. There'll be time for that later." He turned the lantern's light onto the walls of the cave. "And you haven't seen the rest of it."

The cave walls had seemed dark-colored, but now, in the light, Van saw handprints, hundreds, maybe thousands. He stepped closer to the closest wall and saw they were made by hands of all sizes, using dark paint or pigment of some sort, although staring at each handprint, he knew there was only one substance that dried that shade. Spider circled the cave, shining the lantern at every surface. Prints covered older prints until virtually every square inch of wall space had been marked. The form in the back of the cave seemed to pulse stronger.

"How old are these?" Van asked.

"As old as there *is,* I think. Some of them." Spider said, looking at the prints with fascination, as though seeing them for the first time. "Others are much more recent. Amazing, isn't it?" Van found himself unable to speak. "Well, come on, then. You'll have a chance to come up here again." He pointed the way back down the path with a gesture of his hand. Van started down and Davis fell in behind him again. "You alright, sister?" Spider called to her. She was perched where they had left her, staring into the compound below. Her gaze was sharp and cold, and Van found it impossible to read her. She just nodded and fell in with them. They turned and headed down the path again. At the first cutback, Van caught sight of something small and brown with a fat blue tail. It was sunning itself on a crooked rock at the side of the trail. Van smiled at it, and as they walked by the skink did some push-ups on its stubby arms as it smiled back.

The Lodge was the most substantial and sturdy structure in the camp. It was an actual log cabin, built with care and surprisingly good workmanship. Felled and debarked trees were stacked with precision, the corners notched and joined perfectly. The space between logs was stuffed with moss and daubed over with a mixture of cement and sand from the creek bed below. The roof was made of metal and painted to match the surrounding trees. A stone chimney rose several feet above the roof's peak. "A thing of beauty, isn't it?" Spider said to Spot, who was still burrowed into herself. "C'mon in and take a load off, you two." The three of them went inside, followed by Davis. "Ah, Mr. Davis, if you would grab us a few beers, I would very much appreciate it, sir." Davis watched Van enter the cabin and withdrew reluctantly. "It's ... nice."

"Nice."

"Very interesting. A lot of work went into all of this, for sure."

"You got that right, my friend. Many, many years, and many trips across the creek and 'up the cave,' as we say. Those guys outside put a lot of sweat in around here. A few guys that aren't with us any more as well."

Van looked around him. "Looks like your cabin got the best of it."

"Not *my* cabin. It's *our* Lodge."

"But *you* sleep in here."

"Most nights, yes. Sometimes I'm up in the cave."

"Still, a nice place, this. A sight better than those bunkhouses, for sure."

"Well, we started there, with those." He gave a big smile. "Our craftsmanship needed work back then, for sure. We just kind of worked our way in from the entrance of the glade, you know? It's like a story I heard once. My uncle had a friend who moved to Little Rock when he was a young man to take a job at a furniture factory. He was a hard worker, one of those who doesn't need much sleep. His manager loved him. He worked any shift, any hours. All he did was work. He worked so much he never had time for companionship, even. No wife, no girlfriend. No one.

Anyway, when he first moved into the city, he roomed with a bunch of other workers from the factory. Given the number of hours he was putting in, he soon enough had a decent little bit of loot put away. So, he decided to get himself an apartment. He wanted it to be nice, though. He didn't want it to be some smelly dump, like the place he lived with the other guys. He wanted it to be clean, with nice things in it. He wanted it to be somewhere he could invite girls to and be proud of it. So, he looked at newspaper ads and billboard notices, and he walked around the decent parts of town scoping out "For Rent" signs until he found just the place. He walked in and gave his new landlord the first month's rent in cash, and boom, he was in. His very own place. He had absolutely no possessions at all, other than a change of clothes, a toothbrush and a razor, but he didn't care. His first night he curled up on the floor, with his shirt as a pillow and his jacket as a blanket, and he was happy as a clam."

"Is this you? In the story?" Van asked.

"No, damn it. I'm getting to the point. Hold on." Spider took a sip of his beer. "Okay, so this guy, this friend of my uncle's, he has his dream place, right? Good job in the big city, and an apartment all to himself. When he woke up that next morning though, he got all anxious. He realized that he had no idea how to furnish the place. He worked in a furniture factory, but he had never purchased an actual piece of furniture, or a piece of art, or a coffee pot, or anything in his entire life. Now this guy has a very logical mind, you know? He approached things once step at a time. Not a very "big picture" sort of a guy. One step at a time. So, he goes about furnishing his apartment like that. The first thing he did was go to a second-hand store and buy a little table and a, like, small wicker basket to sit on it, and he put them right inside the front door, so that when he came into the apartment, he had somewhere to put his keys. Then the next day he bought a coat rack, so that he had somewhere to hang his coat and hat after he tossed his keys in the wicker basket. Next, he bought a little mat he could wipe his feet on. Then it was some beer, because his refrigerator was only a few steps from the coat rack, and he liked a cold beer when he got home from work." Spider raised his own bottle. "Then it was a comfortable easy chair that he could sit in while he drank his beer, and sleep in at night, because the weather was getting cold, and he didn't want to sleep on the floor anymore. Then it was a table against the wall in front of the chair. Next was a t.v. for the table. Then a set of plates and a fork and a pan so that he could cook his own meals. You see where this is going?"

"Got it," Van said. "Then a couch in case anyone else came by. Then a coffee table. Then some coasters ..."

"Right! And what do you think the last thing he bought was? After everything else was done? He had a bed and sheets and holder for his toilet paper. A vacuum cleaner. He even bought some art prints for his walls off a truck in the parking lot of the local grocery store. What was the last thing?"

Van shook his head. "No idea."

Spot had been trying not to pay attention. Now she asked, "What, already?"

"He went downtown, to men's clothing shop, and bought a nice jacket and some new shoes. And he set out trying to find a girl to spend time with."

Van and Spot quietly stared at Spider. Finally, Van said, "Great story. I think I missed the point, though." Spider laughed.

"No point! I just love that story. It does relate to how this camp came about, though." He waved his hand. "First one barracks. Then another, then somewhere to eat when it rained. Then a real oven. Then some storage. Then this place. We started at the entrance to the glade, and just worked our way back here! All that over a number of years, you know?" He laughed some more. "Have another beer, guys! Help yourselves." Van grabbed another one off the table. The condensation ran across his fingers. Spider turned to Spot. "So, sister, the place has come a long way since last time you saw it, huh?"

She looked confused. "I ... what?" Spider smiled at her.

"Seriously. Did you think you could ride in my truck all the way out here, skulk around the place, and hitch all the way back to town without me knowing? I mean, you're a sneaky little thing, but you're not *that* damn sneaky."

"Well why didn't you fucking say anything to me?"

"I wanted you to see me, to see this! I wanted you to *feel* it!" Lauren looked away, embarrassed and angry. "I never expected you to run, though. You got me there. But I knew you'd be back. I knew it." His eyes narrowed and he smiled like a snake pleased with his menu selection.

"Okay, great!" She said and stood up. "So, you tell each other cute stories and build shit and drink beer. That's nice, but what the fuck is all of this?"

"It's the heart."

"The heart of what? Your gang? Whatever hustle you've got going now?"

"It's the heart of it all, sweetheart. The heart of the land, the heart of nature, the county. *Your* heart! *My* heart! The heart of history. The heart of our people. Right here! It's all right here. 'Blood and Land,' you know?"

"Whose history?" Van asked. Spider spun and snapped his fingers and pointed at him.

"Now *that* is the question. You could have asked 'whose blood' and we could have made it work, but you asked, 'whose history' and that is the point, isn't it?" He looked at Van and Spot for agreement and moved on. "Who does this all belong to, right? I mean who does this," pointing to the table, "belong to? Ownership is history, but it's also possession, right? Look at this table, for instance. The history of this table is that Penske out there made it. Not too shabby too; the boy has a gift. He made it and then I took it. And I invite him in now and then for a drink or whatever, but he knows it is mine."

"So, you stole it from him?" Van asked.

"No. Look don't get all caught up in that. I'm just giving an example. Come on outside, I'll show you." Outside, Davis stood watching the cabin, not a muscle off-duty. Spider walked up the path toward the cave a few yards and turned, so they could get a view of the compound and the woods around it. "There, that!" Spider said with wide arms. "All of that! So, we've decided that part of ownership is history, right? But who writes the history? The most current owners, of course." He looked at Spot. "You! And me! And Mr. Davis! And your friend, there, too."

"At one time, this all belonged to the Osage people. They traveled between here and southern Missouri with the seasons. Who knows how long, but it was all theirs, and they fished it, and hunted it and they used the wood and the plants from here, from all around here! And they gave thanks to the animals they killed, and to the land for sustaining them. But along the way, they pissed off the land, and it didn't want them anymore. Early in the 1800's the Cherokee came along and fought the Osage for rights to the land here. And then in 1808, white men of European descent, our people, started kicking the Osage and the Cherokee out of here. And then the land was ours, and we farmed it and fished it and used the trees for our houses and wagons. And the land loved us. Loved *us*. Am I right, boys?" A few of the other men around the compound had gathered at the sound of his voice. The words drew them.

"That's right!" They yelled. "Blood and Land!"

"See?" Spider turned to Van with sweat fully formed on his brow. "They know. We know. White. Men. That's us! Oh," He turned to Spot, "and our women as well, of course."

"Fuck you," was all Spot could manage.

"So, Native Americans were out then. Just like that." Van asked.

"The land didn't want them, Ryan!" Spider was channeling a bit of the preacher now in his cadence and his tone, or a politician when he was stumping. It was a sales pitch, wrapped in trite phrases and wearing faith and confidence as a uniform. He was charismatic and he was intelligent, and the men standing around raising their fists as he spoke *needed* Spider to make sense of things for them, to offer a pattern from which they could stitch their lives. Offer a justification for their anger, their hatred. Those men like Spider, who found manipulating their fellows as easy as putting on a casual smile never lacked for scared, simple minds to follow them. "Did. Not. Want. Them!" He smacked his fist into the open palm of the other hand with each word. "The land chooses who it wants to live upon it. With it. *Within* it. You follow?"

Van nodded his head, but his face didn't join in. "What about black people? Hispanic people?"

Spider shook his head slowly, with a gesture that said it was all out of his hands. "Where are they? Are they here? I'll bet you didn't know this, but Harrison fought on the side of the Union during the Civil War. That's right! Everyone thinks, 'oh those damn redneck racist Arkansas assholes in Harrison!' Well, that's wrong! General Marcus LaRue Harrison was a Brigadier General in the goddamn Union Army he was! So where are the black folk? Where are the Mexicans? If the land wanted them here, don't you think they'd damn well be here? Some call us '*The Most Racist City in America*,' but that is unfair, I tell you! We just love *our* people! The *land* loves our people. What's wrong with that?"

"It looked to me back in town like you folks were happy to claim that title."

"What, the billboards? Those idiots don't know. They act like they have pride in their race when all they have is hate. There's no need for hatred. There's no need for fear. Those emotions are for those who are *unsure* of their heritage. We ..." he gestured at the men listening, "we *know* we own this land. That's not racism. That's intelligence. That's fortitude."

"I see," Van said. "So, no one in Harrison ever did anything to 'discourage' minorities from living there? It was just 'the land?'"

"Well, the land dictates, and we just follow, see? Don't you think if the land wanted black people to live here, it would have created circumstances that led to that?"

Van laughed. "Like creating a place where they wouldn't get lynched?" But he knew the sound of madness. He knew the danger coming from Spider's mouth. He knew that logic was less than subjective in this world, Spider's world. Van tried to catch Spot's eye, but she was staring holes into the ground. "The land, then."

"Exactly. The land decides who it wants. And if it doesn't want you anymore, then the crops'll dry up, or a tornado will knock your town down, or a plague will wipe your people out. And then the next folks come along and try their luck. And it'll be their land, then." Spider stared at Van silently. He was handsome, Van thought, with smooth, tan skin spread across high cheekbones, and a dark, well-groomed beard. His eyes ...Van couldn't make out the color of his eyes inside whites so big and round they eclipsed his other features. The more Spider spoke, the more the pure white of his eyes grew on his face. It was the color of boiled bones. The eyes seized Van's, digging and extracting, trying to interrogate Van, and in the same moment screaming at Van. *"Get out! Get out!"* The humming noise rose to harmonize with the screaming, and it took every ounce of discipline and effort to continue looking into Spider's eyes as he spoke. They were captivating. They drew attention away from Spider's mouth, full of small, worn, dark yellow teeth. Away from the shine glinting off one gold canine. Van took long, slow breaths and calmed his thoughts, until eventually all he heard, aside from Spider's pedagogical babbling, was the ambient birdsong of the meadow, and a very distant howl riding in on the afternoon breeze.

"But you hunt these woods, yes? You kill the other creatures who also lay claim to this land."

"Of course! The land provides. Blood and land, my friend! We revere life in these woods." Again, he threw out his arms to incorporate what they could see into his narrative. "We give thanks to all of the animals we kill." He looked at Van. "All of them. But we give back also! We give back. Blood circulates, after all. It comes and it goes, arteries and veins, dirty and clean. And it keeps the body healthy, right?"

Van counted five men in attendance below them. Davis stood near, that made six. Add Spider, Van and Spot and the total population of the camp came to nine. "Alright boys! That's enough speechifying!" Spider chuckled. "How about we break for chow? Alright with you, Bobby?" Spider addressed a tall man with round features and a substantial paunch. He had on jeans and a faded camouflage t-shirt, and he gesticulated wildly with tattooed, chubby arms while he talked.

"Good to go, Spider. Let me throw some steaks on. Shouldn't be more than ten or fifteen minutes."

"Outstanding. Mr. Penske?" Spider addressed the squat, red-haired man who had spoken to Spot when they first arrived at the camp.

"Yo!"

"Would you escort Mr. Ryan, please? Make sure he gets something to eat. My sister and I will dine in The Lodge. Bobby? Will you send something over for us?"

"Will do, boss."

Spider wrapped one arm around Spot, and she reluctantly allowed herself to be dragged away. Van was tempted to interfere, but he felt like they were stuck in a narrative now that had been written long before. All that was left now was to let the story tell itself. Maybe the baseball worked backward. Maybe the core was the end of one's life, and the string wound itself around it in reverse, each time around was another year younger until the tip of the string was the day we were born. And life or fate or each person's personal god held the end of the string and threw it or rolled in on the ground and it unraveled as it must until the core was revealed and then there you were. Maybe the story was all written ahead of time, and their only purpose was to live it. Either way, there was always only one end for everyone. Van felt his approaching.

28

SCRUBBING WITH SAND

"COME ON, YOU." STEVE Penske did not relish his assignment. Van climbed down the path and the man turned and headed toward the chow hall. Van saw from behind that he was short, but he had broad shoulders, the muscles showing clearly through the olive-green t-shirt he wore. It was a wrestler's build, and he held his arms out from his sides like someone who had spent a lot of time lifting weights. They walked the short distance to the chow hall and Penske turned to him. "Inside or outside?" He asked Van.

"Sorry?"

"Do you want to eat inside or outside? You're the 'guest.' Where do you want to eat?" He gestured to the handful of picnic tables situated in front of the chow hall.

"Yeah, it's up to you, man. It's your house." Van said.

"Outside it is, then. Have a seat. I'll go get something to drink." He disappeared into the building and came back with a couple of beers. Van opened his and took a sip. It was warm. "Yeah, you probably had 'em cold in there, right?" He pointed toward the Lodge.

Van nodded. "Yeah. This is fine though, thanks."

"Yeah, nothing fancy out here," he said. "Cold beer is just for the big shots." Van could smell meat cooking and turned so he could see the cook working over a grill top loaded with steaks. As he did, Van spotted Davis leaning against one of the storage sheds, staring at him. Van knew he hadn't been out of Davis' sight for a moment. A breeze brought the smoke across their table, and Van's stomach rumbled its approval.

"What's on the menu?" He asked.

"Venison. It's usually venison," Penske said.

"Who does the hunting here?"

"Davis, mostly. He's magic with that bow, man."

"So, no guns, though? Really? Way up here?"

"No. None. Too loud. We want to keep a low profile, you know?"

"I thought it was 'respecting nature' and all of that."

Penske looked at him and rolled his eyes. "Oh yeah. That's it."

"What the fuck, Steve? You giving away all our secrets?" Another man joined them with a chuckle. "Stranger." He nodded to Van.

"That's Holloway. He's an asshole."

"That's me, for sure." Holloway was all angles and straight lines, with a blondish flat top crewcut and a painfully trimmed goatee. His arms started as sharp points on top of his shoulders, and they were long and free of muscle tone. He wore camouflage cargo pants, a stained white wife-beater t-shirt and a gold link chain around his neck. Amateur tattoos stained his arms and neck. "Where you from, son?" He asked Van.

"Georgia. Canton. North of Atlanta a bit."

"Ah, Atlanta! Now there's a city," Holloway said, while he opened his own beer.

"You been there?" Van asked.

"Nah, not me. My cousin lives there, though. Works in hotels. I think he's at the Hilton? The Wyatt? Yeah, the Wyatt, I think. Big place."

"It's the Hyatt, dumbass," Penske said.

"Yup, that's it. The Hotel Dumbass."

"You're an idiot," Penske said to him.

"Your mom likes me, though."

"So how long you and Spot been together?" Penske asked Van, ignoring the other man. As he spoke, two more men sat at the picnic table next to theirs. One was small, mousy even, with small hands and long hair covering half of his face. He wore glasses and a green Army jacket, and when he sat down his hair flipped back away from his face Van saw the long, deep scar running from his forehead to his chin. It was a scar that changed a man's life. Violence gives a man a scar like that, and it either becomes a point of pride, or a source of shame. Either way, it tends to stoke the dangerous emotions in a man.

"Who's with Spot? You?" The man with the scar looked at Van with a mocking grin on his face.

"Well, I'm not really *with* her, not like that ..."

"Sure you are, man! Everyone's with Spot. Or has been, anyway," the man with the scar said.

"Shut the fuck up, Ewing!" Penske yelled.

"You know it's true, you asshole!" The small man yelled. "Hey, you." He leaned over toward Van. "You know why she's called Spot, right?" Van shook his head.

"Ewing, I swear to god, you little fucking piece of shit ..."

"You know, man," he said to Van. "The 'spot?' The wet spot after you get done doing it? We've all laid in it with her, man."

"Motherfucker!" Penske jumped up and ran at Ewing. Ewing's companion was the man who had met Van and Spot with the spear. He stepped in the way and wrapped Steve Penske in a bear hug.

"Just trying to lay some truth on the man here, bro. Calm down," Ewing said, laughing. Just then there was the sound of a cow bell clanging. "Fuck! About time! I'm starving."

After the meal, everyone pitched in cleaning up. The cook had served them each a venison steak, charred and cooked through perfectly, with only a little salt and pepper to season. There was also a baked potato and an ear of corn, grilled in its husk. The meal was served on a ceramic plate, with a stainless-steel fork and knife to eat with. When they were finished eating, Van and Holloway drew dish duty as their share of clean-up. They filled up two grey plastic tubs with the dirty dishes and walked behind the chow hall and down a small path Van hadn't seen before to the creek, which ran north of the camp and fed the larger creek below. Van and Holloway followed the path to the water, and then the lanky man squatted down and transferred all the dirty dishes into one tub. He picked up a handful of sand from the bottom of the creek, grabbed a dirty plate, and rubbed it with the sand until all the leftovers from the meal had been removed. Then he rinsed the plate in the cool creek water and placed it in the empty tub. "Got it?" He asked Van.

"Sure," Van said, and grabbed a dish to help. They took their time. The creek was crisp-cold and smelled of moss and the muddy underside of rocks. "So ... I have to ask, man: is this it? What is there six, seven of you here?"

"So?" Holloway scrubbed forks and didn't look at Van.

"Well, this camp looks like it could accommodate way more than that. Spider said like 15-20 people when we came in."

"What the fuck are you man, some kind of spy?"

"No, I just ..."

Holloway laughed. "I'm fucking with you, brother. Yeah, this is a small crew. We got a team on a big job in Alabama right now, so there's that. Also, Spider wanted to keep things small tonight, on account of your visit, you know?"

"Really?"

"Yeah. 'Intimate' is the word he used. The guys here tonight are some of the oldest. We've all been with Spider for a long time. We all built this place with him. You know?" Holloway had put the last clean dish in the tub, and now he rinsed the tub that had carried the soiled dishes in the creek and put half of the clean dishes back into it. He dried his hands off on his pants, sat down on a rock and lit a cigarette.

"You all work for Spider, yeah?" Van asked. The man looked at Van.

"We work *with* him. I mean, he calls the shots, but ..."

"Spot ..." The name tasted dirty in Van's mouth now. "Lauren told me you guys used to be into a lot of shit."

"Yeah, she should keep her fucking mouth shut. But I guess she's never been good at that." He took a big drag and the lit end glowed brightly. "She's right, though. There isn't much we didn't run around here. Done with all that shit now, pretty much. Fucking set-up now keeps us right with the land and our people, white people, and puts a nice bit of dough in our pockets, you hear me?"

"Must be nice. What ..." Suddenly an arrow shaft sunk into a tree trunk a foot or so from Van's face. He looked back along the vibrating shaft and saw Davis staring at him through the trees.

"Whoa!" Holloway laughed. "Watch it! You don't want to fuck with that guy, man! No sir." He grabbed one of the tubs and motioned for Van to grab the other. "Guess we took a little too long, huh?" He chuckled and headed back up the path toward the camp. Davis met them at the kitchen, and he frisked Van to make sure he hadn't kept any of the utensils.

"So, what do you think of our little operation here?" Spider asked. He and Van were sitting back in the Lodge, at Steve Penske's table. Lauren was sitting by herself in the rocking chair.

"Great, I guess. You've built *something* here. Got yourself a good crew, by the look of it. What are you all into? Banks?"

Spider laughed. "No, nothing like that. Oh yeah, these guys are solid. We've all been through a lot together."

"I do have a question, though."

"Go for it! That's why you're here."

"Is that why? Why I'm here? That's my question: why allow me in here, show me all around?"

"Why not?" Spider held a steady smile on his face.

"You're not on a recruitment drive or something, are you?"

Spider chuckled. "No. No. I'm afraid you wouldn't qualify, being from Georgia and all. We're more of a local organization."

"Well, what then?"

Spider leaned back in his chair. "Well, you brought my beloved sister back to me, for one thing." Spot ... Lauren looked away sharply. She hadn't met Van's eyes once since they arrived at the camp, nor said a word to him. Her face carried a sour mix of anger and embarrassment.

"She doesn't look so happy to be here," Van said.

Spider laughed again. "Really? You don't think so?" He turned to her. "Tell him, little sister. Tell him how happy you are to be reunited with me."

Without looking at Van, she said, "I'm ecstatic. Mind your fucking business, Ryan."

"So, listen, Van, I've got you here. Let's play a little game I like. It's called 'What are you good at?'" Spider asked him.

"What do you mean?"

"I never pass up an opportunity to learn something. You stop learning, you stop living, you know? So, I start by asking you that question: 'what are you good at?' You know?"

"I don't know. I'm no one important."

"Everyone's important, Van! Everyone. And everyone's good at something. Some are good at more than one thing, but everyone has at least one talent. My sister over there is an artist, for example. She has a loft apartment *full* of her own beautiful paintings."

"What ...how did you know that?" Spot ...Lauren snapped at him. Spider just smiled his predator's smile.

"Oh sweetheart. You were never *that* far away."

"I honestly don't ..." Van started.

"Steve Penske is very good at shaping useful things out of wood." He laid both hands on the table in front of him. "Mr. Davis is the absolute quietest person I've ever met. You know the old 'who can stay quiet the longest' game you used to play as a kid? Yeah, he wins."

"I really don't know. There's not much I can do any better than anyone else."

"Come on, man! Weren't you a soldier? Excuse me, a marine?" Van nodded his head, looking the man warily in the eye. Spider seemed to know a lot about him. Van wondered how much he actually knew. "Were you good at it?"

"Good enough."

"Good at following orders?" Spider asked. Van shrugged. "Good at anything else marines do?"

"Leave him alone!" Lauren shouted. "You can play your fucking games with me. Leave him alone!"

"Alright, alright. Goodness. You know, Van, you and I have something in common. Aside from our mutual affection for my sister, of course."

"Fuck you!" She yelled. Spider ignored her.

"Yessir. You and I are both motivated by external forces, aren't we? Forces other folks may not understand." Van felt the humming sound increase incrementally. "I heard about what happened to your friend. On the mountain."

Van's heartbeat picked up its tempo. He felt as though he had suddenly fallen asleep and started dreaming. Like the floor had dissolved beneath them, and they had fallen, table, chairs and all, into a dark pool of water below. Spider's words to him sounded like they were spoken underwater, thick and dead. "So?" Van asked.

"A shame." Spider was staring intently into Van's eyes, so that he couldn't look away.

"It was. It is. He was my best friend." Van felt stuck in Spider's eyes, almost like he had been stuck in the mirror in the bathroom at Elle's Belles.

"Best friend? Shame. Wolves, was it?"

"Yeah," Van said. "Wolves. Why are we talking about this?"

"Just trying to illustrate that we have outside events – outside influences if you will. In common. Maybe not responsible for our actions entirely."

"You and I have nothing in common. Nothing."

"You sure about that, my friend?"

"What's your talent, then? What are you good at?"

"I ...find it relatively easy to ...coax people to do things for me. People *like* to do things for me. Give them a story, or a slogan, and things start happening. You follow?"

Spider's words were spinning. Or it was the room. The table was no longer underwater. They were in the cabin again, but the room was spinning, and Spider's words were being flung from his mouth and were sticking to the walls of the room by centrifugal force. "What's the cave have to do with it?" Van was sweating.

"You tell me. What did your cave have to do with what happened to your friend?"

"Fuck you."

"Whose wolves were they, Van?"

"Fuck you." The letters of Spider's words were getting mixed up on the walls. They began to spell other words. *Get out get out get out ...*

"Who controlled the wolves, Van?"

"None of your fucking business!"

"WHO SENT YOU HERE, VAN RYAN?!!!" Spider bellowed in a threatening, edged voice like a grizzly roar. Van and Lauren stared at him in shocked wonder. The door to the Lodge opened and Davis stepped inside. Behind him Steve Penske leaned his head in.

"Boss? We're all set!" Penske called.

Without taking his eyes off Van, Spider answered, "Yes. Yes we are."

29
THE CAVE

SPIDER LED THE WAY out of the Lodge, and as soon as Van stepped outside, he was seized on either side by Holloway and Steve Penske. Before he had time to react, they had forced both hands in front of him, and Davis stepped forward and bound his wrists tightly with a long leather strap that had been fashioned for that purpose. Van tried to struggle but the men held him fast. Ewing's quiet friend held a spear several yards away from them and made sure that Van saw its point glitter in the last of the evening's light.

"What the hell?"

"Easy, Mr. Ryan," Spider said. "We're moving on to a different part of your tour now. Just relax and enjoy the show." Spider's ringmaster smile had taken on a sneer at the edges. When the men were sure Van's hands were secure, Davis stepped behind him and attached a worn, thick leather collar around his neck and a rope to the collar. "There we are! Comfy?" Spider asked him, and strode off before Van could say anything. Holloway took hold of the rope attached to the collar and pulled Van down the path toward the camp. The man who had made dinner, Bobby, lit two large torches which had been staged on either side of the posts at the east end of the clearing.

Holloway and Davis maneuvered Van until he was between the posts, and suddenly Van felt a kick to the back of one leg, and he dropped to his knees. Davis placed one firm hand on Van's shoulder, holding him down. Steve Penske, Bobby and Ewing walked off in the direction of the storage huts, and the sound of a struggle arose.

"OW! Fuck!"

"Damn kid ..." The sound of a strong slap reached them, and in a moment, the three men walked into the clearing, leading a young boy who was restrained like Van. Penske was limping.

"Fucking towelhead kicked me right in the shin!"

"Shut up! Idiot!" It was almost dark now, and Spider lit a small, hand-held torch off one of the big ones. He held it up to the boy's face. There was a mark on the left side where someone had hit him. Spider glared at Penske. "Are you *trying* to lose us money, dumbass?!" He turned to Bobby. "The drum, please." The man left without a word. "What do you think, Mr. Ryan?"

"Think about what, you fucking psychopath?"

"Think about our friend, here! Isn't he beautiful?" The boy was about twelve years old, and had dark, tousled hair and thick eyebrows. His eyes were dark, and skin was a light brownish tone. They were middle eastern features, and the boy looked familiar to Van. The men had put a gag in his mouth. He showed little fear. Instead, he glared at Spider with a pure and intense hatred.

"What the hell is this?" Van growled from his knees.

"Well, something has to pay the bills, right? I mean, this is fun and all ..." he waved around at the camp, "but a man must make a living. Am I right boys?" The men all chuckled.

"So, what, you're a fucking pimp?"

"Come on, Van. You can do better than that! I'm a purveyor. A facilitator."

"A trafficker," Van said.

"Well, I've always been a trafficker, really. I suppose. Drugs, booze, weapons, cars. We obtain a product, and we sell it at a profit. 'Trafficker' just sounds so ... Hollywood."

"So, your product now is little boys."

"Women ... kids ... A bit trickier than some of the other gigs we've had, but man! There's a *lot* of money in it."

"Yeah, I'm sure. What does your "beloved sister" think about it?"

"Shut up!" Spider snapped. He took a deep breath. "Leave her out of this. I gave her a little something to help her sleep, so she'll miss tonight's festivities, I'm afraid." Spider walked a short distance up the path leading to the cave and turned around where he could be seen by everyone. Holloway turned Van around, still on his knees, until he faced Spider. Steve Penske pulled the boy next to Van and pushed him roughly onto his knees.

"Brothers!" Spider yelled, with his arms above his head.

The men gathered around him responded, "Brother!"

"It is time again, brothers! The land calls to us! Blood and Land!"

"Blood and Land!"

"Brothers, we are gathered here this evening, with two worthy candidates for the land's approval." The men cheered. "We'll take them now and present them to the cave. We'll find out tonight if the land will allow them to continue among us, or if they land will claim them for itself." Another cheer, louder. "Blood and Land, my brothers!"

The men all lifted their right arm into the night sky and yelled in unison, "Blood and Land!" It became a chant. "Blood and Land! Blood and Land!" Spider nodded to Bobby, who began beating on a large wooden drum. It was a slow, strong beat, on the first word of the chant. Van and the boy were lifted to their feet, and Spider led the way slowly and purposely up the path to the mouth of the cave. The men followed behind them. "Blood and Land! Blood and Land!" Van felt the humming sound of the cave join in with the chanting, pulsing with the beat of the drum. Heat rushed out of the cave to meet them as they approached.

They were led to the object, the entity, in the rear of the cave. It glowed fiercely now, pulsing between a dark red and light red color, emitting a searing heat like molten metal. Van no longer heard the drum beating down in the camp. The humming consumed him. The sound was not entering through his ears, but seemed to seep into his head, into his entire body directly. The vibration shook his organs and his bones.

They brought the boy forward first, and Penske loosened his bonds and held his hands out in front of him. The boy turned his head toward Van for a moment, and, for the first time, Van saw the glint of fear in his eyes. Ewing held him from behind while Penske placed his right hand firmly on the entity's form. "Blood and Land!" Spider bellowed, and the men all repeated it. Spider picked up a knife from a shelf on the side of the cave, and while Penske lifted the boy's hand up and held it open, Spider cut the palm of his hand, quickly and deeply. The boy cried out behind his gag. Penske and Ewing walked him to the left and pressed his bleeding hand against the cave wall. It left a fresh, red handprint. Then Ewing held the boy's head still while Penske took his cut hand and placed it on his face, smearing blood thoroughly along one side. When Penske was satisfied, they bound the boy's wrists again and led him out of the cave.

Van felt his right hand growing hot. The bit of the other entity from the Georgia mountains Van was carrying was reacting to the proximity of this one. Now. It had to happen now. Davis and Holloway each held onto an arm tightly, and the man with the spear put his arm tightly around Van's neck, holding him in a headlock. In unison, the men walked Van toward the form at the back of the cave. Van was worried that the men would react when they saw his hand was glowing, but Spider didn't seem to notice as he removed the strap from his wrists. He and Davis forced Van's hand down onto the surface of the object.

The effect was immediate and devastating. His hand, *he,* became fused to the object, assimilated, joined. A force more powerful than any Van had ever experienced surged through his body. Not heat or cold or electric. *More*. Much, much more. It began in the entity's form and coursed through his hand, his arm, down through his toes and up again through his neck. His body became completely rigid in one continuous convulsion. His head was thrown back by the force of the surge and his mouth opened wider than he would have thought possible. A beam of semi-solid light, of energy never seen or felt by human beings, shot through Van's body, out of his open mouth and through the ceiling of the cave. The light reached the earth's lower atmosphere instantly and shattered, traveling in every direction at once as far as there was to travel until it encountered itself again. Then it faded.

In that instant, Van truly *was* one with the aliens. On the mountain in Georgia, that entity had given him a glimpse of what travel through space was like. In this moment of fusion with the alien collective, Van saw and felt what their existence truly was. How, as powerful as they were, they were still just tools used by something more powerful and incomprehensible than they were. They spent eternity alone, listening. Was it any wonder one of them occasionally reached out? Left their programming and began interacting with the creatures around them? Killing their friends? Aiding their descent into degeneracy?

It was over. Van's hand was his own again. He looked at the entity's form and saw it was a pinkish color now, with light red and violet rivulets pulsing gently through it. He slumped into the arms of the men holding him.

"Yo! What the fuck?" Holloway said. "Nobody's ever done anything like that before!"

"Shut up!" Spider growled.

"Did you ...did you see that?" Van asked Spider. "The light?"

"I saw you pretending to have some kind of fucking seizure is all. Get him over here!" The men held his hand out, that had moments ago been joined with the universe itself, and Spider cut him, slowly and deeply. "Blood and Land!" He yelled, looking into Van's eyes while he drew the blade across his palm. The men murmured a response. Van's face was drenched in sweat, but he didn't feel any pain. The four men maneuvered Van over to the cave wall and pressed his bloody palm next to where the boy had left his mark. Then they used his wound to spread blood across his face. Spider took his time with this part also. His eyes were creased into cruel slits and one corner of his sneering mouth twitched while he blooded Van.

Afterward, Van was marched back down the path, back to the posts. He was backed up to one post, the southern one, on the inside, and made to sit down. As soon as he did, someone grabbed his hair from behind, and a strap was tied around his neck, binding it to the post. Another strap was wrapped around his chest and arms and secured around the post. He found himself seated, with his legs out in front of him, his wrists tied in front, bound to the post at his neck and chest. As he watched, the boy was tied to the post directly across from him. Both prisoners faced each other across a distance of fifteen or twenty feet. Once the boy was bound, Penske removed his gag and squirted water into his mouth from a plastic bottle. He drank greedily until Penske stopped pouring, and the last in his mouth he spit in Penske's face. Penske recoiled and Ewing laughed while he put the gag back in the boy's mouth.

"Easy, Steve! That one got teeth!"

Bobby still beat on the drum, although quieter now. "Brothers!" Spider called again.

"Brother!" Came the response.

"Brothers, the land calls to us again! Blood and Land!"

"Blood and Land!"

"Brothers, we have presented these two worthy candidates to the cave, to the land. Now we'll find out what use the land has for them. Blood and Land!"

"Blood and Land!"

Spider addressed Van and the boy. "You two candidates will be left in this sacred place tonight, to see what use the land has for you. If the land decides you don't deserve to live here, it will take you. If you're each here, alive and well in the morning then we will have other use for you."

"What ..." Van started, and someone cuffed him from behind. It was Holloway.

"Shut the fuck up."

"Yes, that was rhetorical, sir," Spider said. "Brothers!"

"Brother!"

"Blood and Land!"

"Blood and Land!"

"Dismissed."

30

Eaten By Wolves

THE TORCHES FLICKERED A nervous light on the ground between Van and the boy across from him. The dirt around and between the posts was dark and bare and Van felt the blood drip from the wound on his hand onto the ground and mix with what had dripped there before. He wished he knew the boy's name. They were cast together in this absurdist, creek-fed theater production, and Van wanted to know who he shared the stage with. He couldn't even talk to the kid; the gag was still in his mouth. The boy looked at him pleadingly, willing Van to wake him from their shared nightmare. "It'll be okay," Van tried to say reassuringly. It sounded ridiculous.

His mission was done. Van had done what he was instructed to do. He had brought the errant entity back into the alien collective. The band was back together. He was himself again, for now. Free to make his own choices, his own mistakes. There was no more hum in the glade. Van wondered if the world was different for Spider and the gang, if they felt the change, felt what was coming. It didn't matter. It was too late for them.

His mission was done. Everything was done. There was no way Spider would let him live now. Van had seen too much. It was comforting, knowing he was near the end. There was a sense of relief, a loosening of the tight knot of muscles in his mind. He didn't have to wonder any more, didn't have to worry. The end of his story wouldn't involve incurable disease, or some fatal accident. He would die here, most likely right where he now sat. The relief came again, a shuddering sigh. He hadn't realized how very tired he had been. For so long. He had been pushing through each day, doing the things he imagined he should be doing, but not really *living* any of it. Not feeling anything. He couldn't remember the last thing he'd enjoyed before the last few days with Lauren. He was so tired.

Van wasn't afraid of death. Death meant no more fighting the world to get through his days. Trying to fit in. Trying to belong. No more hiding with his face the war being fought in his mind. He could rest, go to sleep and dream a long, long dream about confidence. Contentment. Being loved and accepted by the people he adored. All that was left was ignoring the regrets and reminding himself that there was nothing left for him ahead.

Ignore the regrets. But what about ... what would his life have been if Yip had chosen him instead of Will? The two of them always seemed so happy together. He knew they fought. More than one of his trips up the mountain with Will had been about arguments they had. But he knew that she made Will ...better. More than just his shallow, egocentric self. Will grew during the years he had been with Yip. But did he do the same for her? Was it reciprocal? That was the question that ate away at Van's brain like a termite infestation when he thought of them together. Could he, Van, have improved her life?

How? He couldn't have. She was so much more than him. So much more.

Van wished he was at the old home, sitting on his favorite rock by the side of the creek. They listened to him there. They *understood* him. They knew all about Yip. And Will. Van had tried to talk to Yip one time about his friends down at the creek. They were at a football game, Will, Van and Yip, and Will had gone to pee or something. Van had told her in a low voice about the denizens of the creek, and she pretended not to hear him. Then he looked her in the eye and told her again, and she had laughed, nervously, and asked if he was kidding. So, he told her he was kidding, and they never talked about it again. Until the phone call in Harrison.

The phone call. What had Yip said? *I liked you too, you know. You just never tried to get close ... You never paid attention to me.* Van had always assumed he never had a chance with her. That she and Will were destined to be together. It always seemed as though something had pushed her toward Will, while pushing Van away. But in the real world, apparently, Van had pushed *her* away. The whispers in his mind had always told him he wasn't good enough for her. On the phone, at the rest stop, Yip told him that he had always had a chance. Had been wrong about her. He had been wrong about himself.

How many times had he been wrong about himself? About the world around him? How many times had he woken up from a walking dream to see those around him staring, pointing their fingers? He made decisions in those dreams. Ruined relationships. His life had been a series of hi-jacked road trips, interspersed with short periods of lucidity and damage control.

There were events that happened in his life that were outside of his control, no matter his state of mind: his mother leaving, his father dying, the car accident he had been in outside of Birmingham. But what about his joining the Marine Corps? Had that decision been his own? He had been desperate, but surely there were other options at the time. He could've ignored all the foolish reptiles and amphibians that had advised him to join up. He could've gone to college or learned a trade instead. And when the Navy rejected him, he could've taken the bus home and came up with a better plan. Tripping on a broken piece of sidewalk and having a full bladder didn't mandate signing up for combat duty. He could have found somewhere else to piss.

What other choices had he made over the years in his unique, somnambulist state, which seemed normal and logical at the time? His life flowed in front of his eyes as a meandering stream, never slowing, passing in and out of patches of a thick mist while decisions he made along the way diverted and influenced the direction he traveled. Those decisions, those choices, overwhelmed him now, as he looked back. He opened a file drawer in his mind of choices he had made which had influenced the course of his life. While rifling through the files he came upon one which was locked in a secure strongbox, wrapped in thick, unbreakable chains. This decision of his had been hidden from him since he made it, and then forgotten. He pulled the box into the forefront of his mind and chose to open it.

He served as a spotter on a two-man sniper team in a war that no one understood or cared about. Van hated war, hated the desert. He was good at war, good at killing, and he hated that he was good at it. He wanted to go home, to the creek, but the only way home was to accomplish the mission. And the next mission. So many missions. The shooter on his team started targeting children. One kid this day, another a few days after that. This went on for weeks. Or was it months? How many kids? How many died by that one sniper's rifle? Van told himself he couldn't do anything about it. He sighted through the optics of his own scope, laser-sighted on the word "mission." And they died. Dozens? More? While Van crouched right next to the shooter, ignoring the world turning next to him. During debriefings, it was "non-combatants" being killed inadvertently, but that was it. He never reported the shooter. Never even tried to persuade him to stop. When the shooter was hit in the village and Van stood still and watched him die, that was the very *least* he could have done to stop the pattern of murder. For so many years Van had been blaming his teammate, but the truth was that *he*, Van, had made the choice to look the other way, and he had allowed those kids to die.

Van was crying. His chest was heaving, and tears were streaming unchecked. It was a release of guilt and shame that had grown around his spine and heart for many years and had hardened him. Sorrow and guilt had fossilized in his chest until he had grown used to their density. Now it was melting. The shell was decomposing, and its refuse came out of his eyes, his nose and his chest as huge gusts of spoiled air.

He looked at the boy tied to the post across from him and the tears flowed across the dried blood on Van's face. The boy looked like so many boys he had lived and worked around, had fought around in that place in the desert. So many boys that he had allowed to die. Van had been told he was fighting to save children like this one, but he had watched them die instead. Neither him nor the sniper, nor any of the other tens of thousands of killers and oblivious men and women soldiers had any business being in that place to begin with.

"I'm sorry," Van choked through the tears. The boy looked at Van blankly. "I'm so, so sorry." Every word released more tension from Van's chest. "I'm so sorry." The boy either couldn't understand what Van was saying, or he had already written Van off as a madman. Either way, the men had left the gag in the boy's mouth, and he couldn't reply. Eventually, the sobs grew smaller, and gentler. The tears dried. Van breathed more slowly. Breathed deeply. His head leaned forward. His chin rested on his chest.

Van dreamed. He dreamed of a half-pound weight in his right hand. Leather grip. So comfortable. A sunny day in a beautiful mountain meadow. A deer. Voices in his head, *his* voice, screaming at him suddenly, defining a threat to him and his friend. Will was in the process of calmly loosening his pack from his shoulders as the wolf closed on him. His arms were held back by the straps, exposing the most vulnerable, juicy parts of him. Van leapt in two effortless bounds. "Van ... NO!" He drove his knife into the wolf's throat. It was a perfect thrust, trachea and arteries severed. He held the knife there as the creature bled and dropped to the ground. Van stayed that way until the blood stopped pulsing and Will was dead and the threat had passed. He dreamed of a small nod from the deer, of approval. A job well done.

He awoke suddenly, amazed that he had been asleep. It was dark now, and the torches had gone out. He couldn't tell how long he had been asleep. Or was he still dreaming? It was so hard to tell anymore. He wondered if he were still in

Memphis, with Lauren, or home, in his apartment dreaming strange dreams. Maybe he was up on the mountain with Will, in his tent, in his sleeping bag on the mossy ground while his mind had adventures of its own.

A sound caught his attention, and he saw the boy across from him raise his head. He had heard it too. One of the sounds of Van's childhood that was so soft and threatening he wanted to ignore it, to pull the covers over his head and close his eyes and hope it would go away. There was something moving through the storage sheds. The light pad of large but stealthy feet. The sound of deep breathing, of smelling. A grunt. A rumble.

The moon was three-quarters full, and there was plenty of light to see them emerge from the sheds. Van was facing that direction, and they walked into view boldly, with purpose and without fear. There were four of them, and the one in front walked straight toward Van, his head low, his eyes delighted. The boy couldn't see them until they had passed from behind him, and he let out a muffled cry from behind his gag. His eyes in the moonlight were terrified. Two of the wolves approached the boy and sniffed around him while the other two surrounded Van. The leader, the alpha, stood right in front of Van and raised his head until it was level with Van's.

"No," Van said. "No! You're not here!"

The wolf sniffed deeply at Van's hair and his head. Drool ran onto Van's shirt and neck from the wolf's open mouth and mixed with the drying tears there. He heard the boy crying again and again through his bonds. There were no sounds of feeding yet.

"NO! You're not real! You don't exist! You're not real!"

The wolf in front of Van sniffed his head, and finally, with its huge tongue, licked the side of Van's face where the blood had been smeared. When he was a teenager, Van had taken a part-time job at a butcher shop, cleaning the counters and coolers each evening. The wolf's breath smelled like old meat that had been missed during former cleanings. as if this was the only wolf ever and it had eaten all the prey that ever ran and hopped and grazed in the world. And it licked Van's blood from his face, and it marked him as prey that had been allowed to live. It looked into Van's eyes with its own.

"You're not real. You're not real. No ..." And the tears came again.

And then the wolves were gone. As quietly and purposefully as they had arrived, they crept around the camp's storage structures again and returned to their woods. The boy across from Van looked at him in surprise and relief. "It's okay," Van said to him, quietly. "It's okay now." He leaned back against the post and looked up at the three-quarter full moon and took another breath.

"Hey shithead. Wake up." Someone was patting Van on the cheek and whispering a loud, urgent whisper. He had been asleep again. "Come on. Wake the fuck up." It was Steve Penske. He was squatting down, and his round, ruddy, freckled face was inches from Van's. He had his hand over Van's mouth. "Shh. Don't say anything." Penske pulled out a knife and Van leaned back against the post. Penske grabbed Van's bound hands and held them while he made a quick, deft cut with the knife. "Okay, dickweed," he whispered loudly. "Be very careful with this now. I've fixed it so that you can break out, but you have to wait until the right time, got it?" Van nodded. "Keep your hands together like this until then. It'll still look like you're tied up. Then just snap your wrists outward here, go it? Now, I'm going to take my hand off your mouth. Don't fucking do anything stupid." He slowly withdrew his hand.

"Why?" Was all Van had to ask.

"Well, not for your dumb ass, that's for sure. I've known Spot ...I've known Lauren a long time. We go back, you know? We used to date and ..." He looked down at the dirt. "I ... care about her, okay? Fucking Spider's a piece of shit, and its wrong the way he treats her. It was okay while she was gone, but I can't fucking watch this shit happen again." He looked Van in the eyes. "You have to help her. You hear me? Get her the fuck out of here." A noise caught Penske's attention, and his head jerked around. "Fuck. I'm out of here. Do it, man. Save her." He spun and moved stealthily back toward the barracks. He ducked between the storage sheds and moved along the tree line. When he was out of sight, between the chow hall and the trees, there came a sound, an ominous, unpleasant sound. It was a small thumping sound, like meat being tenderized, and then a cough, and a wet choking, and two-hundred pounds of something falling to the ground. Then something sizeable being dragged through branches and leaves and tall grass and being abandoned in the woods.

Van didn't see him move, but soon he noticed Davis standing in the middle of the glade. He stood as still as one of the tree trunks lining the camp. His arms hung loosely at his sides, his legs shoulder-width apart. The moon lit his figure, but his face was only partially visible. Van was certain that Davis was watching him, but he couldn't quite made out the man's eyes. It was a cruel trick, hiding the eyes. Even with his shaded face, and the moon's shadow across the glade, Van felt as though Davis was calling to him. Signaling. What could he want? Van was bound and strapped to a post. What could the man want with him? Davis was there for a long time. Van had no idea how long, but he was sure he had been awake the entire time, and when at last he noticed that Davis was gone, the first tinge of sunrise was teasing the rough edges of Van's last day.

A meadow was a nice place to die. Van had been kind of jealous of Will for dying up on their mountain, in that beautiful place. So much better to die there than on the dirty floor of a bus. Or on a highway, twisted up inside of steel and fiberglass. Or in a hospital, hooked up to machines and tubes and tended to by people who don't even see you. And dying in a meadow was a damn sight better than having holes put in you in some small desert village. An Arkansas meadow was a fine place to die. His reward for reaching the end. He had *made it*, in Riff's words.

Or had he? Riff had dragged himself along to the bitter, bitter end, rolling and pushing and drumming himself along the long highways until his very last, tortured breath. He hadn't let go. Riff hadn't taken the easy way out.

Penske wanted Van to help Lauren. She deserved it. She was the most straight-up, most real person he had ever met, and she had brought him here and now she was stuck. Stuck in a web of emotional and psychological manipulation, stuck there by an evil, brilliant spider who needed her so much more than she needed him. Van saw the hatred in her eyes when she looked at the spider, the murderous hatred, which existed next to the old, impossible, familial love she felt for him, and the shame and greater hate for herself. She deserved more. She deserved better. She deserved to live her own fucked up life, on her own terms, and make her own mistakes without the specter of this greedy, omniscient arachnid spinning his web in the corners of her world, waiting to wrap her up and suck out the creativity and beauty and all that was good about her and leave her a withered husk of self-loathing and anger and doubt. She deserved better.

She and Van had bonded, in a way he had never bonded with anyone before. He trusted her. And he was pretty sure she felt the same way about him. They had shared *everything* in only a few days. It wasn't a romantic intimacy, but in a lot of ways it was better than that. She *understood* him. Van hadn't thought such a relationship was possible. What else was out there? *Who* else was out there? What had he been missing?

"Van Ryan." That familiar voice – the entity's voice he hadn't heard since Little Rock.

"Ah, my old friend. Have you come to see me off?"

"We wanted to express our gratitude. You corrected the fault in the component here, and now the collective is again operating as it should." The voice was everywhere, and nowhere. The entity spoke in his mind alone, and Van was able to respond without speaking out loud.

"Well, that's marvelous," Van said sarcastically. "Glad I could be of assistance. I didn't have much choice in the matter, though."

"No, you did not."

"And I suppose you'll go back to your own 'observe and report' mission now."

"Yes, Van Ryan. You will not hear from us again."

"Well, there's that, anyway. And you'll send your wolves back for me now?"

"No. Those were *your* wolves Van Ryan. They were always yours." And with that the voice was gone. The presence was gone. For the first time in what seemed like forever, Van's thoughts felt free and clear, as though a huge breath of fresh air had blown through his head and refreshed the universe within.

31

THE DANCE

THE SUN ROSE EARLY, and no one slept in that day. By the two barracks buildings there was the rustle and murmur of men's morning routines. The air felt fresh and cool, and Van could smell the young autumn air moving through the woods. Birds called their small, loud songs from their hidden stands, offering witness to the activities of man. The boy across from Van locked exhausted eyes with him. For the hundredth time, Van mouthed the words "It'll be alright" to him. He was sure it didn't reassure the boy any more than it did himself, but he meant it, nonetheless. What would happen would happen, and then it would be over.

"Well! *Both* of our guests are still with us! What a treat!" Spider walked the short path from his cabin. The Lodge. "Congratulations, Mr. Ryan!" He stood at the junction of the Lodge path and the cave path. Van couldn't see him from where he sat. "Gentlemen!" The men all gathered in the middle of the clearing. "Where's Mr. Penske?" Van could see Davis, and he shook his head side to side. "What? Damn. Son of a ... well ... Steve was a valued member ... I think his heart hasn't been in it for some time now." The men were quiet and didn't look at each other. "Well, moving on then. Mr. Davis, if you would please escort our special guest up to the cave, please?"

"Where's Lauren, you asshole?" Van's voice strained against the leather strap around his throat.

"Ah, he speaks! Yes, good question. Where is she? I think she darted off into the woods, to take care of her business. Girl business. I don't know. Has anyone seen her?" No answer. "Well, I'm sure she'll join us at the cave."

"Fucker!"

"THAT IS ENOUGH OUT OF YOU!! *You* have overstayed your welcome, Van Ryan! Now I've lost a good man because of you! Get him up there. The rest of you, take the boy down below. Drive him to town and get him and the others ready to move to Little Rock." Van heard Spider turn and head up the path toward the cave. "Mr. Davis, have someone help you with that one."

Davis strode to where Van sat and undid the strap around his throat. Ewing walked around and untied the one around his chest. Davis reached down and held Van by his shoulders while he lifted him to his feet. Van stomped his feet a few times to get blood circulating in them again. Davis grabbed Van by his shirt front and tried to pull him along, but Van pulled back suddenly, resisting him. Davis pulled harder, and Van suddenly changed direction, and lunged at Davis, knocking him off balance. At the same time, Van jerked his wrists apart and snapped the cord where Penske had cut it. Van used his momentum to push into Davis, keeping him stumbling backwards, off-balance, while he reached down and freed his knife from the sheath on the man's belt. One more step and he drove the blade into Davis' chest. It slid in smoothly, grating very gently as it passed between his ribs. Van looked into Davis' eyes as he drove the blade home, and he didn't see anger or fear there. Only resignation. And possibly an expression of gratitude.

Davis' heavy body fell, and Van spun and drove the knife into Ewing's throat before the other men even realized something was happening. Ewing's face did not register gratitude, but rather surprise. There was no blood until Van pulled the knife out of his throat, and then there was. The blood leapt out of the man's body as Ewing spun and painted the ground with it. The others began to react then, spreading out, looking for something to defend themselves with, spewing useless exclamations. None of them used the last moments of their lives for anything worthwhile. But it didn't matter. What would happen would happen, and then it would be over.

A noise filled his head again, but now it wasn't the grating, torturous cacophony which had issued from the cave the day before. The sound in his ears, in his head and throughout his entire self now was the most beautiful thing he had ever heard. It was relaxing and uplifting and harmonized perfectly with everything that was happening around him. It called for him to dance, and he did. Van spun and dove and lunged, along sublime angles, with gloriously graceful motions. He slashed men's arteries in their legs and throats. He lunged and stabbed and twisted. Near the culmination of the dance, when Van held forth his greatest movements, the performance of his lifetime, he found himself facing the nameless man holding his spear. Van took a breath, listened to the music guide him, and closed with the man in two great strides, charging directly at the danger, and he disarmed and killed the man before the spear bounced off the ground.

It was over in a few short minutes. Breathing hard, sweating blood from head to toe, Van turned to the captive boy. He was loose from his bonds, but stood frozen, unable to flee, witness to Van's beautiful, terrible art. Van opened his mouth to tell him something, and suddenly he was knocked backward by a crushing blow to his chest. Something sticking out of his chest. He took two clumsy steps backward and then fell to his knees, stupidly trying to understand what had happened. He looked up and saw Spider standing above, by the cave, a composite bow in his hand. He was laughing as he notched another arrow.

"Well goddamn, Ryan! I guess we found out what you're good at, huh? Goddamn! That was amazing! Shit, I'd ask you if you wanted to join up, seeing as how I'm going to be shorthanded now, but ...well ...I don't think that's gonna work out." Van tried to look, but he was having trouble keeping his head up. He heard the bowstring draw taught and he smiled a tired smile.

There was a gun shot, small caliber, just one, and Van did look up, and he saw Lauren, her arm outstretched behind the spot where Spider had been a moment before, on the path leading down from the cave. She held her small, shiny, smoking gun, and a lifeless lump of meat slid and rolled off to the side of the path below her.

Van's chest was heavy, made of marble, and spasm after spasm constricted his lungs and tried to cease his breathing. The pain faded, and he was comfortable on his back, in the grass, staring at the afternoon sky. Someone close was breathing underwater, in a small puddle, with a wheezing whistle growing longer on each exhale. Van realized it was him. The captive boy leaned into his frame of the sky above but said nothing. A bird flew high above, headed to or from its home, oblivious to the scene in the meadow below. Lauren was there. She had one wet line on her face. Point A to point B. Van felt a tickle on his hand, and he was glad the skink had found him. He tried to say something to Lauren, but his throat was dry, he needed a drink of water. She touched his face tenderly. On her wrist was a daisy chain bracelet.

It was time, and he was relieved. So easy now to let go. Let it all go. Van opened his mouth to tell the world that he had *made it*, but he saw Lauren's sad face above him, and he thought of all the bus stops, all the rest stops still left on the highway ahead. He wasn't alone. Someone understood. Someone *cared.* He found himself lifting his arm, reaching across the universe for Lauren's hand. A sudden breeze issued forth from Van's chest and mouth and shook the trees around the meadow. The natural world paused in that moment to hear his words:

"Help me up."

ACKNOWLEDGMENTS

I owe the world to my beautiful, patient, supportive wife. She knows where this narrative comes from, and it has been hard for her to read, but she has been there for me throughout its long evolution. She edited, offered valuable insight, helped with the book's format, provided photography and came up with an awesome cover design. In short, she has been essential to this work's creation. Thank you, my love.

A shout out as well to the Darkness that has dogged me for as long as I can remember. It is always two steps behind me and around every corner, waiting in ambush for me to let down my guard. Without this archenemy shading my world, I wouldn't have found those things and people who bring such bright light into my life.

ABOUT AUTHOr

Richard R. DiPirro is a veteran of the United States Marine Corps and holds a BA in English from Armstrong State University in Savannah, GA. A survivor of PTSD and bi-polar disorder, Richard knows what lies at the bottom of the pit, and knows where to turn for help when he feels like climbing in. He finds his greatest joy at home with his wife, surrounded by their three amazing kids.

CPSIA information can be obtained
at www.ICGtesting.com
Printed in the USA
LVHW110213111022
730430LV00005B/382